ABANDONED TO THE PRODIGAL

Season of Scandal
Book Two

Mary Lancaster

DRAGONBLADE PUBLISHING, INC.

Dearest Reader;

Thank you for your support of a small press. At Dragonblade Publishing, we strive to bring you the highest quality Historical Romance from the some of the best authors in the business. Without your support, there is no 'us', so we sincerely hope you adore these stories and find some new favorite authors along the way.

Happy Reading!

CEO, Dragonblade Publishing

CHAPTER ONE

IN THE EARLY morning sunlight, two young
ladies hurried across Grosvenor Square. They
kept their heads down and their faces hidden as
best they could.

At the corner of South Audley Street, they
paused. The younger, Lady Juliet Lilbourne,
glanced up for the briefest moment and
surreptitiously gripped her companion's hand.

"Good luck," she murmured.

"And you. Take care, Juliet."

Their hands parted, and Juliet walked into
South Audley Street. In spite of her hurry to be
safe indoors, her feet seemed to drag. An
ominous weight seemed to crush her whole
being.

About a quarter of the way down the street,
she dared to look up again. At the house of her

betrothed's parents, a maid was scrubbing the front step, calling cheerfully to the girl performing the same service at the house next door. Keeping her face turned away from the neighbor's servant, Juliet took the two steps to the open front door.

"Oh, good morning, my lady," the maid exclaimed, pulling her bucket out of the way. "I didn't hear the carriage."

"Good morning, Sally," Juliet murmured hastily and walked into the hall.

From a room upstairs, she could hear the unmistakable tones of Lady Alford, her betrothed's mother. She sounded agitated, as she often was, though Juliet could not make out the words. A low, soothing male voice attempted to calm her. From this distance, Juliet couldn't tell if it was Lord Alford or his son. Though it was ridiculously early for any of them to be up and about.

As she moved toward the stairs, regal footsteps approached from the back of the house.

Juliet, remembering she still carried her valise, stopped and set it down.

"Good morning," the dignified butler, Johnson, intoned, treading across the hall. "We were not expecting your ladyship."

"No, my plans have suddenly changed. Could you ask Lady Alford to—"

"Her ladyship," Johnson interrupted, "is not

at home."

Juliet blinked. She had just heard her ladyship's voice and was about to point out Johnson's
mistake. And then the truth struck her like a
blow.

She was the Earl of Cosland's daughter,
beautiful, courted, and popular. No one had ever
refused to receive her.

Outraged, she held the butler's relentless
gaze. "When will her ladyship return?"

"I could not say, madam."

"Guess," Juliet commanded.

Only by the faintest twitch did Johnson betray emotion. It looked like irritation. "If I were
to guess, I would say not today."

"But that is ridiculous!" She had nowhere else
to go. Her parents were at their Yorkshire estate.
She had been staying with Lady Alford, who had
always been kind and welcoming. And then she
had been summoned unexpectedly to her duty as
lady-in-waiting to the Princess of Wales. There
was only one possible reason that things could
have changed so drastically between yesterday
evening and this morning.

Lady Alford knew.

And yet, how could she have learned so
quickly?

Panic surged. Lady Alford had been her best,
her only hope to nip this scandal in the bud.

"Johnson, I need to see her ladyship," she said

intensely.

"Perhaps if you were to write first."

From nowhere, a footman had appeared and picked up her valise. He pretended not to see her involuntary grab for it and walked with it toward the front door.

They are throwing me out! Oh, dear God, what do I do now?

In desperation, she threw her shoulders back and glared at Johnson. "Bring Mr. Catesby to me this instant, or I promise you, I shall scream so loudly it will wake the entire street. Then, you may explain *that* to your noble neighbors."

Johnson's eye twitched again.

"You have twenty seconds," Juliet said.

With the gesture of one finger, Johnson halted the footman's progress and sent him scurrying for the stairs instead. Juliet stepped forward, picked up the valise, and walked into the reception room.

"Thirteen seconds," she observed mildly.

But she was shaking with mortification. To be forced to threaten a kind hostess in such a vulgar way! But equally, to be condemned, unheard, as she was being... She had never imagined Lady Alford would treat her in such a way. But hopefully, Jeremy, Mr. Catesby, would be able to reach her when she had calmed down.

She wasn't truly counting and had no idea what she would do if she was simply left cooling her heels for hours in this bare, soulless room. But she did hear swift footsteps on the stairs, then hurrying across the hall. Jeremy strode into the room, his lips tight.

He didn't close the door, and when she started toward him instinctively, he actually raised his hand as though to ward her off.

"What do you want, Juliet?" he asked coldly.

She halted as though she had been slapped. "Want? Why are you treating me this way? What have you heard?"

Only then did she see the newspaper in his hands. It wasn't *The Morning Post* or the *Gazette*. He dropped it with some disgust on the table between them.

Juliet stepped up to it, reached past the vase of fresh flowers, which stood at the center of the table, and lifted the newspaper.

It seemed to be one of the scandal sheets she never read and never wished to. The lurid headline *Orgy in C. Place* caught her eye at once. And below it, words and phrases leapt from the page.

Undaunted by the absence of either propriety or their royal mistress…Lady M.W., Lady J.L., Miss D.S., and Miss H.C. lurk in the midst of the night's debauchery, where also were present vast quantities of finest wines and brandies… and several of London's most prominent rakes.

"Oh, dear God," Juliet whispered, her hand

flying to her cheek while the newspaper dropped back onto the table.

"Dear God, indeed," Jeremy said grimly. "What were you thinking of?"

"Thinking of?" Juliet repeated, bewildered. "Of keeping out of the way, yet protecting Her Highness... Jeremy, you cannot believe this vile fustian? It is all lies!"

"Then you were not at Connaught Place?" he snapped. "You certainly left here with every intention of going there. Or so you told my mother!"

"Well, yes, I did, but—"

"Then you deny any such party took place?" he said with contempt. "That any of these people were present?"

Juliet whitened. "I... No, I cannot deny they were there, but you don't understand!"

"No, I don't," he agreed, swiping up the newspaper with one hand. "I'm glad I don't. But I'm sure *you* will understand that any promises between us are broken and our engagement is therefore at an end. Goodbye. Johnson will see your ladyship out."

Her ears seemed to sing with the impossibility of this situation. The whole world was crashing in on her.

"Jeremy, you can't!" she pleaded. "You cannot so condemn me—"

"You are condemned out of your own

mouth," he said shortly. "I would be grateful if you did not visit my mother again. She is no longer at home to you."

A quick spurt of anger was all that prevented her from curling up on the floor. "Do you imagine my father will not be offended by your treating me in such a way?"

"That is exactly what I imagine. I'm afraid it's *you* who has offended him, your entire family, and mine. Don't make me call for footmen to speed your departure."

It was an empty threat. Probably. But that he would make it, shriveled her to the bone. "But...what will I do?" she said, thinking aloud. "Where can I go?"

"Home. Go to Yorkshire."

"On the ten guineas I have in my purse?"

He hesitated, then delved inside his well-made coat, and retrieved a large banknote which he held out to her. "Goodbye, Juliet," he said firmly.

A fresh spurt of anger saved her once more, bringing with it a moment's pride that was probably foolish but all she had to counter the pain of his massive betrayal.

She stared at the money in his hand, then slowly raised her gaze to his. "The trouble with you, Jeremy, is that beneath your smart coat and your expectations, you are simply not a gentleman."

She picked up her valise and walked past him and out the door, her head held high. As she crossed the hall, Johnson and the footman watched her go. A porter opened and closed the front door behind her, leaving her staring at the open-mouthed maid who had finished scrubbing the steps and stood gawping at her, brush in one hand and bucket in the other.

Juliet would have liked to carry on, stalking up South Audley Street with purpose. But she had no purpose. She thought briefly about going to Lady Meg in Grosvenor Square, but Meg's father, the duke, would not welcome her either. And Meg would have her own troubles if her family had read that disgusting rag which had clearly roused the entire Alford household at such an unprecedented hour.

"Sally," she said slowly, "where would one find a mail coach or even a stagecoach to Yorkshire?"

"The Swan with Two Necks in Cheapside?" Sally said doubtfully. "Or maybe the Golden Cross—the inn at Charing Cross—would be best."

"You are probably right." With a friendly nod, Juliet walked down the steps and set off along the road.

JULIET HAD NEVER taken a public conveyance in her life and had no idea how to go about it. And by the time she had walked to Charing Cross and found the Golden Cross Inn, she felt unaccustomedly exhausted. Her legs and feet felt numb, and she wanted to cry.

It had never entered her head that Jeremey would not stand by her, would not believe her, would not even listen to her. He had simply dropped her like a burning coal without a second thought. This man she had meant to marry and live with for the rest of her life. The man who had made her such exquisite speeches of devotion.

What utter lies! And now my heart is broken along with the rest of my life…

The inn was heaving with people and vehicles. Close by, people were bundling into a coach laden with luggage. Others were climbing up on to the outside seats and onto the roof. Everyone around the yard seemed to be in a hurry, striding about purposefully, bearing boxes and trunks, leading horses, harnessing carts, or shouting instructions or ribald remarks she didn't understand. Delicious cooking smells drifting out of the inn made her stomach rumble.

In the midst of the bustle sat a sleek, black cat, elegantly cleaning itself. Everyone, even men carrying heavy loads, who probably couldn't even see the animal properly, walked around it.

Oblivious, the cat carried on washing its face.

On what appeared to the taproom step, a man sat eating a pie with some gusto, until Juliet approached, and he jumped to his feet. The pie vanished into the pocket of his long coat, and he snatched off his slightly greasy-looking hat.

"Help you, ma'am? Head porter at your service. Let me carry your bag."

"Thank you," Juliet replied gratefully. "I wish to go to York, or at least as close to Kidfield as I can. Is there a coach today?"

The porter scratched his head, "No room on that one," he said, nodding toward the laden coach, which was about to leave. "It's the mail. But there may be space on the later stagecoach. It's slower but does stop at Kidfield."

"Oh, that would be ideal," Juliet said in relief. "What time would that be?"

"Eleven o'clock. Let me see what I can—"

A sudden bark seemed to split Juliet's ears, cutting the porter off. In the same instant, a huge, hairy creature bounded from nowhere across her line of vision, directly at the black cat she'd noticed earlier. People scattered in all directions, dropping loads and bumping into each other.

With an angry squeal, the cat sprang up without apparent hurry onto the balcony wall on the first floor. There it resumed its ablutions while the hairy creature, who appeared to be an extremely large dog, tried to jump after it, landing instead on the porter who staggered under the sudden weight.

"Get away, you cur!" he growled, roughly shoving the animal off.

The dog, however, wagged its tail, immediately losing interest in the cat in favor of the porter's coat pocket. The porter clapped his hand over it, protecting his half-eaten pie from the intrusive snout.

"Get away!" the porter yelled, shoving the dog's head with unnecessary force. He even raised his boot and kicked out, catching the dog a glancing blow on the ribs.

Juliet had seen enough. Barging past the man, she stood in front of the now-wary dog, who was clearly not willing to give up on his pie prospects just yet.

"What do you think you're doing?" she raged. "How dare you hurt your poor dog! If you just fed him…"

"He ain't my dog," the porter said aggressively. "What would I want with a great beast like that eating me out of house and home? And if he don't want to be kicked, he should stay out of my pockets!"

"Brute!" Juliet exclaimed. Even then, she was aware her anger was not entirely on behalf of the dog, who didn't seem unduly upset by his treatment. The rest was her own emotion boiling to the surface.

The porter started toward her, clearly trying to intimidate her. Fury spat from his eyes, and his lips twisted. She glared back, while the dog stuck his hairy head under her hand and growled low in his throat.

The porter made a threatening gesture with his raised boot, presumably aimed at the dog, although it was unlikely he could kick it without hurting Juliet, too.

"Gun! Here, boy!" came a commanding voice, and a tall young man pushed through the crowd that had gathered to watch the confrontation. The dog, who was clearly easily distracted, immediately abandoned Juliet and his quarrel with the porter and instead hurled himself at the young man, jumping up to lick his face.

The man grinned and pushed him off. "Down, Gun," he ordered with not very convincing severity before he turned a scowling face to the porter. "What's going on? You know perfectly well he's harmless."

"Don't you worry, sir," someone in the crowd said, clearly entertained. "The young lady's already told him off for kicking the beast."

The young man's gaze flickered to Juliet and away before it swept back for a longer look. Strangely restless dark eyes fixed on hers and held. For a moment, she had to remind herself to breathe, for despite his youth and somewhat bedraggled appearance, he was extraordinarily good looking. More than that, there was something imposing about him.

He nodded curtly and swung back to the porter. "I'll thank you to keep your feet to yourself," he snapped, bending to run his hands over the dog's fur.

"You keep your *dog* to yourself, sir, and my feet will stay on the ground," the porter said insolently and turned back to Juliet. "Kidfield, for madam. At eleven." The crowd, seeing the fun had finished, began to disperse. The porter stared into her eyes and held out his hand. "Fifteen guineas."

Juliet flushed to the roots of her hair. "B-but I only have ten," she stammered, seeing even this last plan collapsing around her ears.

"You could have an outside seat," the porter said grudgingly.

"She could have a seat there and back for ten," the young stranger interrupted from behind them. He strolled forward, the dog at his heels. "And an inside seat at that."

"Not with extras," the porter said defensively. "I presume the lady wants to eat and have her bag taken care of."

He made an angry grab for her valise once more.

But the stranger was quicker. "The lady will keep her bags for now. And she will pay you when you bring back the correct ticket."

With a muttered curse, the porter strode away.

With no real idea what to do next, Juliet turned her attention to the dog, who had pushed his head under her hand and looked up at her, wagging his tail. She smiled just a little tremulously and stroked him, her fingers curling convulsively in his fur. Suddenly, she wanted to cry again.

"My thanks for looking after him," the young man said. "I hope he hasn't been annoying you, too."

She glanced quickly up at him. Through her slightly blurred vision, he looked tall, dark, and very lean, his dress gentlemanly, but somewhat worn, his expression amiable now that the porter had gone. His stance, though casual to a fault, seemed quite unthreatening.

"Not in the least," she replied. "That horrid porter kicked him, only for sniffing at his pockets. I hope he isn't hurt."

"No, he's fine as far as I can see. He learned self-preservation before I ever knew him. Unfortunately, he's a bit of a scavenger. He *has* eaten this morning, but I suppose old habits die hard. Do you have no friends with you, ma'am? Are you truly traveling alone?"

Juliet tried to look haughty. "I am, sir."

He shrugged. "Fair enough."

By then, the porter was striding back toward

her. With ill grace, he held out his grubby hand with her ticket and waited for payment. Juliet opened her purse and placed the coins in his palm. His hand remained where it was, clearly expecting more.

"Really?" her new friend said softly, and with another muttered curse, the porter stormed off.

"He isn't really the head porter at all, is he?" Juliet asked ruefully. "Is he even a porter?"

"Unofficially, perhaps, but either way, I don't imagine he'll last long." With a quick grin, he tipped his hat, clearly about to walk away.

"Thank you, sir," she said hastily. "I'm very grateful to you. I have never used the stagecoach before."

The corners of his eyes creased as though he were amused. "I didn't imagine you had."

"Does everyone try and fleece you like that?"

"Oh, no. In fact, *he* probably wouldn't have if you hadn't annoyed him by scolding him over Gun. For that defense alone, I'm in your debt, and very glad to have been of any assistance." He bowed, snapped his fingers to the dog, and strolled away. The dog trotted at his heels, leaving Juliet to her unsatisfied curiosity over both of them.

After a moment, she turned away and wondered if she dared go into the inn to find a safe place to wait for the coach. She walked the length of the building, then settled on a bench outside to watch the world come and go.

She wished she was less churned up, angry, and frightened, so that she could appreciate the novelty. But this was not the kind of traveling she'd had in mind when she entered the princess's house in Connaught Place yesterday evening. And she had never imagined being alone.

CHAPTER TWO

ABOUT A QUARTER of an hour later, the dog appeared again, wagging his tail in a hopeful manner. Juliet smiled and patted the great, hairy head. "I'm sorry I have nothing for you to eat," she told him. In fact, her own stomach was rumbling. She hadn't eaten since tea yesterday.

"He's taken a shine to you, ma'am," his master said. "Do you mind if I join you, or shall I take him away? Though without a leash, I suspect he'll keep coming back."

"Please," she said, indicating the space on the bench next to her.

The stranger sprawled on the bench beside her and took off his slightly battered beaver hat. She regarded him with curiosity. He had been kind and helpful, his dog clearly loved him, and he had a rather charming smile, lighthearted and friendly.

The dog laid his head on her lap, and she rubbed behind his ears. "What did you say his name was?"

"Gun," her new friend replied, and the dog wagged its tail.

"Why did you call him that?"

"Well, I know he seems quiet and placid enough now, but you probably saw how he was with the cat. If he hears a noise he doesn't like or gets the scent of an enemy, he goes off like a rifle shot. You'll understand soon enough." He gave her an apologetic glance. "I'm afraid we're on the same coach."

Juliet was not displeased by this news, although she had to warn herself about trusting strangers. After all, if she could be mistaken in her betrothed...

She blinked rapidly.

"I'm Daniel Stewart," he offered.

She put out her hand. "Juliet—" She broke off, remembering the awful words printed in the newspaper. For the first time in her life, she was afraid to be Lady Juliet Lilbourne. Not only might she be subject to insult, but her family wouldn't want it known she'd fled London alone on a public coach. "Smith," she finished lamely.

Mr. Stewart shook her hand. "Miss Smith. Are you going to see family in Kidfield?"

"Near Kidfield," she replied. "I'm going

home. Are you?"

"Sort of. My grandfather claims to be on his deathbed."

She raised her brows. "Claims? Don't you believe him?"

"Not really. But maybe it's time I made my peace with him anyhow. Besides," he added with a quick grin, "pockets to let and nothing else to do."

"Did you quarrel with him?" she asked.

"Never done anything else," he said cheerfully. "We don't see eye-to-eye on anything, and I behave badly."

Juliet gave in to innate curiosity. "How?"

He glanced at her. "I don't believe I should go into details. Suffice it to say, I'm a wastrel."

"Is that what your grandfather says?"

"Very colorfully, too. Though in all honesty, I have to admit he's right."

"So, you're going home to mend your ways?"

A smile flickered across his face. "Well, let's not run too far ahead. I'll do my duty and eat well for a few days until we quarrel again."

"You are alarmingly honest," she observed.

"Do I alarm you?" he asked in apparent surprise.

"Well, no, but I think people aren't terribly frank, as a rule." Her smile felt twisted. "Perhaps I am not used to meeting honest people."

"I don't like the sound of that." He seemed to

hesitate. "You probably shouldn't do anything too hasty."

"Do you mean travel alone on the stage-coach?" she asked bluntly.

"None of my business," Mr. Stewart said. "But I'm happy to help if I can. I'll even escort you home if we go quickly."

"My home is near Kidfield," she said with determination.

"Will someone meet you there?" he asked.

"When I send for them," she said stiffly. "Or I shall hire a post chaise."

Mr. Stewart shrugged, as though he had tried all he was going to. The dog sat on his feet.

"Is he going with you?" she asked.

"Gun? Yes, he'd only chase after the coach until his heart gave out." He pulled Gun's ears.

"Have you had him since he was a pup?"

"Yes, but I didn't know it. He was so big that I assumed he was fully grown. He wasn't."

Juliet laughed. "What breed is he?"

"Who knows? I found him wandering the streets and shared my supper with him. After that, he wouldn't go away."

"Then he's just a stray?"

"Not anymore."

"Will the other passengers complain about him?" she asked. "Will he have to go on the roof with the luggage?"

"Oh, we're both on the roof with the luggage," Mr. Stewart said cheerfully. "He makes an excellent blanket."

She regarded him with some respect. "You don't stand too much on your dignity, do you?"

"Nothing to be dignified about," he replied carelessly, and yet some dark, only half-readable expression flashed across his eyes and vanished. He was not proud.

And neither, in the present circumstances, was she. Although she had done nothing wrong, the world would not agree. Her betrothed had already cast her off. His mother had refused to receive her. This was now her life. Even this easy-going young man would look at her differently once he knew.

"But I am happy to help you in any way I can," he said, and she realized his gaze was still steady on her face.

Her chin lifted in instinctive denial. "What makes you think I need help?" She waved one dismissive hand. "Apart from almost being fleeced by that horrid porter."

"The fact that you're traveling alone by public coach,"

"Lots of people do."

"Not people like you."

"You know nothing about me."

"I know you're a lady of birth and wealth."

"The dress? I could be the daughter of a wealthy cit."

His lips twitched. "But you're not."

She regarded him with sudden dread, searching his face. "We have not met before, have we?"

"I doubt I move in your circles, ma'am."

"Why not?" she pursued. "You are a gentleman, are you not?"

"Opinions vary."

"Well, they shouldn't," she said, perversely annoyed on his behalf. "You have been most gentlemanly to me. And believe me," she added darkly, "I have seen men use the description who clearly have no right to it whatsoever."

"Who?" he demanded.

"My betrothed for one. For another..." She broke off, appalled. She had been thinking of the aristocratic men who had been in the princess's house last night, had nearly blurted the whole to a complete stranger. What was she thinking of?

But Mr. Stewart seemed to have fixed on her first accusation. "Your betrothed?" he said, startled. "Does he know about this journey of yours?"

"Oh, he is not my betrothed anymore," she said airily. "Which is a good thing since he turned out not to be a gentleman at all, except by birth."

"In that case, I wish him an ugly shrew of a wife who keeps him on a very, very short leash. And employs a shockingly bad cook."

Juliet laughed. "Perfect. And I wish you an excellently cooked fatted calf at your grandfather's."

"Unlikely."

"Won't you be treated as the prodigal grandson returned?"

"I would doubt it. My grandfather is a parsimonious old skinflint. Which is another reason he dislikes me so much. Money just slips through my fingers. So, he really doesn't want me to inherit his."

"Are you his heir?"

Her new friend shrugged. "Not necessarily. He has three grandsons he'd like to compete for the privilege."

"Will you?"

"I never have before," he said restlessly. "It goes against the grain."

"But you are going to him," she pointed out.

"I have to think about my mother," he said ruefully. He shifted. "But you don't want to hear my life story. I would rather hear yours."

"I have nothing to tell. I have had a perfect, privileged, and quite trivial life, as anyone will tell you."

"Traveling two hundred miles on the mail coach isn't much of a privilege."

"I shall give all that up," she said with mock grandeur. "I shall retire from the world and go into a nunnery."

He grinned. "How long would you last there?"

"About an hour and a half before the abbess decided I am too frivolous. But at least," she added wistfully, "I would get to travel abroad."

"I'm sure you could come up with a better reason to travel."

"Have you been out outside of England?"

"I was born in India," said the surprising young man. "And I spent a fortnight in Scotland, which I suppose doesn't count as abroad. Pretty, though, if one likes to paint."

"Do you paint?" she asked in surprise.

"I dabble. I've dabbled in most things over the years."

"*Over the years?*" she repeated. "You are not Methuselah!"

"I'm five-and-twenty, which is more than enough years for *considerable* dabbling."

"I used to be considered quite proficient in watercolors," she offered.

"Now who sounds like Methuselah? Is there any reason you shouldn't *still* be proficient?"

"No," she allowed. *But no one will care. No one will look.*

After a few moments, she realized he was rummaging in his satchel. Gun edged closer to him. He came out with a bundle in a folded napkin, which turned out to be a large hunk of bread and cheese. He tore it in two and offered one piece to Juliet.

Her mouth watered. "I couldn't eat your

breakfast."

"It will cheer you up. Everything looks better when you're not hungry."

Stupidly, his casual kindness brought a lump to her throat. She swallowed hard. "Thank you," she muttered and took the ungainly chunk. It tasted better than the finest morsels she could remember.

※※※※

DANIEL STEWART HADN'T expected the girl to be quite so fascinating. Dazzled by her beauty and the spirited way she had defended Gun, he had allowed her vulnerability to arouse his erratic chivalry. He had decided to look after her as best he could on the journey north, but he hadn't supposed he would enjoy her company as much as her appearance. Or become quite so intrigued by what had brought her to this point in her clearly privileged life.

She took off one glove, then the other, and pulled a dainty morsel off the ungainly chunk of bread and cheese he had handed her. She put the piece in her mouth somewhat gingerly. But when she had chewed and swallowed, she had the next piece ready and shoved it in with rather more enthusiasm.

"What?" she demanded when she could

speak. "This is delicious." Another less dainty chunk vanished behind her charming lips.

"When did you last eat?"

She swallowed. "Tea," she admitted. "Yesterday. I didn't even realize I was hungry. When will we reach Kidfield?"

"Tomorrow morning."

"Oh, dear, and I'm eating half of your luncheon! Will we be able to get more with my last two guineas?"

"Of course. The secret of coaching stops is not to shovel your meal in, but to carry away as much as you can." From the satchel, he took out his well-traveled tin bowl with the lid.

She laughed. "But we won't be able to share if you're on the roof. Perhaps I could swap my ticket for an outside one, too?"

"I don't think that would be a good idea," he said hastily. "But we'll find a way."

The time until the mail coach began loading up passed quickly in the kind of lighthearted conversation he most enjoyed. She betrayed nothing further about her life or her reasons for this clearly unfamiliar mode of transport. But she did seem cheered, losing a certain tightness around the eyes that had spoken of worry as well as tiredness.

Escorting her across to the coach, he found himself scanning her fellow inside passengers. A respectable couple with a young daughter, a plump, scowling woman, and an oily young merchant he didn't like the look of at all.

Juliet climbed in without fuss, but he soon saw her head peering out the window, watching as he climbed onto the roof, pushing Gun in front of him. She smiled and waved, and then her head ducked in again.

Dan made himself as comfortable as possible, with his satchel over his shoulder and his traveling cloak at the ready to keep himself and Gun dry and warm. And then they were off. He felt the usual surge of exhilaration at the prospect of speed, fine views, and pastures new. Except, of course, the pastures weren't really new, and there really wasn't likely to be anything different at his grandfather's. A fresh load of insults and scolds about his way of life and threats to leave his money to Colin or Hugh instead.

Dan wished he would—almost. But now his mother seemed likely to marry that imbecile Pilney, just for financial security. And Dan was forced to consider someone other than himself. His mother should have enough to live on, enough for comfort in her old age. And it was up to him, not Pilney, to provide it. If that meant groveling to his grandfather, well, it was a small price to pay.

Really, it was.

When they changed horses at Waltham Cross, Dan climbed down to stretch his legs and let Gun do the same. Most of the travelers stayed where they were, although "Miss Smith"—if that was her real name, he'd eat his hat—stepped outside to join them. Gun welcomed her in his usual boisterous manner. Dan only just managed to prevent him from jumping on her, but fortunately, she took it all in good part.

"Don't wander off," Dan warned her. "They're only changing the horses, and we'll be gone again in five minutes. The coach won't wait for you."

Hastily, she climbed back in and Dan, once they started harnessing the new team, climbed back up to the roof, shooing the dog in front of him. His fellow roof-passenger, who had slept most of the first stage, now woke up and yawned. He proved to be a cheerful young man called Gordon, a schoolteacher by profession, and the possessor of a pack of cards. Since Dan had no money, they played for imaginary guineas. Dan was ten up by the next change.

"You are clearly a lucky man," Gordon said disconsolately.

"Only when the stakes aren't real," he replied, letting Gun jump down.

"Good Lord," Gordon said with awe. "Who is that goddess fending off your beast?"

"Miss Smith," Dan said with a surprising surge of protectiveness.

He managed to send a porter running to

fetch her lemonade, which she drained almost at once before bestowing on him a dazzling smile of gratitude.

"Are you comfortable enough in there?" he asked her.

"Considerably more than you must be," she replied. "Though I suppose you get the better view."

"Your traveling companions pleasant enough?" he asked casually, catching the gaze of the oily merchant striding back from the inn.

"Most interesting people," Juliet said unexpectedly. "Mrs. Harper is going to find her missing daughter, who was last seen in Kidfield of all places. Mr. and Mrs. Brown are taking their daughter to become a nursery maid at a big house near Newcastle. And Mr. George, there, is making a fortune in paraffin oil. Isn't that astonishing?"

"No," Dan managed breathlessly before he saw her own eyes dancing. Clearly, she had a similar opinion of the merchant. He grinned and snapped his fingers to Gun.

"A damnably lucky man," Gordon observed when he resumed his place on the roof. "Any chance of an introduction, old fellow?"

>>>><<<<

BY THE END of the afternoon, for Juliet, the novelty of stagecoach travel had definitely worn off. Uncomfortably cramped, rattled, hungry, and bored, she had too much time to think as her fellow passengers lapsed into silence. Mr. George, the merchant, was reading a newspaper—it looked more like a scandal sheet to Juliet—and sniggering. Mrs. Brown and her daughter were talking in whispers, while Mr. Brown snored gently. Mrs. Harper, of the missing daughter, scowled over her knitting, her thoughts clearly even less pleasant than Juliet's.

By the time they stopped at Stamford for a meal, it was after eight o'clock in the evening. Juliet, squashed against the door by Mrs. Harper's knitting arm, almost fell into the fresh, evening air, her limbs stiff, her stomach rumbling.

Mr. Stewart, dangling precariously off the roof on his front, was shouting something to a porter who ran off, hopefully, to do his bidding. Her friend grinned, rolled, and more or less slid to the ground before her.

"Supper is ordered, but we only have half an hour," he said, offering her his arm.

Just as she took it, a sudden, deafening bark rent the air, and Gun shot past her in joyful pursuit of something. There was indeed justice to the dog's name. Someone yelled, and a crash of falling tin was heard, followed by a tinkle of glass and a roar of wrath.

"Oh, the devil," Daniel said in resigned tones. "Excuse me, one moment…"

He ran off after Gun, and Juliet, amused, accompanied Mrs. Harper into the inn. It was already busy, the noise deafening and somewhat disorienting. But as she sat down, Mr. Stewart strode in with Gun at his heels once more. The innkeeper remonstrated with him over the presence of the dog. Juliet didn't hear what was said, but the dog slunk past her under the table, and his master soon sat down, too.

"All well?" Juliet asked him across the table.

"I had to grovel, but the only breakage was an empty bottle."

A bowl of soup appeared in front of her, and, taking her cue from Daniel, she drank it as quickly as she could. A further course arrived before they had finished—a meat pie of some kind with vegetables. Daniel promptly tipped his into the tin bowl he took from his satchel and passed it across the table to her. Under the shocked gaze of Mrs. Harper, Juliet added her pie to the bowl, though there was no room for any more vegetables. She passed it back to Daniel, who closed the lid and carried on eating his soup.

"Don't give him your food, dear," Mrs. Harper murmured. "He should be ashamed—"

"Oh, no, ma'am, we'll share it," Juliet assured her. "Mr. Stewart shared his breakfast with me this morning when I had nothing."

"My dear, men like him don't give anything for nothing," Mrs. Harper hissed, glaring at Daniel. "They merely take advantage of innocent and trusting young women."

Squashing her spurt of indignation—after all, Mrs. Harper had serious reasons for her jaundiced view of men, her daughter having been enticed away from home by a soldier—she merely nodded peaceably. "But I do believe him to be very kind and good-natured."

"Feckless," Mrs. Harper pronounced. "At best."

Since he had more or less admitted that particular charge, Juliette did not dispute it. She merely finished her soup and accompanied Mrs. Harper to refresh herself. By the time they returned, there were honey cakes on the table, most of the passengers were still plowing through their pie and vegetables, and the coachman was calling for everyone to be back on board.

Hastily, Juliet crammed a forkful of vegetables into her mouth, then seized a cake, and wrapped it in her clean handkerchief before stuffing it into her reticule. Gun kept nudging her with his nose.

"Yes, yes, I'm coming," she told the dog and rushed outside.

Under the fading light, everyone piled back into or onto the coach, and they got underway once more. After little more than a bowl of soup,

Juliet wondered if she should just eat the honey cake now because it looked as if she would not get her pie before the next stop when it would be cold.

However, they were not much farther along the road when a sudden knock against the coach window startled her. Jerking her head around, she gasped. Mrs. Brown squealed, for an upside-down face had appeared outside the window.

Daniel.

With a gasp, she flung down the window. Before she could speak, the tin bowl, complete with lid, was thrust through the window, and she seized it automatically.

"Mr.—" she began, in fear for his safety, but with a last grin, his face vanished upward, and laughter shook her.

The other passengers stared at her open-mouthed, which made her shoulders shake harder. Hastily, she opened the lid and found a slice of pie, and at least half the vegetables that been in the bowl to start with.

"You see?" she crowed to Mrs. Harper. "He wasn't stealing my dinner."

Of course, she had to eat the pie with her fingers, and use the last of the crust as a spoon for the vegetables, and the process was a little messy. Nevertheless, she felt much better when she had eaten and sat back, replete, clutching the bowl on her lap and wiping her fingers on a second handkerchief.

She returned the bowl to Daniel during the next stop. He looked different in the flaring lantern light, his lean face shadowed, his dark eyes somehow mysterious, reminding her that he was a stranger.

"Thank you," she said, "but you should not have risked life and limb to give it to me!"

"Oh, I was perfectly safe," he assured her. "Gordon here was holding onto my legs. This is Gordon," he added, indicating another roof passenger, who smiled and raised his hat to her. "Gordon, Miss Smith. Gordon owes me fifty thousand pounds."

Juliet's jaw dropped. Mr. Gordon looked like an amiable young schoolmaster, not the sort of man who had ever possessed fifty thousand pounds.

"Imaginary pounds," Mr. Gordon said apologetically. "He's been beating me since Waltham. Every hand."

Juliet, who still felt unreasonably guilty that her father had once won another man's fortune at gaming, smiled with relief.

"Here you are, gents," Mr. George said as he headed back toward the coach from the inn. He held out the newspaper he had been reading earlier. "I've read it. Imagine it's more about your friends than mine."

Mr. Gordon took it with a polite thank you.

"Wouldn't waste your time with *that*," Daniel said with distaste.

Mr. Gordon, who had stepped nearer the coach lanterns to glance through the paper, snorted. "What, not even *Orgy at C. Place*? Even when she's… Oh, begging your pardon, ma'am," he added hastily, remembering Juliet's presence.

The blood drained from Juliet's face. She had almost forgotten the reason for this adventure. While the oily, Mr. George had been reading these lies about her, and now Daniel would, too.

Not that either would know Miss Smith was Lady J.L., but the very idea made her queasy.

Daniel was frowning at her, as though sensing her sudden discomfort.

"I believe we are about to depart," she muttered. "Good night, gentlemen."

CHAPTER THREE

LORD BARDEN WAS enjoying a lazy day following the excitement of the party at the Princess of Wales's residence in Connaught Place. He had let loose the first volley of his Great Vengeance Plan, and he meant to complete the next stage by the end of tomorrow, and then have leisure to move on to Lady Juliet.

However, as the afternoon wore on, he couldn't quite resist paying a quick call on the Alfords, just to be sure everything was in place. After all, Lady Juliet Lilbourne was a popular young lady, and people would think twice before offending her powerful father—which was one reason he had chosen to be revenged in this particular way.

So, he strolled around to South Audley Street and discovered Lady Alford was indeed at home, with her eldest son and several ladies of the ton. Thankfully, there was no sign of Juliet, an absence he took care to draw attention to after graciously accepting a cup of tea.

"Lady Juliet is no longer with you?" he asked his hostess, who immediately looked flustered and cast pleading eyes at her son.

"Lady Juliet was called to Her Highness yesterday afternoon," said Lord Alford's heir, the Honorable Mr. Jeremy Catesby.

"Yesterday afternoon?" Barden marveled. "But Her Highness had already left London by then! Did her poor ladyship have to chase after her to Worthing?"

"My mother has not heard from her," Catesby said repressively.

Oh, yes, they had seen the new story and dismissed her as cavalierly as he had hoped.

Barden nodded understandingly. "One hopes she has gone with Her Highness. Because I have to tell you, I had occasion to step round to Connaught Place yesterday—on business for the prince, you understand—and I am shocked to say I found the most vulgar party in progress. Even you or I, sir, would blush to be associated with such an event."

As he spoke, he was aware of being surrounded by avid listeners. Some pretended to be uninterested, but he could practically see their ears flapping. Yes, the word was out, the *on-dit* spreading satisfactorily like wildfire.

Four young ladies were ruined, among them Lady Juliet Lilbourne. And Barden really could not wait to reveal to her haughty father, the Earl of Cosland, the cost of her recovery.

Smiling amiably, he changed the subject, finished his tea, and departed. Somehow, he managed not to crow until he was alone in his own rooms.

≫≫≪≪

FOR JULIET, THE rest of the journey to Kidfield passed in misery. The sight of the newspaper had brought all her woes back to the forefront of her mind, and now she had neither other people's troubles nor the scenery to distract her. The Browns and Mr. George donned nightcaps and blankets and went to sleep. Mrs. Harper dragged a traveling cloak around her and closed her eyes.

Juliet thought of the outside passengers shivering in the chill of the night and tried to be glad she was cramped in here while the horses thundered through the night. In truth, she would rather have been on the roof playing cards for pretend money. However, she fell into a doze, only waking as the horses were changed, and after a while, she barely even noticed that. After all, she hadn't slept last night, either. It was only tiredness that made her despair. Tomorrow would be better.

She woke to someone shouting and discovered Mrs. Harper's head on her shoulder.

"Kidfield!" the coachman yelled again, and she saw the horses sweep into yet another inn yard, this time in the grey light of dawn.

"Mrs. Harper." Juliet nudged her companion awake. "We have arrived at Kidfield."

Mrs. Harper brushed apologetically at Juliet's shoulder. By then, the coach door was opened, and Juliet staggered out into the familiar yard. She had never seen the Black Cat at this time of the morning. Apart from the stagecoach, it was unnaturally quiet. Even the work changing the horses was carried out in silence.

Luggage was unstrapped for Juliet, Mrs. Harper, and Mr. George. Daniel appeared to have only what he stood up in, plus the satchel on his shoulder. Other luggage was put in its place, and the remaining passengers climbed into the coach to go on to York.

Juliet raised a hand to the Browns and to Mr. Gordon on the roof, who was leaning down to shake hands with Daniel.

"What will you do?" she asked Mrs. Harper.

"Take a room here and sleep for an hour or two. And then I shall begin looking for her."

"I shall make a point of asking for her, too," Juliet promised. "And contact you here should I hear anything."

Mrs. Harper's bleary eyes came back into focus on her. "How will you get home from here? Is it far?"

"I'll hire a chaise," Juliet said. "Good luck, ma'am, and thank you for your company."

To her surprise, Mrs. Harper hugged her, a brief, hard embrace, before glaring at Daniel and stalking off toward the house.

Daniel stepped back beside her as the fresh horses began to pull the laden coach away.

"Will you send word to your family that you're here?" he asked.

"No, I can hire a chaise to take me home. What about you? Is it far to your grandfather's?"

He shrugged. "About five miles to Myerly, I think."

She blinked. "Myerly? Is *Lord Myerly* your grandfather?"

"You know him?" Daniel asked, amused.

"Of course not. Nobody under the age of thirty has ever seen him."

"I expect you call him Baron Miserly," Daniel remarked.

"I'm afraid we did," she confessed. She hesitated, then, "My chaise will pass Myerly. I can drop you there if you like."

His lips quirked. "If we like to have the whole country gossiping that you shared a closed carriage with Myerly's prodigal grandson."

"Oh, my goose is already cooked there." She met his gaze and tilted her chin. "My name isn't Smith."

"I didn't suppose it was."

"I'm Juliet Lilbourne."

His eyes were faintly puzzled. "Lilbourne? Then you're related to the Earl of Cosland?"

"His daughter."

"Then, I definitely shouldn't be sharing a carriage with you!"

"His *eldest* daughter," Juliet said defiantly, but clearly, that still meant nothing to him. "I was a lady-in-waiting to the Princess of Wales."

For an instant, he still looked baffled. And then she saw exactly the moment he made the connection. As soon as his eyes changed, she turned away.

"I'm going into the house to see about the chaise." She walked swiftly, trying not to care what he thought of her now, and entered the familiar inn.

A yawning maid was stumbling down the stairs. Mr. George emerged from the coffee room.

"Ah, Miss Smith," he said, smiling hugely as he approached her. "Might I offer you a seat in my carriage, which will be here directly?"

"Thank you, no. I shall make my own arrangements." For some reason, it made her uncomfortable that the maid disappeared toward

MARY LANCASTER

the kitchen, leaving them alone.

"Why bother when you may share mine?" he asked persuasively, halting just a little too close to her.

She stepped back. "I shall not put you out," she said firmly. "My own carriage will be here shortly."

"*Will* be here. You *will* make your own arrangements," he quoted with a hint mockery. Suddenly, he seemed very sure of himself, as though his smarmy desire to please had inexplicably turned into knowledge that he *did* please. "My carriage will be here in five minutes."

"And I wish you well in it," she retorted. "I shall wait for my own."

"Oh, you needn't be shy with me!" His smile broadened, and he actually took her hand. "We are old friends now—having spent the night together."

Juliet snatched her hand free, blushing to the roots of her hair. The blistering retort that rose to her lips froze on the memory of that wretched article, of Jeremy's contempt. Was this all that was left to her?

As though sensing a victory, George moved closer once more. A table jabbed into her back. She was trapped.

"Sir, step back!" she commanded, though she could see in his eyes, he had no intention of obeying. A shadow fell over the front door.

Daniel Stewart.

Juliet's first feeling was relief. And then shame.

George turned his head and saw Daniel, but he didn't move. Instead, he smirked.

Daniel strolled in, the dog at his heels. "I believe the lady made a request." She hadn't known he could sound like that, so cold and contemptuous. She shriveled inside.

George's lips curled in return. "Do you really think that accent entitles you to everything? I'm afraid I've stepped in before you, *old fellow.*"

The dog stuck his head in front of Daniel, staring. He growled deep in his throat, as he had once done to the porter.

"Gun," Daniel said casually. "Fire."

Immediately, the dog leapt forward, snarling. George stepped rapidly backward, all but falling over a chair. Gun came after him, and he turned tail and bolted toward the front door, which Daniel kicked shut behind him.

Gun slid to a halt, whining in disappointment.

"Did that oily little toad dare lay a finger on you?" Daniel demanded, striding toward her. "I thought you wouldn't like a pinch-up in front of you, but give you my word, I'm more than happy to go and beat him to a pulp outside."

Juliet was so relieved that his contempt had not been directed at her that she could only smile tremulously. She sat down a little too quickly, and he immediately dropped to a crouch in front of her.

"Hello there!" he called abruptly. "A glass of water for the lady!"

"No, no, I'm fine," she insisted. "It's just I was afraid he associated me with the article in that horrid paper, and I thought you..." She broke off, grateful to see Mrs. Burton, the innkeeper's wife, emerging from the kitchen, wiping her floury hands on her apron. Daniel straightened and stepped back.

"Why, my lady!" Mrs. Burton exclaimed, hurrying toward her. "Maizie! Bring water this instant! Is your ladyship ill?"

"No, no, just tired. I wonder if you could arrange for a chaise—with two seats."

"It'll be about an hour to wait. Why don't I send instead to Hornby Park..."

"Then, I shall have to wait two hours. Please, Mrs. Burton."

"Of course." Mrs. Burton curtseyed and glared at Daniel while Juliet took the glass of water from the maid. "And what can I do for you, sir?"

"Nothing, thank you," Daniel replied politely, just as Gun trotted across the room toward her.

She squealed in fright and backed away. "What in God's holy name...! Does that beast belong to you, sir?"

"He does, but—"

"I'll thank you to get it out of my coffee room before he eats my guests!"

"He is quite harmless," Daniel assured her, pulling the dog's ears.

"Unless you tell him to fire," Juliet reminded him. Suddenly, she wanted to laugh, and Daniel grinned at her, making it worse.

"Inappropriate humor," he admitted. "But who could resist?"

"Please let him stay, Mrs. Burton," Juliet said, sobering. "He is very well-mannered as you see, and he'll come with us in the chaise. Oh, and this is Mr. Stewart, who is on his way to Myerly."

"Secretly," Daniel said unexpectedly. "So, I'd be very grateful if you didn't tell."

"Mr. Stewart?" the innkeeper's wife repeated, distracted. "Then you are Miss Jenny's son? I beg your pardon, Mrs. Stewart's son. His lordship's grandson."

"Indeed, I am. But for his lordship's health, I don't want anyone mentioning I was ever here."

Surprisingly, Mrs. Burton nodded sagely with another glance at Juliet. "I see. Of course, my lips are sealed. There will be no gossip reaches either of their lordships through my servants or me."

"Thank you," Juliet said as she bustled away. She raised her gaze from Mrs. Burton's back to Daniel. "What on earth were you talking about?

What is the secrecy about?"

Daniel pulled a chair to sit astride it with his arms resting across its back. "Nothing, of course. Just didn't want gossip circulating about you and me traveling together. She clearly knows my grandfather and your father don't talk and why."

Intrigued, Juliet said, "I just thought no one spoke to Lord Myerly. Is there a feud?"

"I wouldn't call it a feud," Daniel said, "And I'm not sure you should look quite so delighted by a quarrel."

"Actually, I was hoping for scandal," she said ruefully. "I need all the ammunition or at least all the sympathy I can muster from my father."

"Sadly, he was pretty much blameless. The scandal was my mother's. She was engaged to your father and then ran off with mine. Your father apparently blamed my grandfather, who would never have accepted any kind of criticism for anything, let alone blame."

"Oh, dear," Juliet said. "And that is the real reason your grandfather quarrels with you? Because he disapproves of your father?"

Daniel shrugged. "To be honest, I never heard of anyone he *does* approve of. I'm actually honored because he has never let my mother in the house since the day she left, while I have been summoned several times over the years."

"Then I can see why your heart isn't really in this reconciliation," she said. "And I'm glad you've decided to come in the chaise."

"Well, someone has to protect you from oily toads and weasels." Slowly, he drew the newspaper from inside his coat. "Is this the reason you fled London on the stagecoach?"

She blinked rapidly. "I had been staying with my betrothed's family when I was summoned by the princess. The next morning, when I returned, they would not receive me. Jer… my betrothed ended our engagement without even listening to me. He gave me money to get home, and I was too proud to take it."

His eyes remained steady on hers. She was sure she saw a spark of anger there.

"Did you love him very much?"

"I thought I did." She dragged her gaze free. "But how could I love someone so shallow, so devoid of feeling or even interest in me?" She cast him a difficult smile. "I believe Jeremy must be one of your oily toads."

"He sounds more like a weasel. Well, we can fire Gun at him later. You are clearly much better off not marrying such a man. What I don't understand is why *anyone* could even be expected to believe this drivel."

"Because enough of it is true," she said ruefully. "The Alfords knew I was summoned to the princess. We all were, apart from Hazel, who was starting her scheduled duty. None of us knew the princess had left that morning, so we just hid from the vulgar party going on downstairs."

"Did you not wonder why she didn't send for you?"

"We thought she was..." Juliet blushed, "...saying goodbye to a friend from whom she was about to part. We all thought we'd been chosen to accompany her abroad and were so excited about it. I suppose we didn't properly consider the rest of the situation. As soon as we discovered Her Highness wasn't there, we fled, hoping our families would be able to douse any suspicion of scandal. I thought Lady Alford would... I never imagined Jeremy... It's this rag of Oily George's! The Alfords had already seen it, and they rarely rise before eleven."

Daniel frowned. "And when did you reach their house?"

"About seven, I suppose."

"So, between that evening and seven the next day, someone had seen you at the party, reported it to this rag, who then printed it among the rest of their nonsense, and delivered it to your betrothed in such a way that he rose from his bed to read it?"

"It doesn't seem very believable," she allowed. "Besides which, we were never in the midst of the party. We never even entered the drawing room, just locked ourselves in the room next to the princess's, ready to guard her if we needed to."

"I think someone has set out to hurt you," Daniel said grimly. "You or one of the other ladies listed here."

"But who would do such a thing?"

"Some jealous lady of the princess's?"

"They had no reason to be jealous. I was to have been married next month and meant to leave her service then. Even if I had been abroad at the time."

He gave an apologetic half-smile. "Jeremy? To give him an excuse to throw you over for some other lady?"

"What other lady?" she said bluntly. "I'm an earl's daughter, and I come with a sizeable dowry. I don't see how he could do much better, and the man I saw yesterday is certainly not capable of the kind of grand passion that might make him oblivious of worldly advantages."

"Perhaps someone with a grudge against your family, then."

Her eyes widened. "Surely not Lord Myerly?"

Daniel's smile was crooked. "He might give you the cut direct, but I can't see him going after you in such a vicious, underhand way. After all, like me, you are an innocent party in his quarrels. Does your father have other enemies?"

"Probably," she said ruefully. "He has dabbled in politics, and he has not always lived well. He gambled away a large part of his fortune and then won it back by ruining someone else entirely. Or so the story goes."

"Who did he ruin?"

"I have no idea. It was just a vague story. And one my mother was never terribly keen on discussing. In any case, this was years and years ago. It would be a very patient revenge."

"The best vengeance always is. Or so I'm told."

Juliet considered that until Mrs. Burton and the maid reappeared with coffee and toast.

"Bless you, Mrs. Burton," Juliet said gratefully, and when the coffee was poured and they were alone again, she said, "I'll talk to my family." After a moment, she added, "I'm glad to have a friend in the neighborhood. Despite my family, I'm bound to be persona non grata, at least until we can prove this is lies."

"Happy to help if I can, but I'm afraid I don't really add to a lady's good reputation."

"I don't believe I care," she said stoutly. "Reputations can as easily lie one way as the other. People may call you a rakehell, although I've no idea if they do or not, but you have been a perfect gentleman and a good friend to me on this journey."

There was a strange expression in his eyes before his lashes dropped down.

"There must have been a scandal," she observed, "if your parents ran away together. How did your mother deal with it?"

He shrugged. "She didn't really have to. She went abroad immediately with my father and followed the drum. It was only after he died that she began to flirt again with polite society." He drained his coffee cup. "But that's all a different matter."

"Perhaps my scandal will just be a seven-day wonder," she said with growing optimism, "and then everything will be as before."

"Especially if your betrothed sees what an idiot he was and apologizes," Daniel said.

Juliet glared. "I would not have him now if he begged on one knee, and my father commanded it."

"Don't blame you," Daniel said, "but it would probably be the best way to squash rumor."

She sighed. "Let us hope there are more palatable ways. After all, my father is not a nobody, and neither is—" She broke off with an apologetic glance. "I suppose I shouldn't really mention the other ladies involved in this. I know you are safe to tell, but I must get out of the habit."

"Actually, you know no such thing," he said bluntly. "As it happens, you're right, but you don't *know* that."

"You think I'm naïve."

"Trusting," he corrected.

"And I shouldn't be," she said bitterly. "I used

to imagine I was such a good judge of character, but I can't be if I liked Jeremy."

Unexpectedly, he nudged her with his elbow, and she realized with a flutter of her heart how close he was. "Cheer up. You are quite right to like me."

"Make up your mind," she retorted. "You just told me not to trust you."

"No, I didn't, but no one ever listens to advice of that nature anyway. I certainly don't."

She regarded him with renewed curiosity. "You must have led an odd life by the standards of most young gentlemen."

He shrugged. "Not so very odd. My grandfather parted with two years of fees for Harrow and then Cambridge, so I do have an education of sorts."

She flushed. "Forgive me. I did not mean to imply otherwise."

"I'm not offended," he assured her. "I'm telling you the good bits before the bad."

"Go on," she urged.

"Since I did what he asked, and even graduated from Cambridge, he invited me to live with him, implying thereby that I would be his heir."

"But that is good, not bad!"

"I refused. He didn't include my mother in his invitation and refused to see her, so I politely declined. Which was foolish in some ways, but I couldn't allow him to slight her."

"Of course not!" Juliet agreed. "So, what did you do instead?"

"I tutored for a bit, but I didn't earn much, so I supplemented it—and often lost it—gaming. And then there was a scandal, and I had to give up the tutoring. I suppose you could say I went to the devil. I ignored this summons from my grandfather for a week, and then I thought, why not? No point in bearing a grudge forever. I didn't tell my mother, but I did come. As you see."

"So, we're both rather scandalous," Juliet said ruefully.

"But you, at least, are innocent."

There was a peculiar pleasure in hearing him say so, perhaps because he was clearly a somewhat scandalous person himself, and a cynic to boot. If *he* believed her, then surely the rest of the country would not think the worst of her.

CHAPTER FOUR

HER SPIRITS IMPROVED by coffee and Daniel's company, Juliet found the time flew until the chaise arrived with a clatter in the yard.

Mrs. Burton herded them outside and into the chaise, hastily dismissing the still sleepy ostlers who had come out to see what was afoot.

"Only a moment's stop at Myerly," she instructed the post-boy. "And then straight to Hornby Park."

"I just told him that," Daniel observed mildly, closing the door and squashing onto the seat beside Juliet. Gun lay on the floor in front of them. "Just rest your feet on him. He doesn't mind."

Juliet suspected the chaise had been designed to be spacious for one person because it was certainly cramped for two and a large dog. She was very aware of Daniel's shoulder and arm, and even the occasional touch of his thigh, as the vehicle weaved around bends in the road and rolled over bumps. He had been such a kind friend to her that it came almost as a shock to remember that he was, in fact, a very good-looking young man.

The realization confused her for a few moments, and she gazed ahead out of the front window, trying to be glad she was in home country. She supposed the butterflies in her stomach were from nerves concerning her family's welcome.

"He must be a total lunkhead, your betrothed," Daniel said suddenly. "Why would he throw over a beautiful, charming girl like you? Just because of lies in a so-called newspaper everyone despises!"

"Well, he has ambitions to follow his father into politics and thinks he needs to be pure as the driven snow, even though Lord Alford won't die for decades yet. I suppose he could stand for election to the House of C—" She broke off as the rest of his question penetrated her nervous brain. "Do you really think I'm beautiful and charming?"

"You must know you are. I can't have said anything you haven't heard a hundred times before."

"People do say such things," she admitted.

"But I've always known it was more to do with who my father is than my own attractions."

"You must have believed your betrothed, surely!"

"I believed in his devotion," Juliet admitted. "He did say very sweet things, not about such nonsense as beauty but about his feelings for me. I felt very lucky, very honored to have won such a man. Only I hadn't. His words were even less honest than the poetical rubbish about my eyes and lips and the way I turn my wrist in a beam of sunshine."

"Your wrist?" Daniel repeated, apparently entertained. He lifted her hand from her lap, pushing back the glove with his thumb to reveal her wrist, which he examined with curiosity. "It's very slender and elegant, certainly. As wrists go, it's a very pretty example. But did someone truly write a whole poem about it?"

"Well, one verse. He wrote it out on parchment and sent it to me with a rose. I thanked him civilly, but I confess I laughed." She smiled painfully. "However, he has the last laugh, since I promptly betrothed myself to Jeremy Catesby."

"Do you regret your poet now?" Idly, his forefinger stroked her wrist beneath the glove. She rather liked the sensation, but her mind was more on his question.

She shook her head. "No. I just regret my own stupidity."

His finger stilled. "It isn't stupid to expect loyalty from friends or family or betrothed husbands."

Tears prickled behind her eyes. "I had all the advantages birth and wealth could bring me. And still, I am not good enough."

"Good enough for what?" he demanded, squeezing her hand in a comforting way. He even dragged it to his lips and dropped a kiss on the back of her wrist. "For some gutless little weasel? Trust me, you deserve much better than that."

She let out a watery little laugh, hastily dashing her hand over her eyes.

Unexpectedly, his arm came around her in hug. "There, don't cry," he said comfortingly. "You've got home by yourself, and I'm sure your family will take care of everything. You are *much* better off without the weasel."

Just for an instant, she let herself hug him back in gratitude. "You have been so kind to me, Daniel. Thank you."

She was about to draw back, and his loosening arm was about to let her, when their eyes met, and she paused. A lock of black hair had fallen across his forehead. It came to her that his dark eyes, serious for once, were extraordinarily beautiful. As was the rest of him, in a careless, masculine kind of way. Her heart gave a funny little flutter.

A frown tugged at his brow. "Would you

mind if I…? Oh, the devil." He leaned closer and kissed her, a brief, sensual caress of his lips that parted hers the instant before ending.

Casually, he released her, dragging his arm back to his side. "A kiss of friendship," he said, "so don't get in a miff."

She blinked to dispel the daze. From somewhere, laughter bubbled up. "A *miff*?"

He grinned. "Well, I wouldn't blame you. Even I know kissing you is not considered proper, but it seemed appropriate at the time. Or at least irresistible."

"I think you are the most outrageous person I ever met, and you don't even know it."

"But I am harmless. Mostly. Do you think your mother would receive me if I called?"

"She'll probably be grateful in the circumstances! But would your grandfather not object?"

"I agreed to go and see him, not be locked in his mausoleum for a week."

Abruptly, Gun struggled into a sitting position, throwing off their feet and squashing their legs while he sniffed the air around the door.

"Don't you dare," Daniel warned him.

"Oh, we are coming up to Myerly," Juliet noticed. "Has he been here before?"

"No. But he'll have caught a whiff of some unknown animal, like a cow or a sheep. I should probably put him on a leash. If only I had one."

Juliet delved into her valise and rummaged

before coming out with a length of blue velvet ribbon. It was of a favorite shade and never worn, but she suspected Daniel's need was greater. "Would this do?"

"It's a bit fine for Gun."

"I don't need it," she assured him.

He took it with a grin of thanks, and as the chaise slowed, he proceeded to tie it around the dog's neck with a stout knot.

The carriage came to a halt at the Myerly cross-roads. From here, she could see the rather grim house through the neglected, overgrown grounds. She and her siblings had used to scare each other quite deliciously with made-up stories about this eerie house and Baron Miserly, who lived there.

Juliet held out her hand to the baron's grand-son. "Goodbye, Mr. Stewart."

He shook it. "Goodbye, but I wish you wouldn't be so formal."

"Daniel," she corrected. After all, she had already called him by his Christian name once.

"Dan is better." He released her hand with a smile and jumped down. Gun leapt after him with great excitement, almost pulling Daniel—Dan—off his feet, and then skidding to a halt and sitting as he felt the unfamiliar pull of his velvet leash.

Juliet laughed, and Dan, grinning, swept off his hat in a hasty bow before the chaise lurched forward again, and she lost them both from view. She was still smiling as she sat back and longed for home. There were still good people in the world, and Dan was right. Her family would support her.

⊱⊰

DAN HAD BEGUN his journey from London, gritting his teeth in order to do his duty. But as he strode along the road, with Gun alternately tying himself in knots, sitting down in bafflement and lunging excitedly in random directions, he found he was grinning to himself.

Of course, he should not have kissed Juliet Lilbourne for any reason, and he knew it as soon as he had given into temptation. Hence his insistence that it had been a friendship kiss.

It hadn't. Or at least, not entirely, but that way led to danger, and he would take better care of his wayward impulses in the future. Not that he regretted kissing her, for she was soft and sweet and smelled delightfully of flowers, but she was a little too heady for the senses of a prodigal young man with no prospects.

Still, he liked her, and he had hope they could continue their friendship and bolster each other's spirits through what was bound to be a difficult period for both of them.

To his surprise, the Myerly gates were open, and he didn't have to bang and shout to be let in, as had happened the last time he'd come. He walked on up the drive, noticing as he drew nearer the forbidding old house that at least half the shutters were open. Normally, the place looked deserted, with the poor servants having to scuttle about in the semi-gloom to fulfill the wishes of their cantankerous lord.

Perhaps the old devil had cheered up. Perhaps he would even speak to his daughter. Or visit his neighbors, like Lord Cosland over at Hornby Park.

Walking across the weed-strewn terrace, he straightened his shoulders and drew Gun to heel by his velvet leash. He knocked loudly at the door, for most of the servants were old and deaf.

To his surprise, the door was opened almost immediately by Griffin, the ancient butler, who beamed with genuine pleasure and flung the door wide. "Mr. Dan! That is welcome, Mr. Stewart, come—"

With a joyful bark, Gun tore his leash free of Dan's too-careless hand and dashed past Griffin, who flattened himself against the door in terror.

"Oh, the devil," Dan said ruefully. "Sorry, Griffin, he wouldn't deliberately hurt a fly, but he is clumsy as a bear. Hold on, I'll catch him."

Dan loped after the dog in the direction of the kitchen, but Gun suddenly swerved, went up on his hind legs to push open the door of the breakfast parlor, and bounded inside.

"Trapped him," Dan said with satisfaction, for his grandfather never used the parlor. He always had his breakfast in bed. However, a feminine shriek mingled suddenly with the unmistakable sound of breaking crockery, and a male yell.

Assuming Gun had startled the servants with an over-enthusiastic introduction, Dan followed, a casual apology on his lips, and stopped dead.

The room seemed full of people, but they were not servants. Two aunts and a cousin around the breakfast table had sprung to their feet in alarm. Gun stood halfway between the table and the sideboard, as though torn between which to ravage first. He was certainly capable of reaching the food on either. The sideboard was unprotected, but Gun liked humans, and he may have imagined these ones could be induced to deliver tidbits and save him from Dan's ire.

Almost mechanically, Dan moved forward and trapped the velvet leash under his foot before reaching for the scruff of Gun's neck. The dog whined and gazed longingly at the table.

Three people glared at Dan.

"I should have known!" his cousin Colin Cornwell exclaimed in disgust. "Is this animal with you?"

Dan ignored that for the thought uppermost

in mind. "Good Lord, the old boy's not really about to croak, is he?"

"I suppose that is why you came!" Aunt Tabetha accused. "And think to frighten us all off with this monster while you steal my poor father's money!"

"Oh, dear," said Aunt Hetty. She generally said this quite a lot.

"Good morning," Dan said wryly. "A delight to see you all again, too."

"Perhaps," Griffin intoned behind him, "the animal would be happier outside?"

Dan held out the velvet leash. "Perhaps in the walled garden. And if someone could find him a bowl of scraps from the kitchen, he'd be very grateful. He won't hurt anyone, you know. Unless I tell him to," he added with an amiable smile at his cousin Colin. "Gun, be good."

The dog wagged his tail and went obediently enough with the wary Griffin, who held the leash at arm's length. Gun glanced back a couple of times, clearly hoping Dan was coming, too. But Dan's stomach was rumbling, and he needed to talk to his family.

"How is my grandfather?" he asked abruptly.

"I'm sure you'll receive a summons and see for yourself," Colin said, holding his mother's chair so that she could sit back down.

Aunt Hetty didn't wait for the courtesy, merely sat and cast a tentative smile at Dan.

"I did receive a summons," Dan said. "That's why I'm here."

"Then I've no doubt you'll receive a second summons to his bedchamber," Colin said. "Always a pleasure. I suppose you had better have some breakfast."

"I suppose I had," Dan agreed. He didn't much like Colin, and he particularly didn't care for the implication that he stood in as host for their grandfather. He even sat at the head of the table.

"Shouldn't you change first?" Aunt Tabetha asked, looking Dan up and down.

"Probably, but I'm starving." He helped himself from the meager leavings on the sideboard—namely two slices of toast, some very thinly cut ham, and the scrapings from a bowl of eggs. But at least there was coffee.

Dan sat down beside the more timid of his aunts and smiled at her. "How are you, Aunt Hetty?"

"Oh, dear. Quite well. Apart from rheumatism, you know, but... How handsome you are, Daniel. Jenny must be so—"

"How did you get here?" Aunt Tabetha interrupted ruthlessly. Normally, their infamous sister was not mentioned in the family except on the very few occasions they met.

"Stagecoach," Dan replied.

Colin blinked. "With that animal? Or did you

buy him in Kidfield, specifically to annoy us?"

Dan took a mouthful of coffee and set about piling some eggs and ham onto his toast. "You might find it hard to believe, but I don't actually consider you at all in the ordering of my life."

"*Is* there order to your life?" Aunt Tabetha wondered.

"Not much." Dan bit into his toast and regarded his relatives while he chewed and swallowed. Tabetha and Colin Cornwell were, as always, immaculately dressed, the former in a severe brown morning gown and a stiff lace cap over her graying locks. Colin's coat was excellently cut, new, and clearly from one of London's foremost tailors. His hair was cut short and brushed forward into the fashionable "Brutus" style. Aunt Hetty looked no less expensive, just with less severity. Her hair tended to escape from its pretty cap, and she trailed several shawls half-falling from her neck and her arms.

Beside them, Dan was sure he looked exactly what he was: the poor relation. Once, it had bewildered him. Now, he didn't care. Except that if Colin inherited the old man's money, he'd make sure none of it went anywhere near Dan's mother. Hetty's son Hugh was better natured. Probably. But Hugh wasn't here, and Dan suspected Colin had come to try and cut them all out of the old man's will. Hence, his consternation at seeing Dan.

"What's wrong with my grandfather?" Dan asked abruptly. "He isn't really dying, is he?"

"If you don't think he's dying, why did you come?" Aunt Tabetha asked with a sniff.

"Because he asked me to."

Colin scowled. "He really did send for you, too?"

They were circling like vultures, Dan thought with distaste, and some unease, for it seemed the old man, who'd always seemed indomitable to the point of indestructible, could indeed be on the way out. Or else, he wanted them all to think that. Old Baron Miserly was a master manipulator.

The door opened once more. Waits, the baron's valet, who was even older than Griffin, entered and bowed.

"His lordship requests Mr. Stewart's company."

Daniel took a last mouthful of coffee and stood, picking up his toast to eat on the way. "I don't imagine he put it quite like that," he said wryly, remembering to bow briefly to his aunts. *"Bring me that wastrel now!* seems more likely."

Waits permitted himself a faint smile. "I cannot remember his lordship's precise words, sir."

"Yes, you can," Dan said, following him from the room. Actually, he was glad to see Waits, who was likelier to have sensible information about the old man. "How is he, Waits?"

"He's been sinking," Waits admitted. "Seemed certain he was going to die."

"Is that why he sent for us all?"

"I believe so. But having done so, he appeared to rally."

"Probably at the thought of us all at each other's throats," Dan observed.

An unidentifiable sound escaped Waits's throat. "I could not say, sir. I *will* say the fact that you did not come agitated him."

Dan cast the old valet a twisted smile. "I told him I wouldn't come back without my mother."

"And yet, here you are," Waits observed.

Dan sighed. "Here I am. Wondering if blood is indeed thicker than water, or at least more powerful than common sense."

Waits was wheezing by the time they reached the top of the staircase, and Dan reflected it was just like his grandfather to send the old man all the way down for him, rather than have a sprier footman or maid carry the message. Dan curbed his impatience and his stride to allow Waits a slow walk along the winding passage to his lordship's rooms.

There was an antechamber, where once Lord Myerly had dealt with barbers, tailors, doctors, and anyone else he chose to summon to his presence. Dan's unease increased to see the old man was not in his chair by the fireplace. Waits led him through to the bedchamber.

It was faintly musty and gloomy since just one shutter had been opened a crack. Dan was sure the old man had only allowed in that much light to save on candles. The curtains of the huge bed were open, and Lord Myerly sat propped up on a fine array of pillows. He looked tiny, causing an uncomfortable twinge in Dan's heart. He really wasn't well.

"You came," his lordship observed in a shaky but still somehow gloating tone.

"Only for your money," Dan said, staring down at the old man.

"So now you'll accept my conditions for making you my heir?"

"Lord, no. Just give my mother a livable allowance, and I'll get out of your hair for good. You can leave the rest of your money where you like."

"Why, thank you," mocked the old man. "I'll bear that in mind. So, you've said your piece. You can go now."

"Thanks," Dan said, sitting on the edge of the bed. "What's wrong with you, apart from spleen?"

"I'm old. I'm dying. I'm allowed to be grumpy."

"You were born grumpy."

"And you were born insolent! What do you

mean crashing into my house with some kind of monster?"

"I thought he'd amuse you. Shall I bring him up?"

The old man's eyes gleamed.

"Don't send poor old Waits," Dan begged. "Send a footman."

His grandfather flicked a glance at Waits, who inclined his head and headed to the door.

"If they're frightened of the dog, tell them just to open the door," Dan advised. "He'll run straight up here—providing the dining room door is firmly shut."

"So," his grandfather asked, fixing him with a suddenly piercing stare, "what have you done since I last saw you two—three?—years ago?"

"I lost at cards," Dan replied. "Won at dice. Then lost again."

"I heard you seduced a cit's daughter."

"Well, I didn't, and I'm surprised you pay attention to such vulgar gossip."

"Why did you lose your position, then?" the old man demanded. "You must have done something to the girl."

"I never touched her. Why would I do anything so stupid?"

"Like father, like son," the old man mocked. "He went in for a bit of seduction, too."

"Actually, he went in for a bit of marriage," Dan retorted. "As you know very well, or you wouldn't even be considering me as your heir."

"Hah!" Lord Myerly said rudely. He regarded Dan thoughtfully. "I've asked the others, so I'll ask you, too. I can't do a thing about the title, or the entailed property at Fallow. That will go to some second cousin none of us have ever even met. But what should I do with *this* place? And the rest of my money?"

"Whatever you want. That's what you'll do, regardless of what I or anyone else says."

"True. But it happens I want your opinion."

Dan shrugged impatiently. "Divide it between your daughters."

"Waste of good property."

Dan regarded him. "See? You didn't want my opinion."

The old man scowled. "What the devil is *that*?"

That was the galloping footsteps and excited wheefling of Gun as he bolted upstairs and along the passage, his claws scratching dementedly on the floor as he slid.

Dan grinned, and the great beast galumphed through the door of the antechamber, where Waits clearly dropped something with a resounding clatter. Gun bounded into the bedroom and straight onto the bed, from where he threw his front paws onto Dan's shoulders and enthusiastically licked his face.

By the time Dan shoved the dog off, his

grandfather was howling with glee.

"I'll say this for you, Dan, you're not boring!"

Dan grinned, holding onto Gun's neck to prevent him from squashing the old man.

Lord Myerly's eyes glinted with malice. "And I'll say this for the dog. I'll bet he scares the devil out of your aunts and cousin."

CHAPTER FIVE

L EAVING THE STATELY if avuncular Abbot to pay the post boy, Juliet ran up the steps and into the house she had always called home. Her mother was rushing across the hall, her cap askew.

Relief flooded Juliet. "Oh, Mama," she said shakily, and flew to meet her.

But her mother's arms did not so much embrace as drag her toward the marble staircase. "Oh, Juliet, where have you been? What have you *done*?"

"I haven't done anything except leave London because I had nowhere else to go. Lady Alford has turned against me. Jeremy—"

"Yes, well, we shall talk about Jeremy in private. Did you post to Kidfield?"

"From Kidfield," Juliet said cautiously, allowing herself to be swept upstairs. Her mother's fingers digging into her arm warned her to stay silent until they reached her mother's boudoir.

There, the countess released her and sank onto the chaise longue in the center of the room.

"What happened?" she demanded. "Were you with the princess?"

"The princess had gone," Juliet said flatly. "Three other ladies and I were tricked into attending. At least I have to assume it was a trick. We didn't discover Her Highness was not there until the next morning."

"Dear God. You spent the night alone in that house without a chaperone? Please tell me you were not seen, that there was no orgy taking place under the same roof?"

Suddenly weary, Juliet sat beside her mother and dragged off her bonnet. "I may have been seen, but by no one who was sober enough to remember. I suppose the four of us chaperoned each other, but beyond that, no."

Her mother took both her hands, squashing the bonnet on Juliet's lap. "Julie, did anyone…any *man* insult you, *hurt* you?"

Juliet shook her head. "No, we locked ourselves in the sitting room next to the princess's apartments in case we had to rush to her rescue. But no one came near us."

"Well, thank God for that, at any rate," her mother said, pressing her hands. "But oh, Juliet, how could you be so silly as not to know…"

Juliet blushed. "It was not unusual for Her Highness to have…private guests."

"Oh, for the love of… I *told* your father I did not want you exposed to such matters, but he said you were all but engaged, and then, of course, you *were* engaged."

"And now I'm not," Juliet said flatly. "I was never more mistaken about anything or anyone than I was in my trust for Jeremy Catesby."

"I know. He wrote your father the most *insolent* letter, kindly enclosing a so-called newspaper I would not use for night-soil."

Juliet giggled, though of course, it was not really funny. Daniel Stewart's irreverent humor seemed to have rubbed off on her.

Her mother didn't appear to notice. "As for Maria Alford! When I think about what I have done for that woman in the past and how she has repaid me… How *dare* she turn you away from the door? Without even troubling to see how you would get home." The countess frowned. "How *did* you get home? Please say post."

"Stagecoach," Juliet admitted. "Jeremy tried to give me money, but I threw it in his face."

"A mistake," her mother said mournfully. "Understandable, but definitely a mistake. Your father won't like this either."

"Is he angry?" Juliet asked with a hint of nervousness, for although she was used to twisting him around her little finger, he was a rather formidable man.

"Furious," her mother said frankly. "With the Alfords *and* with you for putting him in such a position. Apart from anything else, you must know we are to have a dinner party here to celebrate Kitty's engagement and—"

"Kitty is engaged?" Juliet interrupted, distracted by this startling news about her sister. "Who to?"

"Lawrence King. It is a decent match, and there is some expectation from an uncle, I believe, so—"

"Does she love him?" Juliet interrupted. "Because if she isn't *completely* sure, she shouldn't go near him. What's more—"

"What is this?" asked the unmistakable and highly sarcastic voice of her father. "Lessons in marriage from the girl who just lost all chance of a husband?"

Juliet had been so involved with saving her sister that she had not registered the opening of the boudoir door until her father spoke and closed it behind him. She jumped to her feet. "Papa."

Her father threw something onto the sofa, "Is that true?"

She saw at once it was the same scandal sheet she had already seen in the hands of Jeremy and later Oily George.

"Of course not," she said indignantly.

"She was there," her mother said grimly. "Entirely innocent and physically unhurt, but she was there alone with the other three girls."

"God in heaven." He strode across the room to the window.

Juliet swallowed. "Mama says Jeremy—Mr. Catesby—wrote to you. So, you know my engagement has ended."

"Don't worry about Catesby," her father said savagely. "I'll get the little toad back for you. One way or another."

"But I don't want the little toad," she exclaimed, before laughter struck her once more, quite unaware. There was an element of hysteria to this, along with Daniel Stewart. She coughed to sober herself. "I would not take him back if he begged me on his knees."

Her father turned and glared at her. "You no longer have a say in the matter. You are ruined and will take whatever husband we can get for you. At this stage, all we can hope for is that you have not ruined Kitty's chances too."

Juliet whitened, raising both hands to her cold cheeks. "Oh, no. Kitty…"

"Which is why you will stay here, out of sight," her father said grimly. "When we have guests, you will retire to your chamber. You will not even dine with us in such circumstances. Is that clear?"

"Yes, Papa," she whispered.

"There will be no morning calls, no riding, or even walking except within the grounds of Hornby Park."

"But, Papa…"

"Is that clear?" he bellowed.

Her chin came up, though she wanted to weep. "Perfectly."

➤➤➤❰❰❰❮

KITTY, OTHERWISE LADY Katherine Lilbourne, had just endured her first London Season. Pretty but shy, she had not truly enjoyed the social whirl, as she confided to Juliet over breakfast.

"I did not *take* the way you did, and to be truthful, I was glad to come home. Mama was disappointed, I think, but then we received the offer from Mr. King."

"Do you love him?" Juliet asked curiously, for they had known Lawrence King all their lives. His father owned a decent property on the other side of Kidfield, and they frequently met at assemblies and at dinner parties as well as less formal occasions like riding expeditions and al frescoes. Juliet had always liked him, but he had seemed more of an extra brother than a prospective husband.

Kitty blushed. "I always did. He never minds

if I stutter or say foolish things. And he doesn't think me less beautiful than you."

"You aren't," Juliet said, startled. "But these aren't reasons to love someone."

"I don't need a reason. I just do."

"Oh, Kitty, I'm sorry if I have made this difficult for you…"

"Lawrence won't care. Even if you had done something wrong, which I know you didn't, he would still stand your friend."

"Then he is worth a hundred so-called brilliant matches like Jeremy," Juliet said fiercely.

"I'm sorry," Kitty said anxiously. "Is your heart broken?"

"At the moment, I think I am too angry. Even Papa called him a toad. And Da—a friend of mine—calls him a weasel. I would hate to marry a weasel, so I am actually grateful I discovered this before our wedding. But I will keep out of the way for your party."

"I would rather you were there," Kitty said ruefully. "Besides, won't people ask where you are?"

"They probably won't dare, but if they do, I imagine Mama and Papa will have an answer ready."

Kitty nodded sagely. "They may even change their minds. Papa is too angry at the moment. He feels this broken engagement as a slight to himself."

Juliet glanced about the room to be sure there were no servants there. "Did you know Papa had a broken engagement of his own? Which may be one reason he is so angry about mine."

Kitty's eyes widened. "No!"

"Apparently, he was engaged to Lord Myerly's daughter, who then ran away with an army officer. Which I suppose must have been quite humiliating for him. At any rate, he quarreled with Myerly, and that's the real reason we don't visit."

"Well, no one else visits either," Kitty pointed out. "But I suppose they could be following Papa's lead. How do you know this?"

"From the son of the lady in question," Juliet confided. "I met him on the stagecoach. He'd been summoned to the old gentleman's death bed, though he doesn't believe he's really dying."

"Oh, dear... What is he like?" Kitty asked curiously. "The grandson?"

"Not like anyone you've met before," Juliet said with the glimmer of a laugh. "He's very casual in his manners, doesn't give two hoots that he's poor and had to travel on the roof. But he's very kind and funny."

"You like him."

"I do, and I hope he will call here because you will like him, too."

"I'm sure I will," Kitty agreed. "But if Mama

won't let you be with her to receive guests?"

"Oh, they must make an exception for Dan. He already knows everything."

Kitty gazed at her, clearly troubled. "Was that wise, Julie?"

Away from him, it didn't feel quite so wise, but Juliet merely shrugged, and they went to find their brother Ferdy, Viscount Albright, and go for a walk in the garden. However, before Ferdy had even come downstairs, their mother swept Kitty away to visit her betrothed's family.

Kitty's pleas for Juliet to come, too, fell on deaf ears.

Juliet understood. Although she would have liked to see Lawrence again and watch him closely with Kitty, just to be sure he loved her, she appreciated the difficulty. Kitty's engagement stood on a knife edge because of Juliet.

But I am not responsible! she raged helplessly. *What could I have done differently?*

She asked the same question of her brother Ferdy when he ran her to earth in the formal gardens. Dressed for riding, he hugged her with careless, brotherly affection and asked what the devil she'd been about.

"Nothing! I simply sat there till they were all unconscious from drink and then left! I ask you, Ferdy, what else could I have done?"

Ferdy scratched his head. "Hard to see. Even if you'd discovered earlier that Her Highness was gone, the chances are you'd have been seen fleeing the scene. Which might have looked even worse."

"Someone has thought this out very carefully," Juliet said, glaring at a new rose bush. "Made sure we were doomed from the moment we stepped over the threshold."

"Don't see that," Ferdy protested. "You could have stepped straight back out again. I wish you had, to be honest."

Juliet sighed. "So do I. But I had no reason to. None of us did. You're dressed for riding, Ferdy. Do you want to take a walk up to the river instead?"

"Can't today," he said apologetically. "Hunting with the Haretons. In fact, I'm late."

"Hurry, then. I'll see you at dinner."

Clearly grateful not to be pinned down any longer, Ferdy strode off toward the stables, leaving Juliet to her restless pacing and brooding about the garden.

In the end, she went back inside and found a book to read.

Luncheon in only her father's company was not a success either. He barely spoke, and his expression was far too forbidding for her to bring up anything to do with her ruin, or even about his own broken engagement to Daniel's mother.

He left abruptly, and the afternoon stretched out endlessly before Juliet. She found her old watercolor things and eventually went outside with her easel to see what she could paint. But her heart was not in it, and she greeted the sound of her mother's returning carriage with relief. Abandoning her unimpressive picture, she flew to meet them.

"How is Lawrence?" she demanded of Kitty.

"Well, of course!"

"And you are still engaged?"

Kitty laughed. "Of course I am."

"Thank God. Do you suppose they know about me?"

Kitty met her gaze. "Lawrence does."

"But not his parents?"

"I don't know what Mama discussed with Mrs. King. It makes no difference, you know. We will be married anyway."

"It will make a difference to your comfort, Kitty," Juliet said anxiously. "Imagine if you were not received by his family."

"I will imagine no such thing," Kitty said firmly, and Juliet bit her lip, realizing that forcing her own guilt-inspired fears on her sister was neither kind nor helpful at this stage.

Dinner was a livelier meal since Ferdy had an array of hunting stories to share, and the conversation flowed from there. It was good to laugh, and even the countess joined in. Only the earl sat morose and silent at the head of the table.

After dinner, when the ladies were alone in

the drawing room, Juliet said, "You can't keep my presence a secret. The servants will talk."

"Everyone will eventually know you are here," her mother agreed. "But no one will have seen you, and no one will mention you."

"As if I've been painted over."

"Don't be fanciful, Juliet," her mother scolded.

She sighed. "Sorry. But what if people stop calling?"

"I don't believe they will," her mother replied. "Not when it becomes clear we will not thrust your company upon them."

It still came as a shock to realize she was now more of a pariah than the Princess of Wales. She felt herself shriveling from the inside.

⇶⥸⥸⥸⥜⥜⥜

INEVITABLY, PERHAPS, AN early night and a good sleep revived Juliet's optimism. Breakfast with both her siblings improved her spirits further, especially when she realized they had no engagements that day. Even the onset of rain didn't subdue her.

"We can play hide-and-seek," she suggested, and her siblings laughed with delight at the childhood memory.

However, as they were planning it, their

mother let out a shriek from the staircase and bolted into the breakfast parlor. "Juliet, go away. The vicar's wife is here!"

And Juliet had to trail back up to her bed-chamber. She felt the remaining joy in life trickle out of her.

This is my life as a ruined lady. All I have to look forward to is not ruining the lives of my sister and brother... Which was worthy but undeniably dull.

Juliet, go away. How often would she have to hear that in the coming days, months, years...?

I need to get used to humiliation and boredom.

It certainly gave her fresh insight into the princess's life and the effects of the insults she had borne from her husband and his family.

Watching from the window seat of her bed-chamber where she sat with the book open in her lap at the same page, she waited for the vicar's wife to leave. Before she did, the Misses Fairfax from Kidfield arrived in their ancient carriage. The vicar's wife left, and then Mr. Wharton from Hallow Hall rode up.

She began to suspect they had all come to find out what they could about Juliet's scandal. The thought made her face burn.

At least they had all left by the time luncheon was served, although Juliet's appetite seemed to have vanished. She barely minded when another knock sounded from the front door.

"Juliet," her father began, but she was already

on her feet.

"I know, *Go away.*" She walked out of the room and up the side stairs to her bedchamber, just in case she was seen from the front door.

Once more, she took up her position in the window seat, with the unread book in her lap. There was no carriage or horse waiting on the terrace below, so the visitor must have been someone familiar enough to go straight round to the stables. Kitty's betrothed, perhaps. Juliet prayed he hadn't come to end the engagement, or at least to persuade Kitty to do so.

But whoever it was had not been admitted to the house. A man strode impetuously down the front steps. Something about that long-legged stride was instantly familiar, as was the rakish angle of the hat that had seen better days, even the faded shade of his coat.

With a crow of delight, Juliet tossed aside her book and threw up the window, "Dan!" she hissed, and when he didn't hear, called again more loudly, *"Dan!"*

He paused, turning to scan the windows. She thrust her head out and waved. Grinning, he raised his hand in response. She pointed urgently at the drive, mouthing, *Wait for me!* It was anyone's guess whether or not he understood, for he merely tipped his hat and walked away.

Juliet closed the widow, seized her bonnet and an old cloak, and flew out of the room, along the passage to the west stairs which led, conveniently, to one of the side doors. Emerging into the little-used part of the garden, she hurried off in the direction of the wood that bordered the left-hand side of the drive.

She found him at last, seated on a tree trunk within sight of the drive. He held a knife and was whittling away at a piece of wood, but he glanced up at her hurried approach and smiled.

He rose, dropping the knife and the wood into his slightly sagging pocket, and took off his hat to sweep her an elaborate bow. "Lady Juliet."

"Mr. Stewart." She curtsied in the same fashion but spoiled the effect by immediately bursting into a much less formal greeting. "Oh, Dan, I am so pleased to see you! How is your grandfather?"

"I'm not sure, to be honest. He was low yesterday, much lower than I thought he would be. But he seems less…*faded* today. I think I might be annoying him back to health."

"A novel approach."

"I'm surprised it works when I consider all his other annoyances. My relations are circling like vultures. I found two aunts and a cousin already taking root, and now I believe another cousin and an uncle are on their way."

"Perhaps he summoned them as he did you?"

"Oh, he did, at least my aunts and Colin. It's possible he has summoned Cousin Hugh, too, though I know for a fact, the old devil doesn't like him. And I'm as sure I can be, he never summoned either of my uncles. Still, not my place to throw them out."

As he spoke, his eyes had been searching her face, and almost without pause, he asked, "How was your homecoming?"

She wrinkled her nose. "Awful. Shall we walk through the woods? At least the rain has gone off."

He fell into step beside her, listening to her tale of her father's anger with the Alfords as well as with her, Kitty's engagement, and her banishment from all outside company.

"Ah," Dan said, holding an inconveniently trailing branch aside for her. "I wonder if that was why they wouldn't let me in? I didn't have a card, so I asked for you and was immediately told you were not at home. I should have asked for your mother."

"She still wouldn't have let me see you. There have been people in and out of the house all day, no doubt ferreting out the scandal. It's very lowering to think I've known these people all my life."

"Perhaps they came to offer their support," Dan suggested.

"It's possible," she allowed, brightening. "I shouldn't let Jeremy's behavior sour my view of decent people. It just made me realize I don't actually know who *is* decent." She stopped, frowning suddenly. "Gun! Where is Gun?"

Dan grinned. "I left him guarding my family. It struck me he might hinder my attempts to get into your house. Wish I'd brought him now."

She walked on. "You might as well have done so. This path leads around to the top of the woods, or that way down to the gate."

"Or we could carry on to Myerly," he suggested. "You could see Gun and meet my family. Since they won't meet anyone else in the neighborhood, you might as well. And I'd bring you back again."

She was tempted. "I would like to see Gun," she said ruefully at last. "And I am definitely intrigued by your family, but I'm not supposed to leave the grounds. I should at least *begin* by being obedient."

His eyes gleamed with amusement. "That doesn't bode well for future conduct."

"I will break out eventually," she said with a sigh. "It's pretty intolerable already, being excluded from everything and having nothing to do but brood on my own misfortunes and wonder who wrote that dreadful story in the paper. I won't even be able to sneak out to meet you very often, or they will notice." She brightened. "Unless you rise early?"

"Gun does. We could meet you in the same place at seven tomorrow."

"Done," she said promptly, and the day improved miraculously.

CHAPTER SIX

JULIET WAS FORBIDDEN dinner with the family that night since Lawrence King was joining them. Although Juliet was able to accept her dismissal philosophically enough, Kitty cast her several anxious glances and followed her up to her bedchamber.

"I will bring him to meet you at some point," Kitty assured her. "He will be happy to do so."

"No, don't," Juliet said. "We shouldn't give him anything to lie about. Merely pass on my good wishes."

Kitty sat beside her in the window. "You are very good, Juliet. This must be so hard for you."

She shrugged. "I expect it will get harder." *When Dan leaves Myerly, for one thing.*

"Cheer up. Papa might yet manage some miracle with the Alfords. I know he wrote to

Jeremy today."

"I could not marry Jeremy now."

"But if there had been some mistake…"

"The mistake was mine for believing in him," Juliet declared. "He knew exactly what he was doing, and it cost him no more than a moment's inconvenience, not even the twenty pounds he was prepared to give me to make me go away."

All the same, she sat on the stairs to hear the chatter and merry laughter drifting out of the dining room and felt her exclusion like an unjust punishment.

>>>><<<<

THE NEXT MORNING, she rose with the dawn, washed, dressed, and slipped downstairs. She did have to step over the maid scrubbing the hall floor, but that didn't matter. She was allowed to walk the grounds.

She found Daniel in almost the same place as yesterday. This time, he leaned his shoulder against a broad oak, his hat pushed to the back of his head as he raised his face to the rising sun. Gun, attached to his slightly bedraggled velvet leash, sat on his foot, gazing at her as she emerged from the trees, before jumping up in great excitement and tugging his master toward her.

"Good morning!" she said, laughing and bending to make a fuss of the dog before he jumped on her. "How delighted I am to see you, Mr. Gun." She straightened, glancing up at Daniel, while the dog slobbered over her hand. "No carving today?"

"Oh, I finished it." He fished inside his disreputable coat pocket and gave her something. The figure fitted inside her closed hand. It was, unmistakably, a dog with lots of hair.

"It's Gun," she exclaimed.

"I thought you could look at it when you miss him. It's much more peaceful than the real thing."

"You mean it's for me?" She was touched. He did not even mention her inevitable loneliness, just a casual reference to missing the dog, which anyone might take as humorous.

"If you'd like it. If not, just give it to someone else."

"Of course, I would not give it to anyone else. I love it. Thank you."

He seemed almost embarrassed by her thanks, for his eyes dropped to the path before he set off with unnecessary speed. She caught up, and they half-walked, half-ran among the trees with Gun between them.

She took him to the river, which was regarded as the boundary of the home grounds. It was also the boundary between Hornby and Myerly.

There, Dan took a napkin-wrapped parcel from his pocket before removing his coat and throwing it on the ground for her to sit.

"Breakfast," Dan said, sprawling opposite her and opening the napkin to reveal bread, cheese, and two slices of ham. Gun gazed at it soulfully.

"I perceive you have made friends with your grandfather's cook."

"It seemed worth the risk. My aunts and cousin rise early so they can nab all the food before me. To be fair, my grandfather does not keep what you might regard as a generous table."

"What do they do with themselves all day? What do *you* do?"

"My aunts doze and complain, respectively. My cousin reads worthy tomes and writes letters. I've been wandering around the estate with Gun, just looking. It's pretty country. I didn't recognize that when I was here before."

"My father always said that Myerly was good land," she recalled. "But that—" She broke off apologetically and reached for a piece of cheese.

"That my grandfather was neglecting it?" he suggested.

"Is he?"

"Probably. Or ruining it. I'm no farmer, but his tenants don't look very prosperous. That isn't right."

"No," she agreed. Then, frowning, she asked, "What will happen to the land when Lord Myerly dies? He only has daughters, does he not?"

"Yes, but he can will it where he likes. By some historical oddity, it is not Myerly but an estate in the south that is entailed with the title. Some distant cousin will get that. My aunts want Myerly and the rest for their sons."

"Does your mother not want it for you?"

"Probably, but she's a realist. He is more likely *not* to give it to me if *she* asks him to."

"Is he really so unforgiving? Even now?"

Dan shrugged. Swallowing the last of his bread, he picked up a stone, smoothed his thumb over it, and threw it at the river where it bounced a gratifying three times. "He's up to something. Probably just setting us all at each other's throats for his own entertainment. But he's a manipulative old devil, and I don't like to have my strings pulled."

He cast another, slightly larger stone straight into the water. For some reason, this one attracted Gun's attention, and the dog shot after it, trailing his velvet leash behind him.

"Oh, dear, can he swim?" Juliet asked.

"Apparently," Dan said, clearly entertained by Gun's antics. Paddling dementedly, he vanished under the water and popped up again before Dan had made more than a slight movement in his direction. "He's got a stone in his mouth!"

"The same one?" Juliet asked, impressed.

"Who knows?"

Gun was paddling furiously back to them, but it seemed he began to enjoy the water for its own sake, for he changed direction several times, splashing and barking, perhaps following the paths of fish he could see below.

"Oh, no," Dan warned as Gunn eventually hauled himself out of the river and galumphed up to them, the stone still held firmly in his mouth, water streaming from his long hair. Reaching over, Dan dragged the hood of Juliet's cloak over her head and threw one arm over her. "Take cover!"

Gun shook himself mightily. Water sprayed everywhere, which pleased him so much, he thrust his wet face between Dan and Juliet and licked them impartially until Dan hauled him off.

They were laughing so much they didn't hear anything else until it was too late to hide.

A young couple, also laughing, were walking hand-in-hand along the opposite bank of the river. Inevitably, they gawped across the water at Dan, Juliet, and the dog. The man, a farmer of some kind, grinned and tugged his hat. Then, clearly recognizing Juliet, he dragged it off and bowed. The girl, who was nearest the water, sprang to the man's other side in clear alarm, turning her face away until they had rounded the bend out of sight.

"Interesting," Dan observed. "Why would

she hide from you?"

"She wouldn't," Juliet said thoughtfully. "I think she was hiding from you."

"How can you tell?"

"I grew up here. I'm the earl's family. Most of the country people know who I am, like the farmer. He's not one of our tenants, but he knew me. She didn't, but she still hid."

"Perhaps she hides from everyone. I just hope she doesn't blab and get you in trouble."

"I couldn't really be in more trouble."

"Then you'll meet me again tomorrow?"

"We can meet here if you like. Just around the bend is a wooden bridge and a shortcut to Myerly over the fields. So, it's a little bit closer for you."

For a moment, a rare, troubled expression flickered in his eyes.

"You don't need to pander to my boredom," she said hastily. "I am happy to walk alone."

"But it's more fun with a friend," he said lightly. He rose and stretched his hand down to help her to her feet. "For me, at least. I'll walk with you back to the drive."

"No, there will be more people around now, and you needn't add another mile or so to your journey." Suddenly, she was very aware that her hand still lay in his, that they stood close together, and that for some reason connected to those things, she could no longer breathe easily.

In the chaise, he had kissed her.

Butterflies fluttered in her stomach. She whipped her hand free and stepped back with a bright smile. "Goodbye!"

⤜⤜⤜✖⤚⤚⤚

DAN WATCHED HER go with another twinge of unease. She had seemed suddenly eager to be away from him, as though she had sensed his doubts about future meetings. Well, he did have doubts, which had nothing to do with his wishes but with a rare and inconvenient sense of responsibility. He liked her company—too much if the truth were told—and was glad to alleviate the boredom for them both, to give her a little cheer and happiness in the midst of her troubles.

But she truly did not need any further scandal in her life, and being discovered in clandestine meetings would bring just that. However innocent they were. After all, she was innocent too in the disgrace already surrounding her.

Gun thrust his head under Dan's hand, and he turned away from the vital, determined figure hurrying through the trees. Since the velvet leash was soggy, he let Gun lope along beside him. He was too tired after his long walk and swim to run very far.

By the time they crossed the bridge, Dan

knew he could not desert her, as even her family was doing, punishing her for another's crime, for being in the wrong place at the wrong time and trying to do the right thing. In this situation, she needed him, which was a novelty for Dan. He would just have to take greater care that they were not discovered.

It was quite clear when he reached Myerly land. The fields looked different. The scattered cottages were neglected, as was the hamlet where he stopped at the tavern for a mug of small beer. He strolled outside and sat on the bench, Gun at his side. Being friendly by nature, he fell into conversation with a passing laborer and then walked most of the way to the house with a tenant farmer.

The conversations were enlightening, confirming his suspicions about his grandfather's neglect of the land, but providing him with some actual knowledge. It was an interesting problem in its own way, and his mind alternated between farming and Juliet as he strolled up the drive, now holding onto the increasingly stringy, damp velvet. He really needed a length of leather.

Griffin opened the door, his eyes wide and almost popping.

"What's the matter?" Dan asked, amused, brushing past him. "It's only mud. The dog—" He broke off, his mouth falling open as he understood Griffin's astonishment.

It had nothing to do with Dan, or even Gun, but with the lady drifting across the hall, smiling at him as if they had already met for breakfast this morning.

"Good morning, Dan," she said cheerfully.

He closed his mouth and, giving in to Gun's demented pulling at his leash, went forward to embrace her. "Mother."

She clung to him for a moment, while Gun, whining with joy, pressed against her skirts. Behind her usual insouciance, it was not easy for her to be back here, with the old tyrant upstairs and her sisters…

Over his mother's head, he saw his aunts in the doorway of the breakfast parlor. Hetty looked anxious, Tabetha, thin-lipped and grim. Behind them, Colin appeared, looking Dan up and down as though more pained by the state of his dress than by the presence of the scandalous Mrs. Stewart.

"Perhaps the drawing room?" Griffin murmured, and Dan saw that several servants had gathered outside the baize door, smiling hugely but goggle-eyed and avid to see the next quarrel.

"Excellent idea," Dan said, releasing the leash into Griffin's care and offering his arm to his mother. "Have you eaten?"

"Sadly, breakfast is over."

Dan glanced behind him at Griffin, who, having hastily passed the dog to a footman, inclined his head. "Of course, sir."

Colin looked outraged that Dan should give Griffin even silent orders. Aunt Tabetha narrowed her eyes. But they all trooped upstairs and into the drawing room.

"When did you arrive?" Dan asked his mother. "In fact, *how* did you arrive?"

"And why," Tabetha added, not quite beneath her breath.

Dan handed his mother onto the sofa and sat beside her.

"A bare ten minutes ago," she replied lightly. "I traveled post. And as to why," she added, fixing Tabetha with her amiable gaze, "because, like the rest of you, I imagine, I was summoned."

"He didn't tell me that!" Tabetha exclaimed.

"He didn't tell me, either," Dan said, "and we were discussing the matter."

"He always liked to play his cards close to his chest," Jenny Stewart observed. She met Dan's gaze. "I know what else you're asking me. I chose to answer because when I went round to your rooms, I discovered you had gone. I guessed you'd come here. And for the rest, Mr. Pilney kindly provided the post chaise."

Deliberately, Dan tried to keep every expression from his face, but it irked him that she had accepted Pilney's generosity. He didn't want the man owning her. He wanted her able to make a sensible choice. Which, to his mind, was showing

Mr. Pilney the toe of her boot.

"Then you haven't seen him yet?" Dan asked, casting his eyes upward toward the bedchambers.

"Lord, no. I don't expect to be received for at least two days. If at all."

"Then why did you come?" Tabetha asked bluntly. "You know it simply makes everything uncomfortable for all of us. And the servants and neighbors whom you are putting in an impossible position."

"With respect, that's rot," Dan said bluntly. "The servants are paid to carry out their master's orders, and the neighbors haven't spoken to him in twenty-five years."

"But they *have* spoken to me," Tabetha said grandly. "I'll have you know I am on very good terms with the Countess of Cosland, for one."

"Are you, by God?" Jenny said, quite improperly. "What is she like?"

Hetty made a sound like a snigger and fell to blowing her nose.

"I'm surprised you can ask," Tabetha said stiffly, "considering what you did to her poor husband."

"I'm sure Lady Cosland is delighted I jilted her husband," Jenny retorted. "She would not otherwise be his wife, would she?"

Dan grinned. Colin's nostrils twitched with distaste.

Jenny gave her a conciliatory smile. "I'm

sorry if my presence upsets you, Tabby, but the truth is, on the strength of the old gentleman's summons, I have as much right to be here as you or Hetty."

Tabetha sniffed. "Who is Mr. Pilney to be paying your expenses?"

Dan gazed out of the window.

"Mr. Geoffrey Pilney. He is a perfectly respectable gentleman who wants to marry me."

Tabetha snorted. "*Another* so-called respectable—"

But unexpectedly, Colin interrupted her, staring at Jenny. "Mr. Pilney of Broome Hall?"

"You know him?" Jenny asked, apparently pleased.

"We are acquainted," Colin said faintly.

"He's rich as Croesus," Jenny said frankly. "But quite charming for all that."

Hetty emerged from her handkerchief, gazing at her sister in consternation. "Then what do you want with Myerly?"

"Nothing," Jenny replied as the butler opened the door, and two aging footmen scuttled in with trays of food, which they set on small tables in front of Dan's mother. "Oh, Griffin, thank you! This is wonderful!"

"His lordship," Griffin pronounced, "has asked for you to join him at your earliest convenience."

Everyone gaped, except Jenny, whose eyes

twinkled at the butler. "Is that what he said?"

"More or less, ma'am."

She ate a piece of toast with ham and cheese and swallowed. "I shall be up directly, Griffin. I still remember the way."

Dan regarded her with some respect as the servants left the room. "Playing him at his own game, Mama?"

"By keeping him waiting?" his mother replied, reaching for another morsel. "Lord, no. I am starving."

Under the somewhat outraged gaze of her sisters and nephew, much to Dan's amusement, she continued to consume her breakfast with enthusiasm.

"Perhaps," Tabetha suggested. "I should just step upstairs and explain to Papa what's keeping you."

"You could," Jenny allowed. "But unless he's changed hugely, I'd suggest you check first that he has nothing dangerous at hand to throw at you."

"He'll be saving that for you, Aunt, if you don't hurry," Colin observed. "I cannot like my grandfather's temper, but it's something we must all tolerate at this time."

"If you ask me," Jenny said, wiping her mouth on her napkin. "the problem is that you all tolerated it all your lives."

"This from the one who was not here!" Tabe-

ABANDONED TO THE PRODIGAL

tha exploded. "*I* have been the one to care for him, to put up with his foul moods and tantrums!"

Jenny rose to her feet. "Then more fool you, Tabby, for I'll wager anything you like that he's never thanked you for it."

Tabetha's face flushed a mottled red, but Jenny, murmuring "Excuse me," did not appear to notice.

Dan strolled out of the room after her and closed the door. "You are rather magnificent, you know."

"Sisterly banter," his mother said, waving it aside. Reaching the staircase, she glanced at him. "Is she really here so often, looking after him? Has he needed it?"

"I would doubt it. As far as I can get out of Waits and Griffin, the old devil was fine until a couple of months ago, and then went downhill."

Her eyes, for once, were serious. "Then he really is dying?"

"I don't know that he is. Undeniably, he's been ill and much weakened, but...well, see what you think."

She paused at the door of her father's rooms. "You don't need to come with me."

"I know. But I will."

She searched his face and smiled. "No one believes me when I tell them how good you are."

"Not surprised," Dan said as the door

opened, and Waits stood there almost crying with joy.

"Miss Jenny!" He took her proffered hands and hung on to them. "It fills my old heart to see you at Myerly again at last."

"Bring her in here, you old fool!" came Lord Myerly's irascible tones.

Waits sighed and bowed them through.

"Well, well, Mrs. Stewart," the old man mocked from his bed. "I am honored indeed." He scowled, catching sight of Dan. "What are you doing here? Go away. I didn't send for you."

"Nevertheless, I shall stay," Dan said mildly, holding the chair by the bed for his mother to sit.

"And why is that?" the old man challenged.

"To remind her, if necessary, that she doesn't need to put up with your insults."

"Oh, she's never needed reminding about that. Ran away from them twenty-eight years ago and never came back."

"I didn't run away from your insults, as you very well know," Jenny said calmly. "They were merely water off a duck's back. I ran away to marry John Stewart."

He stared. "You still seem mighty proud of such a paltry match!"

"I am."

The old man curled his lip and waved his hand toward Dan. "And see where it's left you."

"I am also proud of Dan."

Lord Myerly pushed back against his pillows. "You're much calmer than you used to be."

"I hear you aren't. How are you, Papa?"

The question seemed to take him by surprise. He dragged his gaze free and looked at his hands on the coverlet. "Weak as a kitten. I suppose that's why you came. You want Myerly for your wastrel son."

"Of course I do," she replied. "But I know perfectly well that makes no difference to you. Tabby and Hetty also want it for their sons. You'll give it where you like. If you want the truth, I came to see if there was any forgiveness in you." She held his fierce old gaze as he glanced up. "For what it's worth, I forgive you."

He glared at his bedside table as if wondering what to seize and throw. "Forgive *me*? Am I supposed to be grateful? You have not even apologized for running away!"

"And I never will. I don't regret it. Though I do regret it was necessary."

"Shameless, disobedient, s—"

"Careful," Dan warned.

"Bah!" his grandfather shouted.

Jenny took her father's hand, an act that surprised him so much, he let it happen. She glanced up at Dan and, reluctantly, he walked out of the room and left them to it.

CHAPTER SEVEN

LATER, DAN COLLECTED Gun and went for a walk with his mother. They headed westward and climbed the hill among some incurious sheep. Dan let Gun grow used to their presence, even sniff one or two before he let him off the leash. The dog bounded ahead, more interested in other smells.

From the summit, they could see over the lower slopes as far as Kidfield on one side and Hornby on the other. The beauty Dan had noticed yesterday struck him again, and although he didn't really want to feel anything for this land, he found he did.

They didn't speak. After a moment, his mother's fingers curled around his, and he squeezed them in return. Because he knew she would prefer it, he pretended not to see the dampness on her face as they turned and began to descend the hill once more.

"I've waited a long time to come home," she said. "I didn't even know I missed it. I'm glad I came."

"Will it be harder to leave again?"

"Not if your grandfather wills it to you," she said lightly. "Because then, I can come back whenever you like."

"He wants us to fight over it," Dan said abruptly. "I'm pretty sure that's what's reviving him. He won't will Myerly to me, because I won't play."

"That's another reason I came," she admitted. "To tell you that if you are doing this for me, you don't need to. You don't even need to do it for yourself. I have decided to marry Geoffrey."

He made an involuntary movement of disgust.

She took his arm and shook it. "Don't be like that, Dan. He is a good man, and he makes me laugh. And he will provide for us both."

"Damn it, Mother," he exploded. "If I want anything from my grandfather, it is so you don't feel obliged to make such a choice!"

"Oh, I never feel obliged to do anything. And you should not feel obliged to toady your grandfather for me."

He cast her a rueful smile. "I came with the intention of trying, but when I'm with them, all that flies out the window. Are you and he friends again?"

She considered. "I would not say friends. He is not a man who forgives easily. But he asked for me. Possibly to spite my sisters, but still, he did it. And I came. That has to mean something."

"Do you think he is dying?"

"I think he could have died. Now...I don't know, and according to Waits, neither does the doctor."

"I think he might have been holding on for you," Dan said. "I think he wanted one last fight, and you took the wind out of his sails."

She sighed. "I was angry too long. It bores me now. I want to be happy and frivolous."

"You *are* happy and frivolous. You don't need Geoffrey Pilney to be more so. You don't love him, do you?"

"Oh, what do you know of love?"

For some reason, Juliet Lilbourne's laughing face drifted through his mind. He banished it. "Nothing," he said crossly. "But I do know you loved my father, and whatever you feel for Pilney is just not the same."

"Of course, it is not. How could it be? I am not the same woman who ran away with your father. Who is this, now?"

A man on horseback was riding around the base of the hill in the direction of the hamlet. Catching sight of Dan and his mother, he changed direction to come and meet them. Gun barked and dashed toward him, clearly giving both horse and rider reason to pause. Used to such situations, Dan loped forward to catch the dog and tie the velvet ribbon round his neck again.

Jenny peered at the silent newcomer. "Why…why it's Patrick!"

The rider, of craggy late-middle years, broke into smiles and dismounted, striding the last few paces past Gun to meet her. "Miss Jenny, as I live and breathe! I heard a rumor you were back but refused to believe it. Well, well, you are still pretty as a picture."

She laughed. "Why, so are you, Patrick! I suppose you must have a *huge* parcel of children by now?"

"Expecting my first grandchild any day," Patrick said proudly.

"Dan, Patrick is my father's steward—" She broke off, frowning. "Or at least, he *was*."

"Still am," Patrick said ruefully. "No one else will take on the wretched position."

"I'm not surprised," Jenny said frankly. "Patrick, this is my son, Daniel Stewart."

Dan offered his hand, and the steward, looking surprised, shook it a trifle awkwardly. "Why is the position so wretched?"

"Dealing with his lordship, for one," Patrick replied. "For another…breaks my heart to work the land to death and put nothing back. Even by the old standards, we could do better than this, and my son talks of all those new-fangled farming ideas that—" He broke off with an apologetic shrug. "But there, I won't bore you with that. I suppose you'll be going back to the big house for tea."

"I suppose we will," Jenny said. She smiled. "Unless your Lizzie would like a guest?"

Patrick beamed. "She would love it."

Dan was happy enough to tag along, both touched and intrigued by the way his mother was remembered after all these years. He had been to Myerly several times and never encountered Patrick, or if he had, he didn't remember it. But then, he hadn't really paid a great deal of attention to his surroundings before.

Gun was slightly miffed to be tied up outside the cottage, though he cheered up when Patrick's younger children burst out of the door to play with him.

Mrs. Patrick came out in their wake and greeted Jenny with tears in her eyes. Proudly, she introduced her children and her heavily pregnant daughter-in-law, who was quickly summoned from her own cottage for the treat of meeting the important visitors from the big house.

While Jenny drank tea and gossiped, Dan got into a conversation with Patrick about the land, bringing up what he had learned from the farmers earlier in the day. He learned a good deal more from Patrick, and more yet from Pat, Patrick's eldest son, who was full of frustrated enthusiasm for new methods that would work wonders. Only Lord Myerly would not countenance the necessary cost.

"Foolishness," Dan said, frowning.

"He doesn't care," Pat burst out. "Because he gets good money from his land in the south. But it's us who live and work *here* that suffer. Not him."

"That'll do, Pat," his father growled.

"No, no, I asked for the truth," Dan said quickly. "I suppose you must both have spoken to his lordship about all this? Urged such reforms?"

"He's not interested," Patrick said again. "It bores him."

"And would cost him money to begin with, when he doesn't see the point," Dan murmured. "Because he hasn't been out of the house in years."

"To be fair, the workings of the land never interested him much before that either," Patrick said.

"Hmm."

It all made Dan very thoughtful as they walked back to the house. He was aware of his mother watching him with something like amusement, but she didn't interrupt the silence.

※》》《《

DAN ROSE AT dawn again the following morning, put Gun on his increasingly crusty leash, and went down to the kitchen, where the cook had made him up another breakfast parcel and a bowl of scraps for Gun.

"Bless you," he said gratefully, letting Gun wolf his breakfast before they started off.

"Hmph," the cook sniffed, but he could tell she was pleased. He suspected kind words didn't come her way very often.

The kitchen door opened, and a young maid came in, yawning prodigiously. She stopped dead at sight of Dan, fear sparking in her eyes. It was the girl who'd walked past on the other side of the river yesterday morning. With her lover.

"Good morning," Dan said, amiably.

The girl blushed a fiery red and bobbed a hasty curtsey.

"Hurry up, girl!" the cook commanded. "Let's have water on to boil and then grate yesterday's bread to coat the fish. A day off yesterday doesn't entitle you to another today!"

Dan watched thoughtfully as the maid rushed to obey. "What's her name?" he asked the cook.

"Susan? Smith, apparently. Why?" The cook glared as though he was disappointing her by planning the seduction of her assistant.

"Oh, no reason," he replied, picking up Gun's empty bowl and dropping it in the basin. "I met another Smith recently."

He left by the back door and lingered a moment, half-expecting the maid to come and speak to him. When she didn't, he set off toward Hornby, cutting across country to the river. Gun was learning manners and had stopped trying to chase the cattle, though he did shoot off at random angles often enough to worry his master. However, he always came back quickly with great excitement. If he was chasing something, he never caught it.

When he crossed the bridge, there was no sign of Juliet. The stab of disappointment took him by surprise, but since Gun dashed happily off toward where they had left her yesterday, he followed. Around the bend, he still could not see her. He hoped he hadn't hurt her feelings by his hesitation yesterday, for she had been hurt enough. Then it struck him it was probably best if she *was* hurt, or at least offended because these clandestine meetings would not be good for her reputation. Still, he would miss her. He had looked forward to seeing her again.

A movement in the trees caught his attention. A young lady standing before an easel, busily painting. In the early morning light, it was a delightful vignette, and he couldn't help smiling with relief as well as pleasure. He turned off the path and strode toward her.

Gun, already investigating the wood, exploded through the trees, throwing himself at Juliet. She laughed, setting down her brush just in time to receive his full weight. She staggered backward before she pushed him off and ruffled his head with both hands.

Still smiling, she straightened to face Dan. "Good morning. I wasn't sure you would come, so I prepared to entertain myself."

She had been painting the sunrise over the river in watercolors. The pink and gold of the sky reflected in the water, the whole framed by the tree branches she had been looking through.

"That's rather good," he said, impressed. "Have you been here since four in the morning?"

She laughed. "No, I always paint quickly, because I have no talent, only instinct."

"They seem to be the same thing in your case. Do you want to finish it before breakfast?"

She considered. "Do you know, I might leave it as it is?"

"Eat, then see what you think," he advised.

She had come prepared this morning, with a blanket already thrown on the ground. He dropped the cook's parcel on top, and Juliet hastily retrieved if before Gun could get to it.

"Did you carry this all the way here yourself?" he asked.

"It would defeat the object to bring a footman. Or my brother. Actually, I thought about bringing Ferdy, but I don't want him to have to lie. I suspect he would like you, though."

"I'm a likable fellow," Dan said with mock pride. "I gather you are still restricted?"

She wrinkled her nose, settling on the blanket while he pushed Gun off and sat in the dog's place. "I am. But Kitty and Ferdy—my sister and brother—are working on my father's sympathies for me. Personally, I doubt he will be in the least receptive unless he gets some kind of reasonable answer from the Alfords. Though, what he would count as reasonable, I have no idea. How is your grandfather? Is he still improving?"

Dan reached for some bread and ham. "So far as I can tell. But you could have knocked me down with a feather when I found who was waiting for me when I got back to Myerly yesterday. My mother."

"Goodness! Did that please or anger his lordship?"

"Apparently the old devil had sent for her, too, but she only left London when she discovered I had. I think she's glad to end their feud. I suspect he is, too, though he'll never admit it. It's my aunts who are infuriated by her appearance."

"Because she is further competition for the estate?"

Dan shifted restlessly. "I told him he should will it to all his daughters on condition they sell the place and divide the proceeds equally."

Juliet swallowed her piece of cheese and found the apple. "Do you still have your knife to cut it?"

Obligingly, Dan cut the apple in two and twisted out the core for her. She smiled her thanks, and he felt a fresh jolt of awareness. She really was incredibly beautiful when she smiled. Several seconds too late, he realized she was gazing at him expectantly, and he tried to remember what he had been talking about before cutting the apple.

"Do you no longer think equal division is the way to go?" She bit into the apple, and he looked hastily away.

"It probably would," he said, dragging his mind back to the conversation. "It would be fairest. And whoever bought the estate would surely look after it better than my grandfather, which has to be good for the people and the land. Only…"

"Only what?" she prompted.

He shifted restlessly. "I don't really know. It seems a shame to remove it from the family. My mother has strong feelings for the place."

"As do you," she guessed, wiping her mouth on the napkin.

He shrugged. "Not *strong* feelings," he disputed. "I can count on one hand the number of times I was ever here. But yes, I suppose I do feel *something.* Still, it isn't up to me, is it? The old man will play his games and do as he wishes. Though perhaps I can get him to listen to reason before that."

"Reason about what?" she asked curiously.

"The state of the land and the improvements that could and should be made."

She blinked. "I did not know you were interested in agricultural matters."

He grinned self-consciously. "I wasn't before yesterday. It's my new obsession. I'm subject to them, you know. Why didn't you think I would come this morning?"

She colored, looking even more adorable. "Because I sensed you didn't really want to. And I had forgotten that while you are my only friend outside of the house, I am not yours."

"Actually, you are." He picked up the remaining half apple. "And as I recall, it was my idea we should meet again." He raised his gaze from the apple to her face. "I'm not used to considering right and wrong, let alone taking responsibility for it. But if you are seen with me, it won't be good. I don't want you to suffer because of me."

"I won't. But I would hate you to feel obliged to come and see me out of pity."

"*Pity?*" He stared at her.

"Well, you do pity me, out of the goodness of your heart. You had never even met me before, but you believed me at once without a quibble and have been nothing but kind ever since."

"I do sound quite a paragon of virtue when you put it like that."

She smiled. "And you make me laugh."

"I endeavor to please." He lay back on the blanket and put his hands behind his head while he gazed up at the sky and the clouds. "Oh, before I forget. The woman from the stagecoach who was looking for her runaway daughter. What was her name?"

"Mrs. Harper? Or the daughter?"

"The daughter."

"Susan. Why?"

"It's probably too convenient, but do you remember the couple we saw yesterday? The girl is one of my grandfather's housemaids. Her name, apparently, is Susan Smith. Which immediately made me suspicious, on account of having so recently met another Miss Smith."

She stuck her tongue out at him, a childish gesture that made him laugh, though she said quickly, "You think she might be Mrs. Harper's daughter?"

"I didn't get the chance to speak to her. I was on my way out, and she was under the close supervision of the cook. I'll talk to her again."

"She ran away with a soldier," Juliet confided.

"Then she's in good company at Myerly. Except that fellow yesterday looked more like a farmer than a soldier."

"He is."

"Hmm."

"But we should definitely find out because the poor woman is worried sick about her."

Dan nodded just as Gun reappeared and licked his face in passing. Dan spluttered and got to his feet, wiping his face, while Juliet laughed and made a fuss of the dog. Dan stood in front of the easel, examining her painting again, now that it had dried completely.

"What will you do with it?" he asked her.

"Nothing, I shouldn't think. Add it to the pile still in the schoolroom, probably."

"May I have it?"

She looked up in surprise. "Really?"

"I like it."

"Then, of course, you may have it. I'm flattered. So long as you don't use it to wrap your breakfast in tomorrow."

He laughed and detached it from the easel. He rolled it into a scroll and slid it into the long pocket of his overcoat. The sun was getting higher, and he knew it was time she was going back.

He folded up the easel. "I'll walk with you part of the way and carry your burden."

"There's no need, you know. I am not such a weakling as I look."

"But I am. I need the exercise." He whistled to Gun, while she looked him critically up and down.

"No, you're not," she argued. "You look very thin, but your shoulders are broad and..." She broke off, blushing. "And I think you're probably pretty strong," she finished in a rush. "Sorry. I'm too comfortable with you. I say exactly what comes into my head."

"Good," he said, then added, "So far."

With Juliet carrying the blanket, and Dan the easel and his overcoat, they walked through the woods, Gun trotting happily at their heels. From their comfortable chatter, he learned little bits about her childhood and her family, which both sounded completely different from his. He had run wild in army camps, and after his father's death, he was brought up only by his mother. Apart from her, his only family stared through him or made rude comments on their very few encounters. Or laid down the law like his grandfather.

As they compared these matters, he said, "You might even know my Aunt Tabetha. She claims acquaintance with your mother, Mrs. Cornwell."

She thought about it. "Does she have a very proper and slightly stiff son?"

"Cousin Colin," he recognized without difficulty.

"Then, yes, I have met them both. Imagine her being your Aunt Tabetha! What of your other aunt? Will I know her, too?"

"Mrs. Ames. She's not as...*forceful* as Tabetha."

"I can't think of an Ames," she said, disappointed. "Except Mr. Hugh Ames, who is positively the height of fashion."

Dan grinned. "All fobs and quizzing glasses and the most outrageous waistcoats."

"He is your cousin?" Juliet exclaimed with apparent delight. "He took tea with Lady Alford one day wearing a pink coat!"

"I was never sure whether the fashionable world regarded him as a leader or a figure of fun," he admitted.

"Neither is the fashionable world, I suspect! I rather like him, though. He is very good-natured and dances most gracefully."

Dan nodded since this was pretty much his own opinion of Hugh. "I prefer him to Colin, but I can't say I really know either of them."

"I wonder if they will call on us?" Juliet mused. "If they—"

Gun's soft growling caught Dan's attention first. His hackles were up. Dan seized Juliet's hand on the leash, and she stopped talking at once.

Someone was approaching along the path, humming to himself.

As one, she and Dan veered off the path into the trees, dragging Gun with them. Juliet dived behind a large oak tree, and Dan propped up the easel there to set about distracting Gun, for the dog, picking up their alarm, was clearly about to have at the approaching enemy with his usual rifle-shot bark. Crouching down, Dan used both hands to ruffle the dog's head and scratch behind his ears. Surprised but grateful, Gun licked his wrist but tried to scrabble toward the threat, the incipient bark rumbling still in his throat.

Juliet caught on, hastily removing one glove and stroking Gun's back. She had her hands well-licked in return, but she didn't stop, and in the end, this game seemed more fun to the witless creature than barking. He sank down and rolled on his back to have his tummy tickled by them both.

Peering through the undergrowth, Dan saw a man stride by with a gun over his arm. It looked like a fowling-piece, and sure enough, Juliet whispered, "It's Campbell, the gamekeeper."

Dan, suddenly more concerned with the effect of her breath against his ear and her soft warmth against his shoulder, could only nod and try to keep scratching Gun's belly. It was difficult, when all his senses focused on *her*, her fresh, feminine scent that reminded him of flowers and orange trees and the spices of the east, and yet was completely her own.

If he just turned his head a little, his lips would touch her cheek, and from there, her lips... He had kissed her before, and his body remembered. Desire curled through him, a heavy, pleasurable ache that he could only ignore. It was exquisite torture he could not bring himself to end.

She did that, up to a point, by standing and peering through the trees after the gamekeeper. The fine muslin of her gown brushed against his face, and he rose abruptly, almost desperately, to stand beside her.

Disappointed, Gun rolled and got to his feet, too, gazing expectantly at Dan.

"He's gone," Juliet murmured. "Maybe we should stay off the path."

Dan nodded as casually as he could and picked up the easel once more. At once, she reached for the leash, and their fingers touched. To Dan, it was electric. Her fingers stilled, her gaze lifted to his face, a tiny, questioning frown on her beautiful face. The world stood still.

With women, as in most other aspects of his life, Dan was used to following his instincts. Usually, it had worked out well for him, and for the girls in question. Undoubtedly, this was the moment he could kiss Juliet—truly, deeply kiss her—and change their relationship forever. He knew she would let him, and if he did it as he wished, with all the sweetness and sensuality of which he was capable, he knew she would like it...

But this damnable new sense of responsibility was getting in his way. She was not just another girl looking for flirtation or a little passion. He could not make her ruin true.

He twisted his lips into a smile and let go of the leash, striding on in the direction of the house.

CHAPTER EIGHT

JULIET WAS SO absorbed in her own thoughts that she didn't notice her brother and sister until they were almost upon her.

Something had changed in Dan. Or in the way she regarded him. It wasn't so much a change in feelings as a change in emphasis. She had always been conscious of his physical attractions—his dramatic, handsome face and charming, easy smile, the casual grace of his long, lean body. Sometimes, when she'd glanced at him, her heart had given a pleasant little flutter. She liked looking at him. She liked being with him, and she had been undeniably delighted to see him walking toward her from the river.

But in those ridiculous moments hiding from Campbell, the gamekeeper, and dementedly tickling Gun to keep him silent, she had found herself pressed against Dan's shoulder. She could smell the soap he used, feel the brush of his hair against her cheek, her lips as she'd whispered in his ear. Her body had responded most agreeably to his nearness, and something about his stillness had spoken of *his* awareness. The emphasis had shifted. He was no longer simply a kind friend who shared her humor as well as her troubles. He was an attractive man who could, who *did*, recognize her womanly charms.

And the moment she'd taken the leash... Touching him had been accidental. Lingering over it hadn't, although she had almost felt incapable of moving. When she had lifted her gaze to his, she had barely been able to breathe for the heat of desire had stood out in his eyes as clearly as the sun in a cloudless sky.

It made her heart soar. Even the fact that he had done nothing about it and had merely walked on, excited her more. And although they had said little on the last part of their journey, she would not have forgone it for the world.

It was only as they had parted with a cheerful promise to meet tomorrow that the doubts had begun. He was a man. Men felt desire all the time, and mostly it had little to do with love— which was why a lady should never complain when her husband strayed, for it had nothing to do with his feeling for his wife and family. According to her mother, who had imparted a good deal of such wisdom upon Juliet's engagement to Jeremy Catesby.

So, she should not dwell on such odd, passing moments with Dan. They meant nothing and could lead to nothing. She was ruined in the eyes of the world and was, therefore, not wife material for anyone. They both knew that. Besides, if she made this into something it was not, she would lose his friendship, this precious time with him and, probably, her sanity.

All the same…

"Juliet!" Kitty exclaimed, right in front of her. "What daydream are you lost in?"

Blinking, Juliet forced a laugh. "I scarcely know."

"You are covered in leaves and mud," Kitty observed. "Where have you been so early?"

"Oh, just for a walk," she said vaguely. "I woke early and had the urge to paint the sunrise."

"Let's see, then," Ferdy said, taking the easel from her.

Drat, I gave it to Dan! "Oh, it didn't work out. I threw it away. What time is it? Have you breakfasted?"

"No, because we went to find you first," Kitty explained as they walked the last few yards to the house. "Only you weren't in your chamber, which worried me because I know how all this must be affecting you."

"You don't need to worry about me," Juliet

said, feeling guilty about enjoying her expedition so much. "Why were you looking for me in the first place?"

"Well," Kitty said, lowering her voice. "Ferdy had it from his valet that Baron Miserly's long-lost daughter has come home, and the whole neighborhood is agog to discover if he is dying, and what Papa might do about it."

Juliet paused with one foot on the front step. "What in the world could Papa do about Lord Myerly dying?"

"Not Myerly, his daughter," Ferdy said, impatiently. "She's the one who jilted Papa and ran away with an officer."

"Yes, but he can hardly do anything about that either," Juliet pointed out, walking on up the steps and into the house. "It was more than twenty-five years ago, was it not?"

"Well," Kitty said with a twinge of doubt, "it seems to be a question about whether or not she should be received by local families. Our people seem to think that Mama and Papa should let it be known that she shouldn't be."

"That would be vindictive, spiteful, and cruel," Juliet exclaimed. "Worse even than was done to me. From Papa, it would also be paltry and mean-spirited. I hope he is not so petty."

"Why such heat?" Ferdy asked in surprise. "We don't even know these people. Well, except Papa, obviously."

Juliet, tight-lipped, gave up her easel to the waiting footman and walked rapidly on.

"Juliet met the son," Kitty explained. "On the stagecoach."

Ferdy's eyebrows flew up. "Did you, by God?"

"Shouldn't you change before breakfast?" Kitty interrupted as Juliet turned automatically toward the breakfast room.

Juliet glanced ruefully at the bits of soil, bark, and grass-stains marring her walking gown, and gave in.

By the time she reached the breakfast room, dressed in a fresh, clean morning gown of sprig muslin, her parents had joined her siblings and were reading their correspondence, while Kitty and Ferdy made desultory conversation.

Her parents bade her a distracted good morning, and she helped herself to coffee and toast and a little smoked fish.

As she passed her father to sit down, she couldn't help noticing the next letter in his pile, and her stomach twinged unpleasantly. It was directed in Jeremy's hand.

"Is that all you're eating?" her mother asked.

Since it was, in effect, her second breakfast of the morning, she really didn't want any more. "For now," she murmured.

"Hmm…"

Juliet sat and drank her coffee.

"I hear," her mother remarked, "that Lord Myerly's daughters are all with him."

The earl grunted. "Dying, is he? They'll be round him like vultures."

"I thought I might leave cards at Myerly," the countess said casually.

Juliet held her breath and picked at her fish while gazing at her father.

He threw down his letter and reached for the next. "You must do as you wish, my dear. I have no quarrel with Myerly's daughters. In fact, if I ever quarreled with Myerly, I've forgotten why."

The last was a lie, Juliet thought. He remembered perfectly well, though it possibly didn't disturb him hugely.

"We are acquainted with the Cornwells in any case," the countess observed.

His lordship did not respond, for he was rapidly scanning Jeremy's letter. He scowled and threw it on the table, then picked it up and read it again.

"It's from Catesby," he said at last. "Jumped-up little..." He broke off, glancing at Juliet.

"Carry on, sir," she invited. "Abuse him to your heart's content."

"What does he say?" her mother asked, hastily distracting his ire from Juliet.

"That he has already told his friends that Juliet preferred to go home to her family than to marry him."

"That's a terrible lie," Ferdy growled. "No one will believe it."

The earl gave an irritable shrug of one shoulder. "Nevertheless, we can believe it was kindly meant. It's the next bit that sticks in my craw. In retrospect, he claims, he and his father regret the haste of his actions—*Jeremy's* actions, note, exonerating his father from blame—but not the decision to end the engagement. Pipsqueak! However, they are prepared—*prepared!*—to keep their promise to attend Kitty's engagement dinner. His mother will attend, he says specifically, *to support Lady Cosland.* Bah! And, he *so* magnanimously leaves it up to me to decide whether or not Juliet will be present!"

"I believe I would like to punch him straight in his smug mouth," Ferdy observed.

"No, no," their mother said unexpectedly. "This could be the very thing for Juliet, Cosland. If they meet in friendship, it will silence some of the talk at least. And who knows? If things go well, the engagement could be resumed, and most people will put the other nonsense down to the Prince Regent's spite. After all, Meg Winter was also named, and who is going to take on *her* father *and* you?"

Juliet opened her mouth to squash this hope, but Kitty kicked her below the table.

"Don't," Kitty warned under her breath. "You needn't marry him, but a resumed engagement is exactly what you need. You may easily jilt him again when this nonsense has blown over."

Juliet blinked at her. "When did you learn so much social wisdom?"

"It isn't social wisdom," Kitty denied. "It's simple common sense. As is not fighting with Papa."

⟶≫≫≪≪⟵

AT THE REQUEST of his aunts, Dan took Gun straight round to the back of the house to stop him from spreading dirt and chaos through the front. To his surprise, he found his mother in the kitchen garden, gossiping with the cook, who, however, raced back to the kitchen as Jenny came to meet him.

Gun gave her his usual boisterous greeting, jumping around her as they walked together toward the walled garden.

"You take a long walk every morning," his mother observed.

"I like to." He pushed open the gate to the walled garden and wrestled with the knot of Gun's makeshift leash.

At last, the dog bolted to freedom, and they shut him in.

Jenny regarded the leash. "Why are you

using a lady's ribbon as his leash?"

Dan shrugged. "I didn't have one at all because he just follows me around. But it struck me
rather belatedly he would be a hazard in the
country until he learned what he could and
couldn't chase. Someone on the stagecoach gave
me this."

"It must have been very pretty at one time."

"Have you had breakfast?" Dan asked.

If she noticed the deliberate change of subject, she made no comment. "Not yet. I think
there might be a little more of it now."

"Now that you have twisted the cook around
your little finger?"

Jenny smiled, though he noted she did not
deny it. They entered the house via the back door
and took the passage past the kitchen and the
servants' hall to the baize door that separated the
servants' domain from the main part of the
house.

"I'll join you in a few minutes," Dan said. "I'd
better wash off some of this dirt first."

As he ran up the stairs, a maid was hurrying
across the landing toward the servants' stairs. No
one else was around.

"Susan," he called, and she paused, glancing
warily back at him. "A word, if you please."

She obeyed with odd reluctance, though
whether because she feared he would take
liberties or ask awkward questions, he could not

tell.

"Don't look so worried. You may walk out with whoever you wish on your day off," he said lightly.

She met his gaze. "As may you, sir."

It wasn't quite insolence, more of a pact, he thought, to keep each other's secrets, although she had no idea, he hoped, of who he had been with at the river.

"Indeed. I wanted to ask you about something else. Why do you use the name Smith?"

Her breath caught. "Same reason anyone uses any name, sir."

"Really? Because I traveled north on the stagecoach with someone who reminds me of you. *Her* name was Harper."

Emotions surged in her eyes, too quickly for him to read. But it was clear the name meant something to her.

"She was coming in search of her daughter, in fear for the girl's safety," he said.

"Oh, no," Susan whispered. "Why did she do that? She was right about Jim, but I don't need my nose rubbed in it!"

"She didn't come to say *I told you so*," Dan said impatiently. "She just wants to know that you're safe and well. You'll find her at the Black Cat in Kidfield, tearing her hair out with worry."

Her gaze fell. "I just wanted to be settled before I met her again. Jim Owens wasn't a good man, but Peter Walsh is, only I haven't known him long…"

"It would not be kind to wait for an offer of marriage before you see your mother," he said flatly.

"I know," she whispered. She raised her head with conscious bravery and took a deep breath. "I'll go on my next day off."

"Which is when? Next week?"

"The week after," she admitted. "I'll get the evening off on Wednesday, but there won't be time to go to Kidfield and back."

"Write to her," Dan commanded.

"I can't write," she confessed.

Dan regarded her with a mixture of amusement and frustration. "Very well. *I'll* tell her."

"Thank you." She flashed him a half-frightened smile and turned away before swinging back and saying hastily, "Sir, you will tell her I'm sorry?"

Dan nodded and strode on to his bedchamber. When he thought about it, he wouldn't mind a jaunt into Kidfield for a change of scenery. Though it would probably be more fun if Juliet came, too.

He smiled to himself at that, for he couldn't really go jaunting about the country with an earl's daughter.

Five minutes later, he entered the breakfast room to find everyone there. He bowed but received little acknowledgment beyond his mother's bright smile and Aunt Hetty's vague one.

He helped himself to the fresh eggs and toast he found on the sideboard dishes and sat down.

"So, will you go over to Hornby today?" his mother asked her sisters.

Tabetha immediately frowned at her. "Why?"

"You talked about it yesterday," Jenny reminded her.

"It depends on whether or not there is time after I have seen Papa."

"Has he sent for you?" Hetty asked in surprise.

"No, but I expect he will, for I didn't see him yesterday."

"Neither did I," Hetty said gloomily.

"The doctor came this morning," Colin told Dan. "He believes his lordship somewhat improved. It's possible you can go back to London."

"Oh, that was always possible," Dan assured him. "Are you leaving?"

"Of course not. I am my mother's escort."

"Why would he go?" Tabetha added. "*He* is not here merely to toady his inheritance out of his grandfather!"

Dan smiled. "More coffee, Aunt?"

She seemed confused by this offer, though

she accepted automatically.

While Dan poured it for her, Jenny said, "Actually, you *should* go to Hornby. There is some calumny circulating in the press about one of the Cosland daughters. It would be kind to show you don't believe such nonsense."

Dan set down the coffee pot, watching the reactions of his aunts and cousin. Hetty's eyebrows lifted in bewilderment. Colin's lips tightened, and Tabetha looked supercilious.

"Yes, I heard about that," Tabetha said carelessly. "Of course, Lady Cosland would never countenance such behavior, but the eldest daughter was always *lively*, and living with the Princess of Wales, you know, must have encouraged such manners beyond what is proper."

"The princess wasn't there," Colin said dryly. "Which is the root of the problem."

"No, it isn't," Jenny said. "The root of the problem is the spite behind such obvious lies."

"Well, you would stand up for someone in the midst of a scandal," Tabetha said maliciously.

She was right, of course, but Dan wasn't having such mud slung at either his mother or Juliet Lilbourne.

"If there was scandal about my mother, it was as manufactured as this was, by those who have nothing better to talk about than other people's lives. It's nothing but envy."

"Envy!" Colin repeated, outraged.

"Envy," Dan repeated, holding his gaze. "But by all means, run up to Hornby and tell the countess her daughter is too lively, and it's her own fault her name is traduced in the gutter press. Which, of course, none of you have ever read."

"Have you?" Colin shot back.

"Naturally," he mocked.

"The point is," Jenny interrupted this locking of horns, "if you wish to support the countess, you should call on her. You might even learn the truth of the matter."

For a moment, Dan could see these arguments weighed with Tabetha, then suspicion returned to her eyes. "You want us gone for the afternoon so you can cozen Papa without us knowing what you are about!"

Dan squashed his surge of temper with some difficulty. "I, for one, won't wait until the afternoon. I shall be off cozening immediately after breakfast."

"You can't," Colin said, staring. "He hasn't sent for you."

"I need to talk to him," Dan said. "He can throw me out of he wants to."

They waited, with some glee, he suspected, for this to happen. But he still strolled alone into his grandfather's dressing room.

"Good morning, Waits. Is he awake?"

"Of course, I'm awake!" came the cantankerous voice from the bed. "What do you want? I didn't send for you."

"I know. So the mountain has come to Mohammed."

"What?"

"Nothing." Dan wandered into the bedchamber where his grandfather was reading the *Morning Post* from two days ago. He sprawled into the chair at the bedside. "I came to ask if I might borrow a horse to ride into Kidfield."

"Farley exercises the only decent horse we have left for riding. You'll interfere."

"Fair enough. I'll walk."

His grandfather scowled. "Oh, take the damned horse."

"Thank you," Dan said. "Also, about Myerly. When did you last look about the place?"

"I don't need to. I keep a steward."

"But you don't listen to him, do you? Do you know, you can tell almost immediately the borders of Myerly land because it's so much poorer than the land that borders it?"

"What do you know about land?" the old man growled. "City wastrel."

"Not a huge amount," Dan admitted. "But I can recognize poverty anywhere."

"It's good land. Always has been."

"And I've no doubt it could be again. With just a little investment."

His grandfather glared. "Are *you* daring to tell *me* how to run my estate?"

"No, I'm daring to tell you to listen to those you pay to run your estate," Dan retorted.

The subsequent quarrel was inevitable, and Dan knew he was doing himself no favors as far as inheritance went. The old man grew almost incandescent with rage until Dan, fearing his grandfather's health would relapse, finally beat a retreat.

However, he wasn't entirely displeased. He had made a few points that he had seen strike home. The old man might never do anything about it. But he might.

And since he hadn't withdrawn his permission concerning the horse, Dan freed Gun and walked round to the stables.

As he rode around to the drive, Gun trotting beside the horse, he heard his grandfather's yells though the open window. He hoped the old man wasn't directing his temper at poor Waits. But in fact, the other slightly strangled, pacifying voice that drifted out of the open window, was Colin's.

Dan grinned with a hint of ill-nature. His cousin seemed to have copied Dan in visiting without invitation. And without realizing Dan had already put his lordship in a filthy temper. Or had he thought to soothe the old devil and win favor that way?

All these machinations and suspicions surrounding the sickbed of a cantankerous and ultimately sad old gentleman left a nasty taste in Dan's mouth. It was one reason he had wanted to spend some time away in Kidfield.

The other reason, of course, was that he had the feeling Juliet would expect him to contact Mrs. Harper now he was sure Susan was indeed her daughter. He wasn't much given to analyzing his motives, but he suspected he didn't often go out of his way to please people. He also knew that while he didn't want Mrs. Harper to suffer further unease, it was his promise to Juliet that took him to the Black Cat.

Mrs. Burton, the innkeeper's wife, remembered him. Or at least she remembered Gun. At any rate, she greeted him with wary courtesy.

"I'm looking for Mrs. Harper," he said. "She arrived on the same coach as I did. I believe she's staying here?"

"She was," Mrs. Burton agreed. "But she left yesterday."

Dan frowned. "You mean she's vanished?"

"I mean, she paid her account and left. She did say she might be back."

"Did she say where she was going?"

Mrs. Burton thought. "Aldergreen."

"What the deuce is there in Aldergreen?" Dan demanded. Then he remembered. "Barracks."

"That's right, sir."

And Mrs. Harper still believed her daughter

was with a soldier. Or was trying to find out from him where Susan was.

He had a horse. He could ride to Aldergreen, although he had no money to change horses, so it would take him forever. And then everyone would be looking for him.

He sighed. "I'll write her a note for when she comes back."

Leaving his note with Mrs. Burton, he took his mug of ale outside into the yard, where a dazzling sight greeted him. A post-chaise had stopped to change horses, and stepping down from it was a young man in a magnificent bright yellow traveling coat. Beneath it, he wore a civilized blue coat, but a striped waistcoat of exactly the same shade of yellow could also be seen, along with a quizzing glass dangling from a yellow ribbon.

The young man stopped, appearing not to notice that the other occupant of the coach could not now alight. Lifting his quizzing glass, he peered at Dan.

"Cousin Daniel?" he exclaimed in amazement, mincing toward him. "What the deuce are you about in this wretched neck of the woods?"

"Much the same as you, I imagine," Dan said, grasping his cousin's gracefully offered hand. "Answering his lordship's summons. How are you, Hugh?"

Hugh had caught sight of Gun by then and

staggered back in alarm. "What in God's name is that?"

"This is Gun. Friendly and harmless, though he will muddy your pretty coat."

"Then he is not harmless," Hugh pronounced. "But where are my manners? Papa, have you met Cousin Daniel Stewart before? Aunt Jenny's son."

The older gentleman, who held a handkerchief to his nose, goggled.

"Dan, my father."

"How do you, sir?" Dan said politely, offering his hand to Mr. Ames.

His uncle took it mechanically, in a limp kind of way, lowering the handkerchief from his face to say, "Poorly, I'm afraid, poorly. I have the most dreadful cold, and the last thing I need is to be shut up in an airless carriage for days on end."

"Days?" Daniel said, startled.

"One day," Hugh corrected, "though it does *feel* like several. Neither of us would be here, to be frank, except Mama wrote and said everyone else was, and I would be missing out. However, I can't imagine seeing me will soften the old gentleman's heart, so not sure of the point."

"To entertain his lordship one last time," Dan said cynically. "I think we're probably meant to fight over our inheritance."

"And how is that going?" Hugh inquired.

"I'll leave that to your own observations. My

belief is, he'll leave everything to an orphanage just to see our reaction."

Hugh considered that doubtfully. "So, he hasn't croaked yet?"

"No. In fact, he appears to be rallying."

Mr. Ames sneezed into his handkerchief and turned away.

Hugh made a comical, long-suffering face. "Offer you a seat to Myerly, old fellow?" He eyed Gun with clear misgivings.

"No, thank you," Dan said hastily. "I'll just finish my ale and ride back when the horse has rested. Good luck."

"Same to you," Hugh said with his unexpectedly sweet smile and assisted his father back into the chaise.

CHAPTER NINE

"DID YOU LEAVE your card at Myerly?" Juliet asked her mother over dinner. They had no guests, so she had been allowed to join the family.

"Yes, I did, but I didn't stop."

"Then you did not see anyone?" Kitty said, disappointed.

"A young man rode up the drive as we were leaving," Mama said. "He was not dressed for riding and wore his hat at a crooked angle, but he had a good seat in the saddle, and he bowed to me."

Dan, Juliet thought with glee. She wondered where he'd been, felt a wistful longing to have accompanied him. Which was silly. She had only seen him this morning. And would again tomorrow.

"Oh, we must remember Lawrence is coming over tomorrow, Juliet, so you must keep out of the way."

Juliet sighed and nodded. She wondered if she could sneak away while everyone was occupied, ride further afield, perhaps to Kidfield. Or Myerly.

"Is that really necessary, Mama?" Kitty argued. "Lawrence knows all about this scandal and believes in Juliet's innocence quite as much as I do. He knows she is here, so it is silly to keep her from him. In fact, it looks positively *odd*."

"You may have a point," the countess agreed. "What do you think, Cosland? Shall we relax the rules, just for Lawrence's visit?"

"I suppose so," the earl said grudgingly. "So long as the Kings don't object."

In her present circumstances, it was enough to give Juliet hope. She looked forward to seeing her sister's betrothed again, of seeing them together, and refused to think about the possibility of Jeremy's presence at Hornby next week.

She went to bed early and rose at dawn. She crammed a book into her reticule in case she had to wait for Dan, but this morning she didn't doubt that he would come.

And she was right. As she came in sight of the bridge, he was already walking over it. Gun shot past him, hurling himself at her with great glee.

When she had fended him off, laughing and ruffling his head, Dan was there, offering his arm in courtly fashion. They walked together, talking like much older friends than they actually were.

"Mrs. Harper has left Kidfield for Aldergreen," Dan said. "I left her a note at the Black Cat, but we can't be sure she will come back."

"And it would be good for her peace of mind to know as soon as possible that her daughter is safe and well. My father is acquainted with the colonel at Aldergreen. I shall write to him and ask him to look out for Mrs. Harper and her inquiries."

"Susan's soldier is called Jim Owens."

She nodded. "I don't think we can do anymore for now."

"And what of your own problems?" he asked.

She wrinkled her nose and told him about Jeremy's letter and Kitty's advice. "The trouble is, I'm not sure I *could* re-engage myself to him quite so cynically, just to dismiss him again when all this nonsense blows over. For one thing, what if it doesn't? For another, although he deserves the humiliation, I don't think I could bring myself to smile at him, let alone accept his offer again."

Dan was silent a moment. "You might feel differently when you see him again. After all, you must have liked him when you accepted him the first time."

"I did." She frowned. "I suppose it's easy to

like someone when you don't know them. Everything was always so formal, not like—" She broke off, taking the stick from Gun's mouth and throwing it for him. It served to hide her embarrassment at what she had so nearly said. *Not like it is with you.*

"However," she said lightly, "it has clearly eased my father's mind to the extent that I am now allowed to be present when Lawrence—Mr. King, Kitty's betrothed—calls on us this afternoon. How is your party at Myerly?"

He grinned. "Growing. My cousin Hugh and his father appeared yesterday."

"Was he wearing his pink coat?" she asked eagerly.

"No, it was plain blue, but his yellow and blue waistcoat more than made up for that. As did the long yellow traveling coat, I first saw him in."

"Like a sunbeam?" she asked.

"Very much."

"Do you know, I think I would like a yellow coat now? Not a pale pastel shade, but a *vibrant* yellow."

"It will look beautiful on you."

"Perhaps Mr. Ames's coat will look beautiful on you, too. Would you wear it?"

"I'll wear anything if I'm cold enough."

Although he spoke in the same bantering tones, the answer made her frown. "Are you often cold? Dan, are you *really* poor?"

"Apparently not if I don't choose to be," he said with an unusual hint of bitterness, which he seemed to shake off with an impatient shrug of his shoulders.

"What do you mean?" she asked. "No one would choose to be poor, would they?"

At first, the deliberate smile in his eyes told her he was about to laugh it off, to change the subject, and then the smile drained away, and he blurted, "My mother has received an offer of marriage from a very wealthy gentleman. She has decided to accept him, and I am afraid it is for my sake. And my fault."

"What does your mother say?"

"That he makes her happy."

"Is she in the habit of lying to you?"

"No," he conceded. "But this is different. She wouldn't tell me the truth if it made me feel bad about not providing for her."

"And you feel *she* is still trying to provide for you?"

"Exactly."

She mulled that over for a little. "What will you do?"

"Tell her I won't take a penny from him. If she still marries him, it's because she wants to. Probably."

Without thinking, she threaded her fingers through his and squeezed. His hand closed on hers in instant response, but his glance was curious.

"What is that for?" he asked.

"Comfort. I'm returning the favor."

His eyes gleamed. "As I recall, I kissed you."

She laughed, although heat surged into her face. "I don't feel your distress is great enough for that."

"It's the best argument I've heard for misery." He swung her hand into the air and drew her back toward the woods.

❯❯❯❯❮❮❮❮

ALTHOUGH IT WAS getting increasingly hard to leave Dan after their walks, Juliet cheered herself with the thought of this afternoon's treat of meeting Lawrence King with Kitty. All the same, she could not help dwelling on her time with Dan, for he had kept hold of her hand for most of the walk through the woods. And she had let him. Which was both foolish and improper. They were not children. He did not wallow in his anxiety over his mother. On the contrary, he was as entertaining as ever. And yet his strong, roughened fingers had held lightly on to hers, novel, exciting, and strangely sweet.

But he was still Dan, her friend. He had taken no liberties as they'd parted near the driveway, merely smiled and said goodbye until tomorrow. She could have imagined the warmth of his eyes. It was likely he had simply forgotten he held her hand. After all, they were very comfortable together.

However, no one seeing them together in that way would have imagined their relationship to be the innocent friendship it was. Dan was just too easy-going and seemed to be infecting her. She had to be sensible, or they would both be in trouble.

All the same, she couldn't help feeling ridiculously happy about life as she ate her second breakfast and helped Kitty choose which gown to wear for her betrothed's visit.

He was expected in the early part of the afternoon and would stay for dinner. "In fact, Mama says he may stay the night," Kitty said eagerly, "to save such a long ride in the dark. And that will be his last visit before the dinner party next week."

"And when will you be married?"

"The first part of September, we think." Kitty glanced at her. "I never thought it would be before your wedding."

"Neither did I." Juliet gave a difficult smile. "My life was perfect, was it not?"

"Do you not think so?"

Juliet shook her head. "No. I think I looked too much at the surface and rarely saw what was beneath."

"You are thinking of Jeremy."

"And other things, but yes, Jeremy is my prime example. I'm not looking forward to seeing him again."

"Do you think Ferdy will punch him on the nose?" Kitty asked.

Juliet laughed. "I hope not. I doubt it would help my rehabilitation! Though part of me would like to see it if he did."

"I don't even know if they will let you come to dinner. And I so want you to be there. I hate that it all depends on the Alfords' attitude to you!"

"So do I. They were so kind to me and then just cut me off without thought or explanation, just because of some vulgar, so-called newspaper."

"Don't upset yourself again," Kitty pleaded.

Juliet smiled. "I'm not upset anymore. To be honest, I feel free and happy. Now, you should dress, or you will not be ready to greet your Mr. King."

Juliet, already gowned for the occasion, stayed and watched critically while the maid helped her sister. But in truth, it didn't much matter what Kitty wore. She was so pretty and good-natured. *Lawrence had better appreciate her.*

The sound of approaching hooves drifted through the open window. In a trice, she and

Kitty had their heads out watching Mr. King's arrival on horseback. He must have heard their voices, for he looked up and smiled spontaneously, before raising his hand in an enthusiastic wave. As a groom hurried to take his horse, he dismounted and vanished out of sight into the house.

"He looks just as I remember him," Juliette said warmly.

"Come, let's go down," Kitty urged.

Juliette was glad to oblige, but as she drew her head in, her attention was caught by some distant movement in the trees that lined the drive, A vehicle was trundling around the bend, traveling toward the house.

She almost let out an exclamation of dismay, but Kitty was already dancing across the room and had not seen. Impulsively, Juliette followed her. Only on the stairs did her heart beat a little guiltily. But she did want to spend some time with Kitty and Lawrence. And in truth, she was too restless, too full of energy she didn't know what to do with. She felt incapable of going meekly back to her room to wait. It could be any kind of vehicle, after all. It could be someone come to see her father privately, or a wagon full of wine or beef or flour…

And if not, she could always hide later.

Both her parents were greeting Mr. King in the salon, but Juliet was delighted to see the way his face lit up at the sight of Kitty. He was a stocky man of pleasant appearance, his mouth ready to smile, his eyes, kind. And there was fervor in the way he kissed Kitty's hand and cheek, not the mere, refined courtliness she now recognized had been Jeremy's idea of love. And hers. *Foolish, so foolish.*

On introduction, she curtseyed to Lawrence's bow and offered her hand. She was pleased to find his grip light but firm, and his friendly smile just as she remembered it.

"Of course, I remember you," she said in answer to his only half-teasing question. "I regarded you almost as another brother, without realizing you would become so, indeed!"

The countess had ordered tea to go with the glass of sherry already provided by her husband, and it was while the trays were being ferried into the room and set before the countess that the other visitors were announced.

Some failure of communication had clearly occurred. Perhaps no one had told the servants that Juliet was present, and other visitors were to be held back until she was removed. Whatever the reason, the earl and countess almost gawped in horror when Abbot intoned, "Mrs. Cornwell and Mrs. Stewart. Mr. Colin Cornwell and Mr. Stewart."

The earl, who had only just sat down, jumped to his feet. Juliet was left in the middle of the room, holding a teacup and saucer designed for him. The countess glared at her so hard, Juliet wondered if she should hide behind the curtains.

And then the regal figure of Mrs. Cornwell, dressed in a fawn gown with matching hat and feather, sailed into the room ahead of a more vital lady in blue. The countess had to leave off glaring and push the table aside to greet her unexpected guests.

"Lady Cosland!" uttered Mrs. Cornwell. "I do hope you don't mind such an onslaught! But my sister was determined to answer your call today, so I felt I should come to introduce her."

"Oh, how thoughtful," said Lady Cosland, always the perfect hostess. "We do not stand on formality here. We are happy to see everyone from Myerly."

Juliet, with Dan's name ringing in her ears, finally saw him saunter in behind his cousin.

"My sister, Mrs. Stewart," Mrs. Cornwell said, not exactly with distaste, yet managing to convey she would not, from choice, have introduced such an inferior person to her ladyship.

"How do you do, Mrs. Stewart?" the countess said warmly. The earl, by comparison, seemed rooted to the spot, having stood at the first announcement. It was hard to imagine he had been humiliated, perhaps even heartbroken by this woman.

Mrs. Stewart was no longer young, but despite the lines of care around her eyes and mouth, she retained the kind of prettiness that comes from a happy disposition. Like Dan, Juliet supposed.

"You know my son, of course," Mrs. Cornwell said regally.

Her son duly bowed and murmured respectful delight.

"And my son," Mrs. Stewart said, her lips twitching as she realized her sister wasn't going to trouble with that introduction. "Daniel Stewart."

Dan stepped forward with his usual casual grace and bowed. "How do you do," he murmured.

For a moment, the contrast between his dress and everyone else's was stark. Colin, perfectly attired in a well-fitting coat of blue superfine and snowy white cravat, stood between the elegantly dressed ladies. Mrs. Stewart, Juliet guessed, had already accepted gifts from her wealthy suitor. Dan, quite clearly, had not. Although his coat was well brushed and clean, it was worn and mended at the cuffs. It was a little too tight across his shoulders, and even a shade too short in the sleeves. And yet, there was something about him that would always draw interested eyes. He felt no shame, no need to pretend. Careless of his outward appearance, he was comfortable in his own skin and not remotely overawed by his aristocratic company.

As the countess turned away, his gaze shifted and found Juliet, still standing in the middle of the room with the tea intended for her father. One of his eyes closed, so quickly and so discreetly, that anyone not staring would have missed it. Her breath caught. She wanted to laugh.

And then her father brushed past her, and the teacup wobbled precariously in her hand. She walked across and set it down by his chair. When she turned back, the earl was civilly shaking hands with the woman who had jilted him, smilingly observed by the woman he had married. The countess's demeanor was as perfect as always, and yet somehow, Juliet suspected she was just a little on edge.

Of course, that could be Juliet's fault. Her moment for escaping through the connecting door and back to her lonely chamber had passed. Juliet went forward with Kitty to greet the Cornwells and be presented to the Stewarts.

"My daughters, Juliet and Katherine." And, of course, not by a flicker did her mother reveal anything other than pride in her daughters.

"Charmed to renew our acquaintance," Colin Cornwell claimed. In the circumstances, he could say no less, but he did sound as if he meant it. As did Mrs. Stewart.

Dan merely smiled, bowed, and murmured,

"How do you do," as if he had never met her before.

Well, Juliet was not supposed to mention the stagecoach, and she had no intention of admitting to their meetings since.

By then, the countess was introducing Mr. King and inviting everyone to sit. "Juliet ring for more tea," she added.

Of course, there was no need to ring. The well-trained servants were already providing another pot and more cups, and Juliet and Kitty ferried tea to everyone.

"Why did you not tell me you were coming?" she murmured to Dan under cover of a smile as she presented him with his cup and saucer.

"Didn't know," he replied. His lips twitched. "I thought it might be a pleasant surprise. If we were allowed to see you."

"You're lucky," she murmured.

"So are you. I almost brought Gun."

At the thought of the dog galumphing among the porcelain, she had to turn away to hide her laughter.

Fortunately, Ferdy wandered in at that point and had to be introduced to everyone. "It's such a beautiful day," he observed. "Can't we move into the garden?"

"There's no reason why you young people shouldn't go out," the countess replied. "I daresay we'll join you after tea."

As they all traipsed out onto the terrace garden, which sloped down to a wider lawn, Ferdy breathed a sigh of relief.

"Don't know how they can bear to be so cooped up indoors," he remarked.

"It's a large, airy room," Mr. Cornwell suggested.

"Not like this," Ferdy said, waving his hand toward the sky and the gardens. "Though I suppose you might be fed up with the sun, Lawrence, since you rode over here."

"I'm content wherever," Lawrence replied, his gaze on Kitty, who smiled back.

"Don't start that, or I'll be sick," Ferdy advised, much to Mr. Cornwell's startlement.

"Do you care for the outdoors, Lady Juliet?" Colin asked.

"Of course," she replied. "Who would not on a day like this?"

"The last time we spoke, you were hoping to accompany Her Highness into Europe," Colin recalled.

"Sadly, she chose someone else, but now that the war is over at last, I suppose we may all go where we please."

"And where would you go if you could decide?" Colin pursued.

"Oh, where would I not go? First, perhaps to Rome, Florence, Greece, Egypt…"

"You are a curious young lady," he said,

apparently amused. "But what on earth would you do there?"

"Look, learn, marvel." She regarded him. "Do you have no spirit of adventure, Mr. Cornwell?"

He smiled indulgently without answering, saying merely, "It is unusual to find it in a young lady."

"There I have to disagree with you."

He looked slightly stunned that any female would disagree with him about anything, even the opinions of her own sex.

Fortunately, Kitty the peacemaker, spoke up. "I prefer the comforts of home. But we are all different. Perhaps, you have been abroad, Mr. Cornwell?"

"Indeed, I have not," he said as though defending his honor. "Daniel, however, was born abroad." He made it sound comparable to being born in prison. "His father was an army captain."

"Colonel," Dan said mildly from where he had stretched out on a wooden bench.

Colin frowned. "What?"

"Nothing. What is rank between cousins?" He sat up and stood. "Will you show me your peonies, Lady Juliet?"

Juliet blinked but walked past him toward the terrace steps. "I did not know you were interested in flowers."

"I confess I don't know peonies from pinks,

but I am prepared to learn. Tempted as I am," he added below his breath, "to stay here and see which of us punches my cousin first."

"I didn't realize you let him upset you."

Dan cast her a rueful glance. "I don't usually. I didn't realize he was quite such a condescending prig."

"And you don't mind him picking on you, but he should give your father the respect he deserves?"

His lips quirked. "Something like that."

"This is the peony. It is quite beautiful this year."

"Ah, *that's* a peony," he said, fortunately before those following came close enough to overhear his ignorance. "What are those bands on the grass for?"

"Pall mall," Ferdy said, opening the wooden box at the side of the lawn to reveal the wooden balls and mallets withing. "Want a game?"

Dan smiled.

It was, in the end, a hilarious game with a hotch-potch of rules and no one keeping proper score. Even Colin relaxed enough to smile, while Dan and Ferdy outdid each other with amusing trick shots and silly wagers, which saw Dan losing his handkerchief to Ferdy and then winning Ferdy's cravat. Ferdy tied the handkerchief around his neck instead. But it was Juliet who won the game, in time to receive the applause of the older people who had wandered down to watch.

"Brava," Mrs. Stewart exclaimed. "A notable female win!"

Juliet laughed. "Hardly. They only declared me winner because no one was counting the scores."

"You should still have a prize," Dan declared.

"Then I shall have a peony from the garden. If you can still remember which that is."

Dan grinned and walked off to return with a luscious, red bloom, which he gave to the countess to present to Juliet. After which, the servants brought out some freshly made lemonade, and everyone sat informally on walls and cushioned benches according to taste.

Juliet saw Mrs. Stewart sit beside the earl. She wondered if her mother noticed it, too. Mrs. Cornwell certainly did, for she looked as if she would like to drag her sister away by the ear. However, after only a few moments, Mrs. Stewart moved and sat on the wall beside Juliet instead.

"I heard about your trouble," she murmured. "Allow me to say, you handle it very well."

"Thank you," Juliet said faintly. "I think."

"Oh, yes, it was a compliment," Mrs. Stewart assured her. Her eyes twinkled rather like Dan's did. "I'm sure you're aware I speak from experience."

"Did you also handle it well?" Juliet asked. She hadn't meant to. It just slipped out.

"No," Mrs. Stewart said. "I ran away. I admire you for meeting it head-on. But then, you are innocent."

Perversely, Juliet said, "You don't know that."

"Oh, I think I do. Tell me, did you lose a velvet ribbon?"

"A velvet..." Juliet broke off with sudden uncertainty. Did she mean Gun's unconventional leash? "Not recently," she said in a rush. "Why?"

"Oh, I am curious by nature. As, I think, are you." She smiled amiably and rose. "Tabetha, do you think it is time we left these good people in peace?"

Tabetha looked anything but gratified to be reminded of manners by her scandalous sister, but there was little she could do except agree and stand up, opposing the polite objections of her hostess.

The carriage was summoned, and everyone trooped round to the front of the house to wave the visitors away. Juliet still clutched her peony, and halfway to the carriage, Dan suddenly paused and came back to her.

She smiled, about to offer her hand, but unexpectedly, he took the peony from herand began to thread the stem through her hair, reusing several hairpins to hold it in place.

Flushing under his ministrations, she murmured, "What are you doing?" For though the brush of his fingers in her hair was curiously pleasant, even exciting, she was very conscious of being in full view of everyone else.

"I don't know." His hands fell away, and his gaze dropped to hers, and then to her lips. Her heart gave a funny little lurch, and she couldn't breathe. A reluctant smile flickered across his face. "I never know."

Then he stepped back, bade a civil farewell to everyone else, and jumped up into the carriage.

"He is a little forward, that young man," her mother observed. "But there, I daresay he is merely unconventional. Or would you say eccentric?"

"I'd say both," Juliet replied. And the strange thing was, she wouldn't have him any other way.

CHAPTER TEN

SINCE SHE HAD come home, Juliet had left the shutters and curtains in her bedchamber open, so that she was more likely to wake at dawn. When she opened one eye, it still seemed pitch dark, so she closed it again.

Only then, the unmistakable sounds of pattering rain filled her ears, and she sat up. It *was* dawn, but the sky was cloudy, and the birds were quieter than usual.

Drat the rain! She and Dan could hardly have their al fresco breakfast in such weather. In fact, he probably wouldn't come, which was lowering. However, *she* would go as usual. If nothing else, she would have a good walk.

She donned an old walking dress, sturdy old boots, and her traveling cloak, then picked up the umbrella from the stand by the side door.

However, the rain was relentless. There was little chance she would not get soaked and covered in mud.

The umbrella was useless in the woods, so she had to fold it up, but at least the trees gave some protection.

She saw him at the edge of the path, silhouetted against the lightening sky and the river. At least she hoped it was him, for he looked different hunched under the trees, his collar standing up and rain streaming off his hat.

Fortunately, he heard her coming and turned, and she immediately hurried on to meet him. Unfolding the umbrella, she reached up to hold it over him, too. He laughed and took it from her.

"Not a pleasant day for a walk," he observed. "I passed a disused hut on the other side of the river."

"There's a cave closer by," she replied. "Along the riverbank. Come."

As they broke from the trees, he threw one arm around her shoulders, presumably to keep her steadily under the umbrella. She was not used to such easy contact. Even waltzing was more formal. But Dan seemed to be a very *physical* man. It excited her in some inexplicable way, but she didn't dislike the feeling in the slightest.

The riverbank was slippery, and twice they almost ended in the water before she located the gap in the bank, overhung by willow roots.

"It seemed much larger before," she said as he crawled in after her.

"When you were ten years old?" he suggested. "But it is dry, and I'm not complaining." He took off his hat carefully and emptied the water collected in the brim outside the cave. He glanced at her. "Actually, I didn't think you would come."

"I almost didn't. I nearly went back to sleep, but I would miss the walk."

"Me, too," he said vaguely.

"But where is Gun?"

"I left him at home, much to his outrage. He's impossible in weather like this. I'll take him later when I hope the rain will have gone off."

"I got some honey cakes from Cook last night," she said, fishing in her reticule. "They might be a little stale."

"But very welcome. A cup of hot coffee would be good, too."

"It's not very civilized," she agreed.

"Do you want to stop?"

Her eyes flew to his. "Do you?"

"I asked first."

"I'm here in the pouring rain," she retorted, "so I suppose I don't." She bit into her cake and considered. "Though after yesterday, I presume we can call at each other houses in the normal way."

"Not sure my grandfather would agree," he

said wryly. "Mind you, I saw Patrick, the steward, coming out of his rooms yesterday, and he didn't look unhappy, so it's possible the old devil is softening in some ways."

"Does he receive you all in his bedchamber?"

"He won't allow anyone in unless he summons them—one at a time, of course, to lessen the chances of rebellion. But I don't think he's seen anyone more than once. Except me, because I barged in and took him by so much surprise that he forgot to throw something at me."

"Maybe the others should do the same."

"Colin tried. He threw the teapot at him."

She couldn't help her hiccup of laughter. "The secret is clearly to judge one's moment."

"Or duck and keep going, though that's certainly a risky tactic."

"Perhaps he just likes you."

Dan appeared to consider that. "No."

"Why not? People do, you know. Besides, he probably prefers people who defy him. He must be bored with servants and toadies. In fact, he sounds a very sad, lonely person to me."

"Sad, lonely, and very bad-tempered."

"Maybe he didn't bring you all to Myerly to fight, but to provide company."

"Well, he doesn't take much advantage of it."

"But he must hear your voices sometimes, your footsteps, all the bustle that comes with extra people. And even though he's improving, he hasn't asked anyone to leave Myerly, has he?"

"No," Dan allowed. His lips quirked upward. "You're quite wise and compassionate for a social butterfly, aren't you?"

"I don't know about any of that," she said hastily. "Except that I'm not a social butterfly. I just like people. They interest me."

"I know. It's part of your charm."

She couldn't help her flush of pleasure, though she said, "Stop. I'm always suspicious of flattery."

"Why, in case I kiss you again?"

Butterflies jumped in her stomach. "No," she managed. "That was a kiss of friendship. Friends don't flatter."

"But they do tell the truth."

"Hmm." She brushed the crumbs off her hands. "You just like teasing me."

"I do. But much as I hate to say it, you should go home and change into dry clothes before you catch a chill."

"So should you. And you have further to go. You shouldn't come with me this time."

He shifted position and stretched one long leg out under the tree roots. "I'll come part of the way and see if the sun comes out."

"Optimistic," she commented. "It looks to me as if the rain is on for the whole day."

"At least there's no wind. Or lightning."

Dan crawled out of the cave first and clapped

his hat back on his head, while she drew up her cloak hood and they scrambled up the bank, sometimes sliding backward again until Dan dug the point of the umbrella into the mud to hold them in place. The rain, if anything, was even heavier.

Eventually, laughing, they staggered over the top and ran for the shelter of the trees, Dan's arm around her shoulders once more and the umbrella over their heads. She tripped over a gnarled tree root that crossed the path and stumbled back against the trunk. Only his arm prevented her from falling, but it still seemed exquisitely funny as she laughed up at him.

His eyes never left her face as he folded the umbrella. Gradually, the laughter in them died, leaving an expression of something very close to wonder. His gaze flickered to her mouth, and her stomach dived, much as it had yesterday. Rain ran off his hat and face. It trickled over his parted lips, and she couldn't look away.

He bent his head and kissed her. It was gentle and brief, and she thought he was smiling as he did it. But her heart hammered as he raised his head. From pure instinct, she reached up to his damp cheek and drew him back.

His mouth closed over hers and began to move, caressing, exploring, and the world stood still. There was only Dan, the wonder of his kiss, of his arms around her. Rivulets of rain ran down into her hair, into her mouth. The kiss deepened, and she gasped, following his lead and her own blind desire. She flung her arm around his neck, tangling her fingers in his wet hair, and wished this moment would go on forever.

It seemed it would. She no longer knew if it was the same kiss or if had turned into others, just that she seemed to have melted in his heat and that a sweet, heavy ache was forming in her stomach, in her whole body.

With a groan that was almost laughter, he broke the kiss, holding her tightly against him with his cheek pressed to hers. That was wonderful, too.

"Dan," she whispered.

Slowly, he raised his head and met her gaze. His eyes were warm and clouded and yet faintly rueful.

And then she heard the voices, clear, easily recognizable, and almost upon them.

"Surely, she wouldn't have come so far in such weather?" Kitty said, almost pleading.

Juliet stared at Dan in horror. Something very like laughter flashed in his eyes, but he drew her slowly around the tree, which might hide them from the path, especially in the rain.

"She might have gone to the cave to wait for the rain to go off," Ferdy replied.

"She won't even remember the cave. I don't think *I* could find it."

"Hmm. She's probably warm and dry at home while you and I…" Ferdy paused, and Juliet was afraid to breathe.

Then she saw the umbrella lying in the grass where they had been standing before. Ferdy picked it up.

"It's ours!" Kitty exclaimed.

Their feet came closer, rounding the tree as she and Dan slid farther around—and came face to face with Ferdy. Juliet swung the other way, and there was Kitty.

"Found," Dan said cheerfully to Ferdy. "Now it's your turn to hide. Since you seem to be playing."

Ferdy looked as if he wanted to be stern and ended by appearing merely bewildered.

"You're playing hide and seek?" Kitty demanded. "In this weather? At this time of the morning? Juliet, is this an *assignation*?"

"Oh, don't be silly," Juliet said crossly. "Dan is a friend, and you know how bored I've been. In—"

"Why doesn't he just come to the house?" Ferdy interrupted in a flat, hard voice.

"I did," Dan said. "But I wasn't received until yesterday. Look, you're right to be concerned, but I would not hurt your sister, and you're probably right that today was a mistake. Come, we can talk as we walk back toward the house."

"Why do you seem too reasonable to be

ordered off my land?" Ferdy wondered.

"Feel free," Dan offered. "I'll go if you ask. And let's face it, my grandfather would happily throw you all off his. It seems to be up to us to behave like adults."

"Adults!" Kitty exclaimed. "Playing hide and seek in the rain before seven in the morning?"

"Even adults play games," Dan said. "I should know. I've lost money at most of them."

Ferdy gave a crack of laughter. "You're an amusing rogue, I'll give you that. But you shouldn't be meeting my sister in secret. And Julie, what the devil are you thinking of? You're not even out of the last scrape yet, and you're getting into another. How is anyone meant to believe this orgy business is lies if you're—"

"How dare you compare the two?" Juliet said furiously. "Dan is the one who—"

"No, he's right, Juliet," Dan said ruefully. It felt like a slap in the face. "I always knew it was wrong. It just seemed the lesser of two evils for you at the time. Now, it isn't. We've had a good run of luck, but it's time to change games before we're caught by someone who could hurt you with gossip. I'll call like the gentleman I'm supposed to be."

"That would be best," Ferdy said, though he spoiled it almost immediately by asking, "Did Juliet show you the cave?"

"We nearly ended in the river several times."

The rest of the walk home passed in pleasant chatter, leaving Juliet baffled and hurt that Dan had given in so easily. He had kissed her—kissed her in such a way—and now he was shuffling her off. Did he imagine he would be forced to marry her?

And dear God, what had she been thinking of to allow such intimacy? To kiss someone she had no intention of marrying... But that line of thought seemed far too confusing.

"Join us for breakfast?" Ferdy offered, having apparently forgotten his original ire. Had that been Dan's plan all along?

"Thanks, no, I won't. I want to see the Myerly steward, and I need to take my dog for a run if he'll still acknowledge me." And with that and an amiable bow to her and Kitty, he trudged back the other way, kicking up mud and puddle water as he went.

She turned resolutely away in the other direction. "Why were you looking for me in the first place?" she asked her siblings.

They glanced at each other.

Reluctantly, Kitty said, "I saw you go out early yesterday morning and the one before. You always veered off the drive to the woods. Then I saw you with Mr. Stewart yesterday, and it seemed to me you were friendlier than acquaintances who had met on a dull stagecoach journey. And then this morning, you weren't in your room, and it was bucketing with rain. So, I woke Ferdy and made him come and help me look for you."

"Oh, dash it, Kitty!" she exclaimed and broke off to take a deep breath. "I know you meant it well, and it is just your good nature. But this…this whole situation *stifles* me. It's as if I have no control over anything anymore, and Papa is as likely to marry me off to the weasel after all as to send me to a nunnery or lock me in the attic!"

Ferdy grinned. "He won't lock you in the attic. You'd make a shocking row."

His sisters ignored him.

"So, Mr. Stewart is your way of controlling your life? Is he not a little…erratic for such purposes?"

"Entirely," Juliet said helplessly. "He is simply *fun*. And he may not be rich, but he *is* a gentleman." *A gentleman who kissed me in the rain, and dear God, I want him to do it again.* She swallowed. "But thank you for looking after me."

"Then you won't do it anymore?" Kitty asked anxiously.

She shook her head. He would not be there anymore. She wanted to cry.

They entered the house by the side door and went their separate ways to change out of their wet clothes. Clean and dry at last, Juliet made her way down to the breakfast parlor, where she almost bumped into her father coming out.

He was frowning over a letter while he walked but pulled up short at her murmured apology. Unexpectedly, his brow cleared. "Ah, Juliet, just the person I was looking for. Come into the library for a moment."

It was something of a relief that he didn't appear to be angry with her. After all, he had been so since she'd come home.

"This letter is confusing me," he said, closing the library door behind them. "Perhaps you can shed some light on it."

"Oh, dear, it's not from the Alfords again, is it?" she asked apprehensively.

"What? Oh, no. They will come tomorrow when they said they would. This is from Lord Barden. Are you acquainted with him?"

"Very slightly. He had some place in the Prince Regent's household, and he occasionally carried messages to Her Highness when I was there."

"Did he show any special interest in you?"

"No, I don't believe so. In fact, I rather thought he disliked me for some reason. But I never paid him much attention, and then the princess refused to receive him because he'd shown too much interest in Ha...one of the other ladies." She frowned. "But oddly enough, he was at Connaught Place the night—*that* night—and he was still there in the morning."

Her father frowned. "You mean, he saw you there?"

"I think so, yes."

"He must know what happened and that you are innocent."

"Then I wish he would say so," Juliet said tartly.

"Perhaps he intends to. He is proposing to visit us while we are holding Kitty's engagement dinner, in fact, and I don't believe I have time to put him off. But then, it may work out for the best."

"What may?" Juliet asked, bewildered.

"His assurance. If you are there. He writes quite cryptically, but if I'm reading it aright, he is implying he might offer for you. And if he does…and if Jeremy Catesby stops behaving like a nincompoop, you may yet have a choice of suitor. Which cannot be bad."

"Can't it?" she said, gawping at him.

"No…Odd who your friends turn out to be sometimes."

"*Is* Lord Barden your friend?" she managed.

"I didn't think so. Well, not after I won most of his fortune off him at hazard one night."

Her eyes widened. "That was Lord Barden?"

His eyes refocused on her face. "I'm not proud of it. But he would keep playing." He shrugged. "Debt of honor. He had to pay, though it left him damnably short. But at least he got the place with Prinny, so he didn't starve."

"You would consider a poor man for me?" she blurted, her mind for some reason on Daniel Stewart.

"It's true I wouldn't have up until a week ago," her father replied. "But if it gets us out of this scrape, I'll give an even more handsome dowry. I'd never let you want for anything." He waved the letter at her. "Go and eat, girl. You look half-starved."

CHAPTER ELEVEN

DESPITE THE RAIN, Dan spent most of the day outside. After a quick breakfast with his mother, he rescued Gun from his makeshift kennel in the garden and trudged over the fields with him to meet Patrick and Pat.

The older man was delighted that Lord Myerly had finally agreed to some basic repairs and to look again at plans he'd shown him two years ago. Young Pat was furious because his lordship hadn't gone nearly far enough to save the estate.

"You'll never get it all out of him at once," Dan said when Patrick had ridden off to report again to his lordship. "And at least he's talking to your father now. We have to start somewhere."

"Well, I have to hand it to you," Pat admitted. "No one else has ever got him as far as the desperate repairs before."

"We'll see how much further we can get him before he throws me out the house," Dan said cheerfully. "But if I'm going to talk him into things, or at least try to, I'll need a better understanding of what I'm talking about. Will you show me?"

"So that you know I'm not talking rubbish?"

"That, too," Dan admitted, but Pat didn't take offense, merely set off toward the ditch at the foot of the field. The rain had slowed to a mere drizzle.

By the end of the afternoon, Dan knew more than he'd ever imagined about drainage, enclosures, and crop rotations, and had grasped the sense as well as the scale of the improvements Pat wanted to make.

Exhausted, but with his mind buzzing around the problems and possibilities, he arrived home with Gun in time for dinner. The rain had gone off altogether, so he was more or less dried off as he walked upstairs and straight into his grandfather's rooms.

Waits looked wary. "His lordship's just preparing for dinner, sir."

"Who's that?" the old man yelled from the bedchamber. "If it's that blithering, prancing idiot, send him about his business."

Dan, who had no difficulty in recognizing his cousin Hugh from this description, grimaced as he sauntered over to the bedchamber. "I might be an idiot, but I don't think I prance. May I come in?"

"You *are* in, are you not?" his grandfather snapped.

"I won't keep you," Dan promised.

"Damned right. You look as if you've been dragged through a hedge backward."

"If I haven't, it's only because Pat didn't think of it. He did drag me through several ditches, though. There's quite a science to this farming business, isn't there?"

The old man regarded him with contempt. "How would I know? I'm a gentleman, not a damned farmer."

"You're a poorer gentleman than you need to be," Dan said, frankly. "Which brings me to what I wanted to ask you. Do I have your permission to look at the estate books?"

The old man's jaw dropped. Then he rallied. "Checking up on the inheritance I won't leave you?" he snarled.

"You're not dying, Grandfather," Dan said wryly. "Not yet. I want to see what there is, to see where and by how much it can be better."

"Why?"

Dan shrugged. "Got nothing better to do," he said honestly. "And besides, it's actually interesting. I like this place. You have good people."

His grandfather goggled at him, and he wondered what the devil he had said wrong. Then the old man let out a bark of laughter. "Very well. Tell Patrick to show you what you like. When you've looked, talk to me again. Now go away so I can enjoy my dinner in peace."

>>>×<<<

THE NEXT MORNING dawned a little cloudy but fair. Dan and Gun stepped into the fresh air and loped together toward Myerly hamlet. The people there had got used to seeing them over the last week and now generally waved or exchanged greetings with him. Some would even make a fuss of Gun, although the tavern cat kept a safe distance. It was too early for most people to be about, so he skirted the hamlet and paused.

For days, even in the pouring rain, this was where he had cut across the fields to the river and crossed the bridge to Hornby. To Juliet. He wondered if she would come, despite their discovery. If she would be waiting for him among the trees, reading, painting and ready to greet him with the smile that made his heart turn over.

He could just go and see. He would hate to disappoint her.

But this wasn't his usual type of flirtation. For one thing, she didn't flirt. They were friends, and for the second time, he had endangered that relationship by being unable to resist kissing her. Worse, they had almost been seen, which had brought home to him the seriousness of their clandestine meetings. There was no need for them if he could call at the house.

It won't be the same.

His mouth twisted into a sad smile, and he turned away from Hornby.

The instant he moved, a loud crack filled the air, startling him out of his reverie. Gun immediately went off like the rifle shot he was named for, barking and bolting straight ahead. Then, when he could find nothing to chase, he ran in circles, as though searching.

Eventually, the dog trotted unhappily back to Dan, sniffing the air with a look of disapproval.

Dan didn't blame him. Even he could smell the gunpowder. Someone was up early shooting foxes or rabbits. Or poaching, perhaps. Whatever the victim, the shot made Dan feel oddly exposed.

⟫⟫⟫⟪⟪⟪

JULIET WOKE AT dawn as she had done for most of the last week. Her heart felt stupidly heavy that she had no need to rise to keep her assignation.

I could just go and see if he is there…

And if Kitty is watching me again? If she tells Papa? For my own good, of course...

Determinedly, she closed her eyes. Dan's laughing face seemed to dance across her vision. And then came closer, his eyes warm and serious. She remembered his lips on hers, the novel sensations of deep, passionate kisses and heat spread through her belly. Her whole body tingled.

Almost with surprise, she realized she liked everything about Dan, from the way he talked to the way he moved. From his casual kindness to his unexpected passions for matters like farming. His care for his mother, the reluctant affection she sensed for his grandfather, and his growing interest in the Myerly people. Dan was a good man.

And no one had ever kissed her as he did.

Juliet had always been curious. In her first Season, she had allowed a fervent suitor to steal a kiss, which had so utterly underwhelmed her, she had immediately lost interest in him. Jeremy was more a man of devoted speeches and gifts, which she had mistaken for respectful love. And she had been comfortable with him, had looked forward to learning about physical love with him when they were married.

Dear God, what an escape! From the shallowness of his affections—*and* hers, if she was honest, for what she had imagined to be love had died instantly that last morning at Alford House when she had asked for his trust and been offered twenty pounds. But also, it had clearly been an escape from future boredom. Jeremy was an excellent partner for dinner or dancing, a welcome guest to one's box at the opera, or to tea, but to live with him...her spirit would have shriveled and died. One touch of Dan's finger excited her more than...

And she should not be thinking like this.

In desperation, she threw off the bedclothes and rose. She was thinking about Dan, she told herself, to avoid thinking about the arrival of the Alfords, who were expected by dinner time this evening. Her father anticipated much of this visit, although at least he had become less intense about it since the letter from Lord Barden. He imagined either Jeremy or Barden would come up to scratch and save her from utter ruin.

Juliet, on the other hand, was wondering how to play them off against each other until the whole scandal blew over.

If it ever did. Either way, the next few days and Kitty's engagement dinner were going to be a strain on her nerves. And she did not even have her time with Dan to look forward to, to sustain her.

Yes, I do, she told herself. *He will call at the house, as he did before...*

However, the only visitors from Myerly were

Colin Cornwell and his cousin Hugh Ames, and they did not stay long.

"We come merely as messengers from our mamas," Hugh explained, presenting a letter to the countess.

Colin bowed and handed her a similar one with an apologetic smile. "The upshot is, we are all honored by your invitation to Lady Katherine's dinner and are delighted to accept."

That they had been invited was news to Juliet, whose spirits immediately lifted.

"Mr. Stewart is not with you today?" she asked politely.

"Alas, we could not drag him away from his dusty books," Hugh mourned.

Juliet blinked. "Dusty books?"

"Estate ledgers," Colin said disparagingly. "He must imagine it will impress my grandfather."

"Do you think so?" Hugh sounded surprised. "I've never known Dan try to impress anyone. Strange fellow. I would die of boredom, and as for inhaling those decades of dust, I believe I would be ill for a month."

"Do you care to read, Lady Juliet?" Colin inquired.

"Yes, though I have yet to try ledgers!"

"I imagine no one will force such dull matter upon you. Perhaps you have read *Waverley*?"

It was a short, slightly ponderous discussion

that lasted a quarter of an hour before the gentlemen took their leave.

"I look forward to seeing you again on Saturday," he said to Juliet, smiling.

"Do you know," Kitty observed when the door had closed behind them, "I think he came just to see you, Juliet."

"Perhaps he doesn't read the same newspapers as everyone else."

"Or perhaps he thinks he'll try for an earl's daughter while her stock is low," Ferdy mused.

"Don't be vulgar, Ferdy," the countess snapped.

"Or insulting," Kitty added, glaring at her brother.

"Not insulting at all," Juliet said tiredly. "Papa told me he is now considering poor suitors. It is not Ferdy but the suitors themselves—if they exist—whom I find insulting."

❯❯❯❯❮❮❮❮

AS EVERYONE EXPECTED, greeting the Alfords when they arrived just before six o'clock that afternoon, was something of a trial. The original plan had been to welcome them as almost-family who would spend a few days with them, allowing Juliet and Jeremy time together while their fathers put the final touches to the marriage agreements. And of course, they would have been honored guests at Kitty's betrothal.

But trust and goodwill had vanished. Now it was strictly business, with Lord Alford and Jeremy holding the upper hand. Lord Cosland's chief concern was to marry off his elder daughter at almost any price that would have a chance of saving her reputation and, therefore, the entire family's.

Fortunately, it was deemed best for Juliet to stay very much in the background. Perversely, now that she was called upon to be present at all, Juliet rather wished she could hide in her chamber instead.

It was her mother who saved the day. Being the perfect hostess, she greeted them hospitably and immediately swept Lord and Lady Alford upstairs to their rooms.

"Ferdy, take Jeremy up," she called over her shoulder. "And make sure he has everything he needs."

Jeremy eyed Ferdy somewhat warily. Ferdy looked back without friendliness.

"This way," he said at last.

Only then did Jeremy's gaze actually meet Juliet's. Surprise flickered across his face. *At what?* she wondered. That she had not gone into an obvious decline? That she was dressed in fine sprig muslin and jewels rather than sackcloth and ashes?

She inclined her head very slightly and walked back into the drawing room with Kitty at her heels.

"That could have been worse," Kitty observed with relief.

"It will be," Juliet assured her.

>>>><<<<

"I HOPE YOU don't mind," Dan's mother said to him during dinner that evening, "but I accepted Lady Cosland's invitation to dine. On behalf of both of us."

Dan, who had been performing complicated calculations in his head, dragged himself into the real world with a start. "What invitation?"

"Lady Cosland's," his mother replied patiently. "They are holding a dinner party for all the important families of the area to celebrate Lady Katherine's engagement."

"Oh, that. But we're not an important family of the area."

"Apparently, we count because of our connection to Grandfather," Hugh explained.

Dan's eyebrows flew up. "What, did they invite the old gentleman, too? Is he going?"

"How could he when he cannot get out his bed?" Aunt Tabetha demanded.

"I'll wager he could if he wanted to," Dan

remarked. "But I take your point."

"He wouldn't go to Hornby if he could," Colin said. "He hasn't spoken to Cosland in decades."

"Don't suppose Cosland has invited him in decades either," Dan replied.

"I'll tell you what, though, Dan," Hugh said, frowning in his direction. "Think you might need a better coat for the occasion."

"This *is* my better coat. I'm hurt you didn't notice."

"I noticed it was black and not blue. And I know you're not remotely hurt. I could lend you one."

"It wouldn't fit," Hugh's father said vaguely.

"I won't care so long as it's pink. Or yellow," Dan said, grinning at Hugh. "Is it?"

"Of course not, dear boy," Hugh said, apparently affronted. "Colors are for morning wear. Evening clothes are black. Apart from waist-coats."

"I can't wait," Dan assured him.

He sat back while the servants cleared away the dishes and brought in an apple sponge pudding with vanilla custard.

Griffin, overseeing matters to his satisfaction, bowed to the table. "His lordship has asked me to pass on his invitation that you take a glass of wine with him after dinner. In his rooms."

"Who?" Tabetha demanded.

"Everyone, ma'am," Griffin replied. He bowed again and left.

"All of us?" Hugh said doubtfully. "Not sure I care to have a glass of wine thrown at me."

"You've got to be quick," Dan acknowledged.

"Is there even room for us all up there?" Mr. Ames demanded.

"I daresay Waits will *make* enough room," Aunt Hetty said doubtfully.

"There is nothing worse than being forced into a crowded room with a sick person," Mr. Ames said with a frown of worry.

"Then don't go," Aunt Tabetha retorted. "I doubt he meant you in any case."

"Why would he not?" Hetty demanded with unexpected spirit. "I suppose my husband must count among *everyone*!"

Dan's mother reached for her spoon. "If he doesn't want us all, I imagine he'll weed us out at the door in no uncertain terms. We should all go and be prepared to run."

"Your levity is inappropriate," Tabetha said grandly. "Have you considered he wants to see us all because he is actually dying?"

"No," Jenny replied.

Hetty laid down her spoon. "Suddenly, I am not hungry."

"Save it for later," Hugh advised. "Think I will, too."

After a day spent among numbers and riding about the various farms, Dan was not about to give up any part of the somewhat meager meal. Eventually, realizing everyone was staring at him, he shoveled in the last spoonful and rose, still chewing, and gestured with his hand toward the door.

"What's got into the old devil?" he murmured as he walked upstairs with his mother.

"Who knows? You saw him last. How was he?"

Dan shrugged. "He let me prattle on for a bit but didn't shout. Threw me out when his man of business turned up from Kidfield. I hope he wasn't trying to dismiss the Patricks because I've been nagging him…"

Lord Myerly was discovered in his dressing room. Wrapped in a startlingly fine embroidered dressing gown, little worn but probably dating from the previous century, he sat in an armchair by the empty fireplace. Other chairs had been brought in, and he waved everyone toward them with surprising cordiality. Naturally, there weren't enough. Hugh stood somewhat nervously behind his father's. Colin leaned his shoulder against the side of the mantelpiece farthest from the old man. Dan, after helping Waits to distribute glasses and wine, rested his hip on the arm of his mother's chair.

For a recluse, Lord Myerly seemed to enjoy

being the center of attention as he gazed around his family.

"Don't look so worried," he said at last. "I won't keep you long. Just thought you'd all like to drink a toast with me."

"Your continued good health, Grandfather," Colin said politely.

The old man glared at him. "*My* toast!" he snapped. "Which is to my heir. Yes, I've made my decision."

"May we know what you based it on?" Hugh's father asked mildly—and rather bravely, Dan thought.

Oddly enough, Lord Myerly didn't annihilate him, either verbally or with missiles. "Good question," he allowed. "I have three grandsons. Colin is the eldest. Dan is the son of my eldest daughter. Hugh is...Hugh. I couldn't make the decision based on age or birth, so I asked each of them what they would do with the land if they got it." He glared around each of his grandsons. "None of you said anything remotely sensible, let alone practical."

Dan smiled faintly into his glass. His grandfather was unlikely to recognize a sensible suggestion rammed under his nose.

"But Dan went and found out," the old gentleman growled. "He talked to people, my old steward and his fiery son. He looked at the land, looked at the books, and nagged me to utter boredom!"

"Not Dan then," Hugh murmured, and Dan cast him a quick grin.

"Why not Dan?" their grandfather demanded. "Because I quarreled with his mother? Because his father was a mere army captain?"

"Colonel," Dan said mildly.

His grandfather ignored him, glaring instead from Hugh to Colin. "Well, here's one in the eye for you, popinjay! And you, Master Ramrod. Dan will get the estate. Everything that is not entailed." He thrust his glass out. "My heir!" he declared and drank.

Dan's mouth fell open.

Jenny began to laugh.

"Well, that's that," Hugh said, sounding almost relieved.

"Papa, you cannot have considered…!" Tabetha spluttered.

"At least consider a three-way split of the estate, Papa," Hetty wheedled.

"Three-way split?" her father repeated with contempt. "You never mentioned such a thing before, just how it would benefit Hugh, who apparently has this powerful affection for me! No, I've considered and considered well. He speaks his mind, and he cares what happens to the place, not just for how it will boost his standing. It's done. My will is made and signed, and Dan is my heir. To Dan."

He drank again. This time, Jenny echoed him. "To Dan!" she said and raised her glass to him before drinking.

"To Dan," Hugh agreed, with a sigh. "At least now, you can get a new coat."

"On my expectations?" Dan asked.

"He's not even taking it seriously!" Tabetha exclaimed.

"I'm stunned," Dan said frankly. "I'll take it seriously when I can think again."

"Oh, don't pretend," Colin flung at him. "You've been all over my grandfather since you got here, whispering in his ear, turning him against the rest of us…"

"Idiot!" Myerly roared, making everyone, including Colin, jump. It was as well Gun was not present. "Do you imagine I am incapable of independent thought? Or reason? Bah!" He knocked back the rest of his wine and waggled the glass at Waits, who walked over and refilled it before effacing himself.

This seemed to restore his lordship to good humor. "Well, I've said my piece and made my toast, and now we all know where we stand. However, seems to me I'm not dying yet after all, so you can go if you wish. On the other hand, you can stay on into next week, just in case I have a relapse. After Wednesday, there will be no more food until my funeral."

"And by then," Jenny said innocently, "we

shall all be sponging shamelessly off Dan."

»»»«««

DAN LAY AWAKE long into the night, his head full of the totally unexpected news. He was his grandfather's heir. Myerly would be his. Unless the old man changed his mind again, so he should not set his heart on it. Nor should he sit back and wait for it to fall into his lap before he tried to bring about the improvements that would make such a difference to the lives of the people here.

But still, to be master of Myerly. To be able to run his own life instead of being dependent, to give his mother all the choice he wanted for her, to give her a home if she needed one...

It was odd, but until he had come here a week ago, he had never thought of Myerly as home. Coming here had been a chore, a dull chore, seasoned only by resentment on his side and on his grandfather's. Now, of course, the resentment was all with his aunts and cousins, and he didn't seem to care.

I will be a landowner. I will be respectable enough for...

For what? he asked himself severely, banishing Juliet's laughing face from his mind.

But as his brain went over and over possibilities with the land and the village and the house,

Juliet kept intruding into his thoughts. And he liked her there. She was gladness, sunshine…and desire, that too.

It was a heady combination to fill his thoughts, but eventually, his mind gave up and slept.

He woke with the sudden jerk of Gun's body on the bed. The dog did that frequently at night, and it often woke him. But it only meant some sound or smell had caught the dog's erratic attention, and when he felt only a thump of a tail on his leg, Dan merely closed his eyes again.

But something moved in the room. A faint, scuffling sound on the wooden floor. Surely there weren't mice in the bedchambers? Even his easy-going mother would not tolerate that…

But mice did not breathe so audibly.

Dan's eyes flew open once more, peering blindly into the darkness. Was that a person-shaped patch of deeper blackness? He sat up, reaching for the flint on the bedside table, and knocked the candle off on to the floor.

As it clattered, Dan swore, and the patch of blackness moved, no longer shuffling but bolting to the door.

"Wait, what is it?" Dan demanded. "I'm awake now."

The bedchamber door open and closed with a sharp click. Dan threw himself out of bed, aiming for the door and all but falling over Gun, who had elected to accompany him. But when he finally opened the door, the passage was dark and nothing moved.

Dan scratched his head and went back to bed. Clearly, it had been no one threatening, for Gun had only looked up and wagged his tail. He had known who it was. But who the devil would come blundering into his chamber in the middle of the night? And what the devil had they wanted? Whoever it was hadn't even answered him.

Perhaps someone walked in their sleep.

He shrugged and closed his eyes. All the same, he couldn't quite shake off the uneasiness caused by his silent, unknown visitor, and his dreams for the rest of the night were full of ominous shadows.

CHAPTER TWELVE

FOR JULIET, THE following day was even more difficult.

Her father spent a good deal of time in serious conversation with Lord Alford, and they both rode out with Jeremy during the afternoon.

"Showing Alford and Jeremy what they've missed out on," Ferdy said sardonically.

"Don't be silly," Juliet replied. "It's not as if Jeremy would have inherited any of this if he'd married me."

"No, but it's all wealth and power, isn't it? Wealth and power, they will no longer be connected to if they reject you."

"They *have* rejected me," Juliet said flatly.

"Perhaps not for good, Julie," Kitty suggested.

Juliet shrugged. "It no longer matters. I can't

bear to be in the same room as Jeremy, which hardly bodes well for marriage."

"Oh, I don't know," Ferdy said cynically. "Seems to be a requirement for some. I suppose we should go back down to Mama, do the pretty with Lady Alford."

"I thought you would have gone riding with Papa," Juliet observed.

"So did I, but apparently I'm too frivolous and am better employed entertaining the ladies."

"Or he doesn't want you telling me what they're discussing," Juliet said darkly.

"Now *you* are being silly," Ferdy observed.

He was right of course, but Juliet could not help feeling tense and oppressed by the Alfords' presence. Even walking into the room where her mother and Lady Alford sat at their needlework, making quiet and apparently companionable small talk. It infuriated Juliet, who, after the briefest of greetings, sat in the corner with her own embroidery. She could barely bring herself to speak to the woman who had once welcomed her as a daughter. And then turned on her in an hour of need, merely on the word of an unreliable scandal sheet she would never admit to reading.

Everyone makes mistakes. I have made many.

But she has never once apologized for what she did or even acknowledged it.

Juliet hated such bitter, unforgiving feelings,

but she could not seem to shake them off. She wanted to see Dan, to laugh it all away, to feel like herself again.

"Oh, Juliet," Lady Alford said suddenly, laying down her embroidery frame and fussing inside her work bag. "This arrived for you in a bundle of letters sent on to us from London."

"That's odd," Juliet's mother observed. "Who would be writing to you that didn't know you had come home?"

Juliet walked across the room. "I have no idea. Thank you, ma'am," she added, taking the letter. "I don't believe I know the writing."

"It looks like a lady's hand," her mother said. "Open it."

Juliet broke the seal, retreating to her own chair while she unfolded it and glanced at the signature. "Why, it's from Hazel."

"Who is Hazel?" her mother asked, bewildered.

"Miss Curwen. She was one of the princess's other ladies who was…" She paused, not so much at the difficulty of bringing up that night of shame at Connaught Place but because of what Hazel had written. "Dear God. It *was* malice. Hazel has discovered who tricked us that night."

"Who?" her mother demanded with a mixture of hope and dread.

Juliet knew how she felt. Kitty arrived at her side with a gasp and a demand to read the letter.

But along with the euphoria of vindication, came a new wariness, for Hazel's letter was more than information. It was a warning.

Lord Barden had set out to harm them, for spite. And Lord Barden was already on his way to Hornby. This was the man who had lost his fortune to her father, and who was coming here tomorrow with some kind of offer. He could prove her innocence or confirm her ruin, and for that reason, she could not yet reveal his name in public.

She refolded the letter and stuffed it into her work bag. "I shall give it to Papa," she said.

"But this must be such good news for you, Juliet," Lady Alford said with a hint of timidity.

"My innocence, ma'am, is not news to me," she said and picked her embroidery back up. For once, she found the awkward silence soothing.

⤚⤛⤜⤝

HER FATHER JOINED her in the library almost as soon as he returned from his ride.

"I've made them think," he said. "There's definitely regret in both of them at losing you. Whether or not anything comes of it..." He shrugged and sat in the armchair. "Now, what's this about a letter from your friend?"

Juliet gave him the letter, and he read it,

frowning. The frown turned into a scowl. "The blackguard!" he exclaimed. "Absolute scoundrel!" He went back to the beginning and read it again. "She has no proof apart from the fact he called her out in public and is trying to meet with her in private. This is her word against his. Although the Sayles seem to be on her side, which counts in her favor."

Juliet sat down heavily. "Then this means nothing? You still don't believe me?"

"I always believed you," he growled. "It's the world's opinion that bothers me."

Alford's opinion. Jeremy's.

"No one around us cares," she observed. "No one has canceled on Kitty's dinner. She is still engaged. Mama still receives callers. The people from Myerly did not snub us. Do we need to care for the rest of the world's opinion?"

"Yes." He looked up from the letter. "You must be creditably married, Juliet. You are in something of a-a *bubble* here, but the world is larger than Hornby, and a scandal affects all of us, not just you. And God knows I wish you a better life than that of a recluse."

She swallowed. "So, what will you do? Will you receive Lord Barden?"

"It would be dangerous not to."

"Can…can he hurt you, Papa?"

Lord Cosland's lips twisted. "He's already proved he can hurt all of us. He already has."

><<

TEA WAS THE next test of endurance. Conversation moved politely around the fine scenery of Hornby to the prosperous land and, from there, to other comparable estates and the growing importance of additional sources of income.

"I'm not suggesting we all give up land and buy mills," Jeremy said, "but investment in banking and industry, in the Exchange, those will be our future and our fail-safes in bad years." He smiled. "But I suppose I am preaching to the converted here, for I know you already have interests in these areas. I am trying to convince my father."

"Your father's political interests keep him quite busy enough," Cosland said vaguely. He hated to discuss business.

"As do yours," Jeremy replied.

"Oh, no, I'm strictly a dabbler," Cosland said modestly, though with some truth. He was just a rather influential dabbler, which had, probably, been the point of Jeremy's courtship. It had never been about Juliet.

She rose, moving toward the open French window and stepped outside onto the terrace.

"Are you well?" Kitty asked, following her out.

Juliet glanced behind her to make sure no

one else had come out. "Yes. I just feel I can't breathe in their company. I know Papa still wants me to marry Jeremy, and even if Jeremy was willing, I'd rather eat my own boots."

"Not recommended," said a voice that had her spinning around in delight. "Unless your cook is even worse than ours."

"Dan!" She hurried forward to meet him, both hands stretched out in welcome. He was strolling up the terrace steps, looking as he always did: relaxed, mildly disreputable, and wildly handsome. Gun, pulling on the end of his bizarre lead, had his tongue lolling in ecstatic welcome.

"Good day, Mr. Stewart," Kitty said more properly.

Hastily, Juliet dropped one hand, holding it out to the dog instead, while letting Dan take the other. But she couldn't stop smiling. "I am so glad to see you! Have you come for tea?"

"Oh, no, not with Gun here. Just dropping in with my regards and my mother's, to see how you are. Sit, boy," he added to the dog. "Now greet Lady Katherine in a civilized manner. Lady Kitty, this is Gun."

"Because he's liable to go off like a rifle shot," Juliet explained, and Kitty laughed, patting the dog's big head from a safe distance.

"How are you?" Dan asked, looking directly at Juliet.

She wrinkled her nose but smiled. "We're

getting through the days. The Alfords are here."
But, of course, he knew that. It was why he had
come. "Oh, and I had a letter from a friend who is
also caught in this scandal, and we now know
who is responsible. We were indeed tricked with
malicious intent."

He frowned, all laughter gone from his dark,
steady eyes. "Who?"

She shook her head. "I can't say until Papa
has spoken to him, not even to..." *Not even to you.*
Fortunately, she broke off before she said the
words, for she suspected Kitty wouldn't
understand. She wasn't sure *she* did. "Anyone,"
she finished lamely. "How is your grandfather?"

"Cock-a-hoop," Dan said wryly. "Because he
has set everyone at everyone else's throats. Mine,
mainly, because he has made me the heir to
Myerly."

Juliet's eyes widened. "But that is splendid!
Have the others departed in high dudgeon?"

"No, they have stayed put with their dudgeon since my grandfather has condescended to
feed us all until Wednesday."

Kitty said faintly, "Congratulations. Oh, dear,
is that the right thing to say in the circumstances?"

"I have no idea, but I'll take it in the spirit
you intended."

"So, what will you do now?" Juliet asked.
"Go back to London?"

"Nothing to do in London," he said casually. "I thought I might skulk here a bit longer, annoying the old gentleman's steward. If he'll let me."

"Well, you've already got around the cook," Juliet reminded him.

He smiled faintly, but his eyes had gone beyond her. She and Kitty both turned to see Jeremy standing just outside the window. Her stomach tightened unpleasantly as he walked toward them.

"Kitty, your mother is asking for you," he said, giving Dan a nod of acknowledgment before turning expectantly to Juliet for an introduction.

"Mr. Stewart, Mr. Catesby," she murmured, wondering how she could make Jeremy go away.

"Catesby?" Daniel repeated in response to Jeremy's elegant but minimal bow. "Good Lord, is this the weasel?"

Her laughter was sudden, almost hysterical, and she had to choke it back with a somewhat unladylike sound.

Jeremy, quite unused to such blatant rudeness, flushed and looked down his long, aristocratic nose at the shabby stranger. "I perceive you mean to insult my name, sir."

"Not your name," Dan said frankly. "Your person."

Fresh anger flashed in Jeremy's eyes. "I cannot recall ever meeting you in my life before, so I fail to see why you imagine you may insult me with impunity."

"I don't ask for impunity," Dan said at once. "But a man who treats a lady whom he is supposed to love, honor, and cherish, in the shameful way you treated Juliet, is most certainly more weasel than gentleman."

"Dan," she protested breathlessly, for the laughter still lurked very close to the surface.

"You know nothing of the matter!" Jeremy exclaimed, flushing under Dan's contempt.

"I know more than you," Dan retorted. "Because you didn't trouble to listen to her."

Jeremy turned furiously on Juliet. "Have you been gossiping to strangers about our private—"

"Don't you dare," Juliet interrupted, glaring at him. "Don't you *dare* lecture me on *gossip*."

To her surprise, he dropped his gaze with the first hint of shame.

"Oh, it's you, Stewart," came Ferdy's cheerful voice. He strolled toward them, holding his hand out casually to Dan. "Come to be trounced again at pall-mall?"

"I trounced both of you at pall-mall," Juliet said, relieved to change the subject.

"Only because I wasn't playing seriously," Ferdy said. "Come in for tea, Dan?" He eyed the enthusiastic Gun who, forced to sit on Dan's foot, seemed likely to wag his tail off. "Not sure about the monster, though."

"Oh, don't worry, I'm taking the monster away. I won't come in, but give my regards to your parents." With an airy wave and a smile at Juliet, he set off down the terrace steps once more.

She couldn't help feeling lost.

"Who the devil is that?" Jeremy all but exploded. "I beg your pardon, Juliet, but I have never encountered anyone of such insolence."

"Don't you like him?" Ferdy asked in surprise.

"The man called me a weasel!"

Ferdy's gaze flew to Juliet's. The laughter surged so hard, she couldn't speak.

"Have to…" Ferdy began in a strangled voice and then simply turned and strode back to the house.

Since her laughter seemed too likely to turn to tears, Juliet combatted both with anger. "What do you expect, Jeremy? You did not behave well. And you still have not even asked me how I got home that day. A housemaid is entitled to better conditions of dismissal than I was accorded. You believed some filthy scandal rag rather than even ask me, and more or less threw me into the street with nothing."

"I offered you—"

"Twenty pounds," she said with contempt. "I imagine it would cost you considerably more to pay off an opera dancer."

"Juliet!" he protested in shock.

"I am an earl's daughter. And you broke not only your promise to me, but every rule of human decency I can think of. You *are* a weasel." She walked past him and back into the house without troubling to see if he followed.

❈

INEVITABLY, HER MOTHER was still trying to build bridges between them and placed her beside Jeremy for dinner. Fortunately, Ferdy was on her other side, so the silence between them wasn't too noticeable.

It was only when the fish course had been taken away and the meat course was being placed on the table that Jeremy said suddenly, "I do owe you an apology."

Surprised, she turned her head to find him gazing earnestly at her.

"You are right. I acted cruelly and without thought, merely giving in to my pain with no thought of yours. Or of the truth of the matter."

He appeared to mean it, so she replied, "I accept your apology."

"It does not mean," he added hastily, and broke off, biting his lip.

She raised her eyebrows. "It does not mean what?"

"That our engagement is resumed," he muttered. "It will take time."

For a moment, she could only gawp. "No, it won't, Jeremy," she said flatly. "For it will never happen. There is nothing you or anyone else can say or do that would make me marry you. Pass the sauce, Ferdy."

"I have made you angry again," he said miserably.

"Oh, I am beyond anger. It doesn't matter. I am glad to be on civilized terms with you, Jeremy, but under no circumstances imagine I want or will tolerate, more than that." She put a forkful of food into her mouth, barely even tasting it, though when she'd swallowed it, she said, "You should have some sauce with that. It's really very good."

CHAPTER THIRTEEN

O N HIS JOURNEY north into Yorkshire, Lord Barden had plenty of time to reflect on his Great Plan of Revenge.

The first part—the presence of the young ladies at Connaught Place after the departure of the princess and anyone else who might have counted as a chaperone—had gone better than he had hoped. The girls might have hidden, but several people had glimpsed them, and many people knew they were there. And he had personally seen to the circulation of the newspaper in the right quarters. Such as to the Alfords and to Lord Cosland up in Yorkshire.

Oh yes, the women were ruined. But that was only the beginning. Taking advantage of that ruin proved to be somewhat more difficult.

He had begun the journey north in a filthy

temper because he had been forced to abandon his plan for Hazel Curwen. This annoyed him on many levels, not least of which was that he had wanted Juliet's father to be aware that the Curwen girl had recently become his mistress. It would all have added to the insult and humiliation of the offer he was about to make. The offer which the mighty Earl of Cosland could not refuse.

Only when the horses were changed at Kidfield and he began the last stage of his journey to Hornby Park, did he begin to think much about Lady Juliet. He had paid little attention to her, avoiding her at both ton parties and the princess's residence. Her only interest to him was as Cosland's daughter. It was Hazel Curwen who had stirred his blood as well as his ire.

But now he thought of Juliet, he had the impression of a beautiful, vital young creature, courted and toadied. Why her father had placed her with the princess, he had no idea. It wasn't as if Cosland had need of the salary, which Prinny rarely troubled to pay in any case. No, it must have given the earl some political advantage, which Barden had every hope was now shattered with the girl's ruin.

Enter Lord Barden, their only hope.

He smiled out of the window. They were almost there. He was ready. He knew his lines.

But then, he had known his lines at

Brightoaks, and it had all gone horribly wrong. He shuddered at the memory of his departure and swung his attention to his valet, Rogers, whom he had allowed to travel inside the vehicle.

"You will not gossip with the servants at Hornby Park," he commanded.

"Of course not, my lord." Rogers sounded shocked.

"You will say merely that we have just come from Lady Sayle's party at Brightoaks."

"We have."

"And the mode of that departure will never be brought up."

"Never," Rogers agreed, clearly bored.

Barden eyed him suspiciously, but no sign of amusement was visible in the valet's expression. "Good. You will soon have cause to congratulate me. And with the rise in my fortunes comes your own comfort, Rogers."

"You mean I will be paid?" Rogers inquired with a hint of sarcasm.

"Liberally, my good man, liberally. Look, ahead, over there, that must be Hornby..."

Of course, it was as impressive a house and grounds as one would expect of a wealthy earl. It riled Barden, but only a little, for he would have his share. He thought with longing of his own ancestral pile in Hertfordshire, mortgaged to the hilt and rented out to some wealthy cit. Soon, it would be his again. Soon, he would be the one inviting people to stay for week-long parties with his beautiful wife playing hostess to everyone he chose to invite. *Everyone.*

He smiled. *Oh yes*, the great earl and his family would be brought low. There was no way out for them, though he would make it appear there was.

The gracious, tree-lined drive swept up to the house, where the carriage pulled up. Well-trained servants appeared to carry baggage and deal with the horses. Leaving Rogers to instruct them, Barden walked up the steps to the open door. Satisfied, he stepped inside to be greeted by a very superior butler. Barden had once had one of those.

"Welcome to Hornby, my lord," this individual said with a bow, without even glancing at the card in Barden's fingers. "His lordship is expecting you. Her ladyship wonders if you would care to be conducted straight to your chamber? Or if you would care to join the party in the salon?"

"My chamber, if you please."

A footman was summoned with one flick of the butler's eyes and led him across the entrance hall and up the grand staircase—grander than his own—two flights and then along wide but winding passages to a large apartment with two windows and comfortable furnishings.

His bags were already there. And a few moments later, Rogers joined him to dig out a fresh cravat. In truth, he did not have so many clothes that he could change several times a day, but a wash, a brush down, and a clean necktie made all the difference.

He sauntered downstairs and had a footman direct him to Lady Cosland in the salon. Here, welcomed most civilly by the earl and countess, he discovered he was not the only guest. The earl's brother, Lord Stephen Lilbourne, and his family were also present.

"We are having a few guests to dinner this evening," Lady Cosland explained. "By way of marking the engagement of our younger daughter. I hope you will enjoy the company, but if you are tired after your long journey—"

"By no means, ma'am. I should be honored to join you," Barden said politely. "I can only apologize for intruding on a family occasion."

"Not at all, my lord," Lady Cosland assured him. "It is a pleasure to welcome you here, and several of our neighbors will be present, too. We have even set up the drawing room so that the young people may dance afterward."

At that moment, several young people entered the room from the open French windows. Lady Juliet really was a beautiful girl, he saw with fresh pleasure. She outshone her merely pretty sister and the other young lady who must have been a cousin. On the other hand, he wasn't best pleased to see her in the thick of company, as bright and vital as ever. He had assumed she would be punished for her indiscretions, or at least kept out of view. But then, apart from himself, only family members were present.

And then, behind them, came a young man Barden had never expected to see here.

Jeremy Catesby.

For an instant, Barden's world tilted. Dear God, had this plan gone wrong, too?

Behind Catesby, came Cosland's youthful heir, Lord Albright, and a few moments later, Lord and Lady Alford.

Damnation!

"Do sit down, sir," Lady Cosland invited him, "and let me give you a cup of tea. Was your journey very horrible?"

"Why no, not at all," Barden babbled, seating himself beside her. "Surprisingly smooth and trouble-free. The roads are much improved from the last time I was in the north. Is that young Catesby? I must say I am delighted. I had thought the engagement was over."

"Oh, well, young people, you know," Lady Cosland said vaguely. "They may or may not sort out their differences."

A closer look showed Barden that Catesby looked anything but happy. He did put on a pleasant expression when he and the others greeted Lord Barden, but Catesby and Juliet were definitely stiff in each other's company.

Parental pressure, he realized. Cosland was squeezing Alford to fall back into line, and Catesby didn't like it. Obviously, no one, least of all Barden, cared what Juliet liked. The avoidance, or at least reversal, of scandal, was the important thing, as he had always understood.

He barely glanced at Juliet as he bowed to her and her sister, but as he sat down, he realized she had not offered her hand. On leaving him, she retreated to a chair in the corner, and that pleased him more.

Making civil conversation with Lady Cosland and Lord Alford, who had joined them, he finished his tea. The young people began talking about a game in the garden, and the party was about to split up until dinner. Now was Barden's time.

"Perhaps your lordship has a few moments?" he suggested as he rose from his chair.

"Yes, of course," Cosland replied with gratifying promptness. "Come along to the library, where we won't be disturbed."

Barden's heart beat with anticipation. As he took a seat in the opulent library, without waiting to be asked, he watched Cosland close the door, and thought, *This is the man who ruined my life, who took everything from me but the shirt on my back. And now he is about to pay, with interest.*

"I was surprised by your letter," the earl admitted, walking across to join him. He sat in the chair opposite. "Not quite sure what you meant, but I'm very happy to hear you out."

"I knew you would be. May I be blunt, my lord?"

"Preferably."

"I am aware—frankly, who is not?—of your daughter's...fall."

"My daughter did not fall," Cosland barked. "Vile lies perpetrated by some rag I'll see shut down before the month is out."

"I have no doubt you will, and of course, I am well aware of Lady Juliet's *actual* innocence. However, we are both men of the world. We both realize it is not *fact* that governs such frail matters as a young lady's reputation. An unmarried lady found discussing the most unexceptionable topics two yards away from a gentleman but behind closed doors, is compromised. A young lady who spends a night in a house without her family or a chaperone is ruined. Add an orgy to that night, and there is really no hope. I am surprised she is even visible when you are entertaining guests."

Barden was delighted by the effect of this speech. Cosland's face flushed with anger and his lips thinned. His eyes darkened under a growing frown.

"You may leave my daughter's care to me," the earl snapped.

"Apparently, I can't," Barden said insolently.

"You placed her with a royal lady of questionable morals, to say the least." Here was where he had hoped to make clear his own illicit intimacy with another of the princess's ladies. Regretfully, he let the line go, enjoying instead the narrowing of the earl's furious eyes. "It was surely only a matter of time before something went horribly wrong."

"And if you imagine I don't know why or how it went wrong," Cosland growled, "you are very much mistaken!"

This part of the discussion was not meant to come until later when Barden revealed it, but it was no matter. He could adapt.

He smiled. "Then that is one matter I don't have to spell out. Between these walls—although, of course, I shall deny it elsewhere—of course, I was responsible for your daughter's fall. And you should know, I am also prepared to lift her back up."

The earl's hand clenched on the arm of his chair until his knuckles whitened. "How?" he asked between his teeth.

"I am prepared to marry her."

Barden had hinted as much in his letter, in order to be sure of his welcome to Hornby, so the earl did not look particularly surprised. Slowly, his hand unclenched.

"You have an old and respected name," the earl allowed, just as if he still imagined he could negotiate. "But your fortune is...lacking."

Barden's eyes narrowed at the temerity. "Only because you took it from me."

"You *lost* it to me, Barden, in two nights of foolishness neither of us is proud of. Which is why your offer surprises me. Why offer for her now? She has had two London seasons and only became engaged a month ago. Yet now, when you have made her damaged goods…"

"Why, I hoped to provoke you to greater generosity," Barden replied. "The girl does not interest me." Here, again, was where he had hoped to add the extra insult of his relationship with Hazel Curwen, but it didn't matter. The point was still made. "Her dowry does."

Cosland's eye twitched. "If she were to accept your offer, you would not find me ungenerous. However, as you saw, Jeremy Catesby is also here."

Barden smiled. "And neither he nor your daughter look very pleased about it. That bird has flown, Cosland, and we both know it. The Alfords are here in a futile attempt to salvage a little of Juliet's reputation, in the hope of keeping any of your favor at all. They don't want the marriage, and judging by Juliet's face, neither does she. It's insulting. I, however, have never insulted her."

Cosland's jaw dropped. *"Never insulted…* What do you call that damned newspaper piece?"

Barden examined his nails. "Do I control such

a scandal rag? Or any other newspaper?"

"You may drop the act. Both she and I know you are responsible for the story. Her friend, another lady-in-waiting to that princess of questionable morals, has already written to her. From Brightoaks, where the girl appears to be under the protection of the Sayles."

Barden was annoyed, for he hadn't considered the girls would be on such terms of friendship that they would correspond with each other. But he managed a smile. "Indeed, she is. Sir Joseph appears besotted. However, he is not besotted with Juliet. And neither is Jeremy Catesby."

"Nor you!"

"No. But I have terms."

Through his inevitable shame and anger, Cosland tried hard not to look interested. "You had better tell me what they are."

"I'll take her for half of what you promised Catesby for her," Barden said carelessly and waited for the relief to lower Cosland's shoulders before he added, "plus the return of everything you took from me ten years ago."

Cosland's head snapped up. "You lost that fair and square. It was a debt of honor, and you cannot ask for it back."

Barden smiled. "I can, and I do. I deserve it back, not for the ten years—*ten years*—of poverty, at the beck and call of that fat, petulant fool who will one day be king. I deserve it for taking your ruined daughter off your hands and saving her reputation. It's possible I can even get the newspaper in question to retract Juliet's name from the story."

"I tried that," Cosland snarled.

"As I said, it's possible I will succeed where you failed. Either way, your daughter ends up a viscountess with a comfortable life. Society will forgive her in time. You may even get a better husband for your second daughter if you hold off."

"Hold off what?"

"Palming her off on the first gently born bumpkin who came her way."

"We are not speaking of Kitty," the earl said firmly.

"No, we are not. Our men of business can meet as soon, but you could do worse than announce Juliet's engagement along with your other daughter's. I can still make the damage worse if you weasel out."

The earl shot to his feet. "How dare you, sir?" he raged.

Barden laughed. "I dare because I finally have what I want. The return of my property, with a little extra. And a very cold but pleasurable revenge."

CHAPTER FOURTEEN

"HAVE YOU SEEN the dining room?" Kitty asked in dismay, swirling into Juliet's chamber in a waft of gauze and perfume. "Mama must have invited the whole county!"

"Hardly," Juliet said calmly.

"They have opened the partition so that the table stretches across two rooms."

"They often do when they have guests."

Kitty looked very pretty in her gown of pale yellow muslin, with pearls around her throat, dangling from her ears, and threaded through her hair. However, her face was flushed with more anxiety than excitement. She sank onto the edge of Juliet's bed and sighed. "Mama asked me if I would like to do anything to mark the occasion, and I suggested dinner. I was thinking perhaps my aunt and uncle and cousins, and a few of our closest friends. A cozy dinner. But this is a-a *banquet*."

Juliet smiled. "I know. It has been taken out of your hands a bit, but that was inevitable. I think Mama is so determined to prove to everyone how they value Lawrence that she has forgotten your preference for smaller parties."

"Because he is not a great catch by the world's standards?"

"Exactly. But he is a great catch for *you*. You mustn't worry about everyone else. Lawrence will be beside you. Your friends will be there, and you will enjoy it."

She groaned. "And then I will have to worry about the wedding breakfast! If this a mere engagement, what kind of fuss will there be over the wedding?"

"None," Juliet soothed. "Let me just fetch my reticule, and we'll go down together. Once you're with Lawrence, you won't care about anyone else." It was true, and yet another reminder that she had never felt like that about Jeremy. She had been pleased to see him once. She had enjoyed his company, but it had never shut out the world for her.

Snatching up the reticule, she glanced back at her anxious sister and smiled. "You do look particularly beautiful, you know."

"So do you."

Juliet glanced doubtfully in the glass as she

passed. She had made no effort to shine this evening. She wore no jewels, but the dainty diamond set her parents had given her as a coming-out present two years ago. Her gown, of a subtle, icy green silk, was a favorite, but it needed emeralds to bring it to life. But her intention, as well as her parents' wish, was to remain in the background.

And in truth, she had no idea how she would be greeted by these friends and neighbors. No one had refused to come, and no one would be rude to her in her father's house. But no one could deny her name was tainted. Those who had called on her parents in the last week had not brought their daughters. Old friends of her own age had made no effort to see her.

If it had not been for Dan's anticipated presence, she would have felt even more uneasy than Kitty. As it was, she felt rewarded when they descended the stairs into the gallery where the guests were gathering to be greeted by the earl and countess. It was not yet crowded, and Kitty's face lit up like a beacon as soon as she caught sight of Lawrence. And Lawrence, moving instantly toward them, had eyes only for his betrothed.

This made Juliet smile as she moved aside to exchange a few words with Lawrence's kind parents. After a few minutes, she moved away, unwilling to take advantage of their shelter, for this was something of a triumph for them, to have won the earl's daughter into their family. Juliet thought they appreciated Kitty for herself rather than her birth and was glad.

She caught Jeremy's gaze on her once but pretended not to. Unlike Kitty's, her engagement had been for political ends, both her father's and Jeremy's. Only she had been unaware of it.

Lord Barden bowed over her mother's hand, and with a jolt, she remembered Hazel's letter. That the man responsible for her downfall should be here at this moment... She still didn't know why he had come. On impulse, she moved forward, placing herself on a course to intercept him.

He saw her coming and bowed. "Lady Juliet."

"Sir."

"You must be delighted for your sister," he remarked politely.

"Of course. I know she will be very happy."

He smiled, reminding her for some reason of a cat playing with a mouse. "Still, you cannot have expected her to marry before you."

"I never considered the matter," she replied coldly.

"Allow me to offer my sympathies on the ending of your own engagement."

"They are not necessary, sir, but I thank you for your kindness."

"I confess I am surprised to see Mr. Catesby here. Someone is not taking their dismissal well."

With shock, she realized, he did not mean Jeremy, but her. Of course he knew, despite the polite fiction that Juliet had done the jilting, that it was Jeremy who had cried off. But that he should refer to it, when he had, in effect, caused it, flabbergasted her.

"I suspect you are not regarding the unfortunate situation in quite the right way."

"Do you?" she said deliberately, meeting his gaze with all the contempt of which she was capable. "And how do you advise I do regard it?"

"As an opportunity," he replied.

"To do what? Bring to justice the...*person* who traduced me?"

"There is no chance of that," he stated, with frightening confidence. "But you should marry him. There is some justice in that." He smiled at her stupefaction and bowed before moving on. "Lady Juliet."

So that *was* the offer he had made to her father? No wonder Papa was looking tense. Although at the moment his expression could have something to do with the fact that he was greeting Mrs. Stewart and Dan.

Her heart lifted at the sight of Dan, and she found herself already moving toward him as though to her only source of comfort. Fragments of conversations reached her as she walked.

"… Myerly's eldest daughter, you know. The one who jilted Cosland and ran away with a soldier."

"…her name is Stewart now. Do you suppose Cosland still carries a torch for her?"

"…her son?"

"According to rumor, old Myerly made him his heir."

"Hush…"

"How do you do, ma'am?" Juliet greeted Mrs. Stewart, only too aware of the avid listeners.

"Very well indeed. How beautiful you look— does she not, Dan? Oh my, is that Amelia…" She drifted away, and Juliet had to concentrate in order to prevent herself from grabbing Dan's arm and dragging him off to a quiet corner.

"Yes, she does," Dan said, his eyes gleaming as he looked down at her.

She could only smile distractedly and begin to walk, knowing he would fall into step beside her.

"What is it?" he asked, low.

She drew a deep breath. "Nothing really. But that man is here, the one responsible for the vile piece in the newspaper."

"Is he, by God," Dan said softly. "Point him out."

"No, for I don't want you getting in a fight or even a quarrel with him. I think he is dangerous, and I'm afraid…"

"Afraid of what?" he asked, frowning.

"I don't know. But he's also the man whose fortune my father won at cards."

Dan's eyebrows flew up. "Then this business is simple revenge?"

"Not simple. He named four of us, and Hazel seems to have thwarted him somehow with the support of the Sayles. Which is odd in itself, for she never had a kind word to say about Sir Joseph." She drew in her breath. "I'm babbling. I've been needing to talk to you."

"I miss our walks," he admitted. "But, at least tonight, we can enjoy ourselves."

She glared at him. "How can I enjoy myself when I have Barden in one corner, Jeremy in the other, and half the county avidly watching my every step to see if I'm a fallen woman?"

He smiled. "That's my girl."

A moment longer she scowled, then she had to smile back. "You are abominable. How dare you make me laugh when I'm trying to be a tragic heroine in a melodrama?"

"I thought you'd prefer to laugh. It would do me good, too."

"Are things difficult for you? Has the rest of the family not left yet?"

"What, before Lady Cosland's dinner? No, we just couldn't all fit in the one carriage, so we came ahead with Hugh."

"Oh, where is Hugh?" she asked eagerly.

"He is quite soberly dressed, sadly, although there are yellow butterflies on his waistcoat, which he is very proud of."

"And do the others quarrel with you?"

He shrugged. "They gave up when I wouldn't quarrel back. But you could still cut the atmosphere with a knife. Silly, really, because we all know he'll change his will again as soon as I annoy him too much."

"Do you think so?"

He shrugged. "He is capricious."

"So, what have you been doing?"

"I keep out of the way, spend most of my time with Patrick, the steward. Am I allowed to monopolize you like this?"

As it turned out, he was, for he had been earmarked by the countess to take Juliet into dinner. Of course, it was largely to keep the scandalous daughter away from more important people, but the countess could not have chosen a more congenial dinner partner for her.

"Actually, now I think about it," Juliet murmured as he sat beside her at the massive table, "it makes perfect sense. As Lord Myerly's heir, you are an important man and quite worthy to take the earl's daughter into dinner. And yet, you will not be insulted or alarmed by being obliged to talk to me."

"What rot," Dan countered. "You are obviously here to tell me which cutlery to use."

The meal was long and magnificent, and Juliet was glad to see her sister smiling and contented. Ferdy was making up shamefully to the squire's daughter. Jeremy, seated with her cousin Anne, cast Juliet occasional glances, perhaps because she was laughing too much for someone not engaged. She also caught several curious and shyly admiring glances cast by young women—married and otherwise—at Dan.

But it was Barden's observation that made her flesh crawl. So much so, that Dan drew her attention away by asking, "Are you sure you don't want me to take him outside and punch him?"

"Not yet," Juliet said hastily. She glanced at him. "Besides, I've never thought of you as violent."

"I'm a peaceable man for the most part," Dan agreed. "But I'm happy to make an exception for the oily, the weasely, and anyone else who upsets you."

"Oily George," she remembered, almost with fondness. "That seems so long ago, and it is only about ten days!"

He regarded her thoughtfully for a moment, then politely turned to speak to the blushing girl on his other side.

A little later, he turned back to Juliet, asking, "So what happens after this?"

"You will not be encouraged to linger over

your wine, for Mama has hired a fiddler, and there is to be dancing."

"Will you dance with me?"

For some reason, the casual question made her blush. "Of course."

>>>>«««

THE PARTITION BETWEEN the small and large drawing rooms had been folded back and both cleared of excess furniture. The result was a miniature ballroom with seating for chaperones and others not dancing. The room connected to the large drawing room had been set up for card players. Candles blazed in the chandeliers and in several wall sconces.

The overall effect was a fine balance of splendor and coziness, although it was all on a rather larger scale than Kitty had wanted.

"What utterly charming rooms," Mrs. Cornwell remarked, sitting unexpectedly beside Juliet. "And what a delightful way to mark your sister's engagement."

"You're very kind, ma'am. I believe Kitty is enjoying it."

Kitty was the center of a group of young ladies, including several old friends they had both known all their lives. Normally, Juliet would have been part of the same group. Now she felt awkward and unwanted, as well as bound by her parents' strictures that she stay in the background.

"Ah, here are the gentlemen," Mrs. Cornwell observed. "You must be looking forward to dancing."

"I love to dance," Juliet admitted, looking toward the door. She couldn't see Dan at first and then was glad to glimpse him laughing with Ferdy and Lawrence King, before they all sauntered off in different directions.

"Lady Juliet," Colin Cornwell said in front of her, and she looked up to see him bowing. "Mama."

"Mr. Cornwell," Juliet replied, smiling. "I hope your evening is agreeable so far?"

"Most agreeable. Charming company, an excellent dinner, and dancing to follow—what man could ask for more?"

The inviting scrape of a fiddle struck up from the corner of the room, and Colin bowed again. "Perhaps, Lady Juliet, you would honor me with the first dance?"

Surprised, for Colin struck her as something of a high stickler and he must have known about the scandal breaking over her head, Juliet said, "Thank you, of course I would."

The country dance was just what she needed to lose the tensions of the evening. Colin smiled and chatted, as did everyone in the set, and when it was finished, she was quite happy to take his arm and go in search of refreshment, which the footmen were offering.

"I should escort you to Lady Cosland," he observed as they sipped champagne.

"Oh, the party is too small and informal to worry about such niceties," she replied. "In this setting, everyone is a chaperone."

Rather to her surprise, they were joined by two neighbors' sons, old friends who seemed delighted to see her. She wondered cynically if they would be so happy to escort her to their sisters. However, this situation was even less their fault, so she merely asked after their families and their latest news, while Colin tried to look interested but didn't, oddly enough, excuse himself.

The fiddler, having given them a few minutes to recover, struck up a waltz. Her old friends amused her by getting in each other's way to prevent the other asking her to dance. She rather thought Colin would win simply by offering his arm. But then the worst happened.

Lord Barden loomed over the more youthful heads. "Lady Juliet," he said, extending his hand in a languid manner. "Will you do me the honor?"

It reduced her old friends to chagrinned silence. Colin frowned with something very like frustration. Juliet shared it. She would have danced with anyone, even Jeremy, to avoid this. But in all politeness, she could not. He had asked, and she had no reason to refuse that would not cause an unsightly quarrel and upset Kitty's party.

"Gladly, sir," she replied, trying to smile. She placed her hand on his sleeve. Dan advanced onto the dancefloor with her cousin Anne, and she desperately wanted to swap partners. He was bending toward her as if to hear her better, a smile lurking about his lips. Just so had he often smiled at her. Her stomach tightened.

Dear God, am I jealous?

Of course not. I just have no desire to dance with Barden.

But she has to suffer his arm at her waist, his fingers lightly clasping hers. There was something cold, almost reptilian about him, and yet behind this ice, his eyes swirled with anticipation. Or was it triumph?

It didn't matter. Convention, manners, and care for her sister might have forced her to dance with him, but she had no intention of conversing with the man who had so casually ruined four innocent young women.

Over his shoulder, she saw Dan dancing as she'd known he would, with careless grace and a shade too much enthusiasm. Anne seemed enchanted.

Barden broke the silence at last, in a bored voice. "You are enjoying your sister's party?"

"Of course." She did not return the question.

"You need not worry. You will still be married before her."

She met his gaze. "I have no plans to marry. And frankly, the order of such events is immaterial to me."

"Won't young Catesby come back up to scratch?" he said sympathetically.

"Mr. Catesby and I do not suit."

"The trouble is, my dear, in your present predicament, you do not suit anyone. But you will do very well for me."

"Why, because you are no one?" she flashed back before she could bite her lips.

His eyes narrowed. Then he smiled. "My, my, the kitten has claws. Those must be clipped."

She ignored him, gazing straight ahead at his chin. She hoped she looked as disdainful as she felt. And trusted she was hiding the surge of panic. He sounded too sure of himself, as though he knew more than she did. And he made her flesh crawl.

"I suppose you know," he drawled, "that these opulent surroundings, the exquisite dinner we have just enjoyed, even the expensive silk gracing your lovely person, all were bought with money stolen from me."

She curled her lip. "You lost a game of cards. Or was it dice? Whatever, I suggest you grow up, for you are not a child to complain now about the fairness of the game."

A mottled flush stained his cheeks. His eyes spat. "Fairness? I was little more than a child. He fleeced me."

"A child? By my reckoning, sir, you would have been around five- or six-and-twenty and well able to take responsibility for your own bad decisions."

Deliberately, it seemed, he calmed himself. He even smiled, although it was not pleasant. "As you take responsibility for yours? You should not have stayed in that house, you know."

"What difference would it have made? You already had the piece written and printed before any of us arrived."

He could not quite hide his surprise. The suspicion had been Hazel's, and clearly, she was quite right. The princess's ladies were the only people named, or at least initialed in the newspaper. And yet more famous people, including two well-known singers and a notorious actress, had been present. They could have added juicier meat to a very generalized description. But nowhere in the article were they mentioned.

He forced another smile. "But at least the Alfords might have stood by you. Don't misunderstand me. I'm glad they didn't. I now find you back on the marriage mart, heavily discounted."

"You are insulting, sir," she said between her teeth.

"Get used to it, little girl. I am already your master, and you should know it."

No one had ever dared to speak to her this way. The combination of rudeness and blatant insult was flabbergasting. She resolved not to open her mouth again and didn't, even when he spoke to her. But she endured until the end of the dance.

Even then, he would not let her escape at once. "Some champagne to celebrate your new fortune," he said, retaining her hand and placing it on his sleeve. Stiffly, she walked off the floor with him and was handed a fresh glass of bubbling wine.

She wanted to throw it in his face. She contented herself with murmuring thanks to the waiter and removing her hand from his arm at last.

"Another dance, Lady Juliet?"

She stared at him. And, again, was reminded of a cat playing with a mouse. He was torturing her for his own entertainment. Well, that was not a game she would allow him to win. He was relying on her good manners. Since people must have heard him ask, and two dances in one evening was unexceptionable, he thought she was obliged to accept.

She tilted her chin. "I am a little fatigued. I

would rather sit this one out with—"

Before she could add her mother, sister, or any other member of her family, he interrupted. "Excellent choice. I am happy to sit with you. Here, perhaps?" He indicated the vacant chairs closest to where they stood, still well within the hearing of other guests where she could not deliver the blistering set-down on the tip of her tongue. He smiled, offering his arm once more. "Or perhaps my lady would rather dance after all?"

She didn't want to be anywhere near him, and he knew it. She could plead a sudden headache and flee to her mother, but such spiritless conduct appalled her. It would still let him win.

"Don't be a hog, man," a familiar voice said at her elbow. "The lady is promised to me."

CHAPTER FIFTEEN

*D*AN. HER RELIEF was dizzying.

"Really?" Barden drawled, amused. "Since when?" He still thought he had won.

"Since dinner," Dan said.

Blindly, she took his arm before he offered it and walked away with him.

"Juliet, you're trembling," Dan murmured in quick concern. "Where can we go?"

"Out of here," she said intensely.

He let her lead them toward the open drawing room door. Flicking the fan dangling at her wrist, she tried not to waft herself with too much agitation. Other people, mostly the older men, were standing around in the gallery, talking. On the other side, a small salon was being prepared with extra refreshments and supper.

"More food?" Dan said. "Where on earth will

we put it?"

"The evening is young," she babbled, leading the way in.

The servants were busy there, of course, but at least there were no guests to see as she pushed open the connecting door to the salon beyond and closed it with a gasp of relief.

"Juliet, what is wrong?" Dan demanded, urging her away from the door toward the window seat. The moon through the window was the only light in the room. "What did he do?"

"Do? Nothing, I suppose. It's what he says. He assumes I will marry him and be grateful because there are no other options!"

"There are always other options."

"Jeremy," she said in despair, sinking onto the window seat. "Or ruin."

"Oh, no, that card is played. If your ruin is declared somewhere, no one's paying any attention. Your life is not over, Juliet. You don't need to choose between the weasel and the snake."

She gave a shaky laugh and dashed the back of her hand across her eyes. "You're right, of course. Barden has done his worst, and I'm still dancing."

"That's my girl. We'll make sure he doesn't get near you again this evening, and then you must tell your father about his behavior. Nothing, surely, would induce any father to give his daughter to such a man."

"Barden looks upon it as justifiable revenge because my father won most of his fortune from him. But you are right. I do need to talk to Papa. I don't even know what was said between them, though they went into the library together this afternoon." She straightened her shoulders and cast a quick smile up at him. "I'm sorry. I'm not usually such a-a *drippy* person."

He grinned and put his arm around her shoulder in a brotherly hug. "I know you are not. You have an indomitable spirit and brighten everyone's life."

"Even yours?" she teased.

His lips quirked in an expression she didn't quite understand. "Even mine."

"Nonsense. It's you who always brings cheer, even when I know you're not cheerful yourself."

His smile faded. "And whatever leads you to imagine that?"

"I don't know," she admitted. "But I know you feel things deeply."

Subtly, the character of the once brotherly embrace had changed. "Do you?" he said deliberately. "Such as what?"

"Concern for your mother, care for your grandfather's people…"

"And for you?"

She searched his face. "You have been a good, kind friend to me."

"Have I, Juliet?" He threw his head back against the folded shutter with a half-laughing groan. "I have to stop acting from impulse. Look, I shall go back first and watch for you from the door so that you're never alone where Barden can get to you. Wait about five minutes so no one connects our reappearance."

He was right, of course, Being discovered here was fresh ruin. She tried not to be disappointed and simply nodded. "Very well."

He put his finger under her chin, tilting her face up to his searching gaze. "You will be fine now?"

Her gaze dipped to his lips, fascinated by their texture, and their movements as he spoke. "Of course I will."

"And the next dance is mine?"

"If you still wish it."

His breath caught. The finger under her chin moved, caressing, and was joined by his thumb. "Oh, the devil," he muttered and kissed her.

She opened to him with a sigh that was almost relief. She touched his face with wonder, loving the faint stubble beneath her hand. It was a gentle kiss, sweet and exploring, and her whole being seemed wrapped in its glow.

He raised his head.

She swallowed. "Was that comfort also?"

Slowly, he shook his head. "That pretense is long gone." He swooped, capturing her mouth again in a swift, sensual kiss that parted her lips and then left them.

"Stop putting ideas in my head, Juliet Lilbourne," he said with mock severity.

"I never said anything."

"You don't need to. That's the trouble. Five minutes and I'll be watching."

When the door closed, she reached up and touched her lips. They were smiling. And somehow, she no longer cared about Barden's distasteful talk, or his vile assumptions, or even about his villainy. Because somehow Dan's kisses raised her above it all.

⟫⟫⟫⟪⟪⟪

HE WAS AS good as his word. She spent a moment in the supper room with the servants, deigning to approve their arrangements, then poured two glasses of lemonade, one of which she would pretend was for her mother since it was a good excuse to be out of the drawing room alone.

She arrived back just as the country dance was ending. Dan stood with Ferdy and a couple of other people near the door. Anne was hurrying toward them.

Dan smiled at Juliet, just as if he hadn't kissed her only minutes before. "My dance, still, I hope?"

"Of course, let me just take this to Mama—"

"I'll take it," Ferdy offered, taking one glass off her hands.

She thanked him and sipped from the other, smiling at Anne. Beyond her cousin, she noticed her mother. She wore a faint smile, as she often did when she had stopped listening to the conversation but wanted to pretend she was still interested. Her eyes darted now and again, always in the same direction.

Juliet followed her glance and saw her father, seated beside Dan's mother, deep in conversation.

She dragged her gaze back to Dan. "Is it a waltz?" she asked brightly.

"I hope so," Dan said. "I bribed the fiddler with a secret glass of champagne."

Juliet laughed and set down her glass to accompany him to the dancefloor.

The contrast between her last dance and this one could not have been greater. Both comfortable and thrilled in Dan's presence, she welcomed his embrace for the dance, rejoiced in his nearness, the very scent of him.

And of course, it was fun. They exchanged banter and simply talked together as they hadn't been able to since the days of their secret walks. And all the time, her heart beat faster, and her whole body thrummed with awareness of him. Some huge idea was forming in her mind, but she refused to dwell on it for fear of spoiling the moment. After all, on either side of the present lurked all the disagreeable anxieties involving ruin, Barden, and her broken engagement.

But for now, she lost herself in the exhilaration of the dance, turning and swaying to the beguiling rhythm in the arms of the man who made her feel safe and alive. Her friend.

Toward the end of the dance, he was silent and thoughtful, glancing often toward the curtained windows.

"What is it?" she asked at last.

He sighed. "I'm talking myself out of my current impulse."

"Which is what?"

"To dance behind the curtain, kiss you, and dance out again with no one noticing."

Her heart skipped a beat. "Could such a thing be done?" she wondered while excitement and pure mischief soared at the possibility.

"The first part could." His gaze rested on hers, warm and unusually intense. "Which is so desirable I don't want to consider the inevitable discovery. I don't know whether you're making me staid or insane."

"I don't believe you can blame me for either. Though I doubt anyone would call you staid."

Somehow, it thrilled her that he did not laugh. "It's a bit of a novelty, this," he observed. "Thinking ahead. Thinking of other people. I expect I'll tire of it, soon."

"Is that a warning?"

He considered. "Yes. But you don't need it, do you? You think for yourself."

"I'm not quite sure what you mean."

A breath of laughter escaped him. "Neither am I. But God help me, I do like dancing with you."

She smiled up at him, and his fingers tightened on hers before relaxing again. And then the music came to a close. He bowed with a flourish, and she curtseyed in the same style before taking his arm without thought.

Her mother announced the refreshments in the supper room while the musician enjoyed a rest before the final dance of the evening. Which gave Juliet an excuse to stay longer in Daniel's company.

In the supper room, they encountered Hugh Ames, resplendent in a sky-blue waistcoat with bright yellow embroidered butterflies.

"Lady Juliet," he beamed. "I hope I have not missed my chance of dancing with you. Have you promised the final dance?"

"Why no, not yet,"

"Then, may I?"

"Of course. I would be honored."

"Oh, and have you met my father?" he added, indicating the older gentleman next to him who was systematically filling his plate.

"I believe we were introduced in the crush of everyone's arrival," Juliet said. "I hope your evening has been agreeable so far, Mr. Ames?"

"Most agreeable," he replied, pausing to bow over his plate to her. "It is the first evening I have been able to enjoy since I arrived. I have had a terrible cold. But this is most pleasant, most pleasant indeed." His gaze flickered over Dan. "May I help you to supper? Better still, let Hugh while I give this to my wife."

"Oh, no, carry on, sir. I prefer to help myself, and if I can't reach, I shall command Mr. Stewart."

"Good luck," Mr. Ames said vaguely.

"It always amazes me," Dan observed as they strolled back to the drawing room with their plates, "how two such vague creatures as my aunt and uncle, could have given birth to someone as precise as Hugh."

"Your uncle does not like you," she observed.

"None of them ever liked me. They like me even less now I'm supposed to inherit Myerly. Except, Hugh, who is the best of them, in my opinion."

"I danced with your other cousin. He was most amiable."

"I'm very glad to hear it."

Since Kitty waved to her, she went to join the group of young people surrounding her. In an informal huddle, she finally felt part of her old

group of childhood friends again. But somewhere, she knew that her contentment had much
to do with the man at her side.

Dan's cousins joined them for a time, but
Jeremy did not. Neither did Barden, who had not
come near her again, although he did not look
remotely downhearted as he sat talking to her
mother, or strolled about the room with Lord
Alford.

And then came the final dance, which Kitty
had chosen to be a waltz, of course. She stood up
first with Lawrence, and Juliet smiled to see them
so happy. She gave her hand to Hugh and
enjoyed the final dance of the evening. Apart
from the rocky patch in the middle, with Lord
Barden, it had gone so much better than she had
expected.

In fact, as her gaze fell on Dan, who was
clearly amusing Mrs. Coates, the vicar's wife,
with some tall tale or other, her heart filled, and
she wondered if she would ever be this happy
again.

"Do you know," Hugh said, "the shade of
your gown is perfect with your eyes?"

"Thank you. I have to compliment you on
your stunning waistcoat."

He smiled. "Delicious, isn't it? I have a coat
the precise shade of this yellow, but it is more
suited to morning calls."

"Then I hope you will grace us with one

before you leave Myerly."

"Anything for you, dear lady."

Juliet laughed. Like his cousin Dan, Hugh did not take himself too seriously. But unlike Dan, she sensed he was playing a role, that of empty-headed dandy. A social convenience, perhaps, to cover a natural shyness?

The dance came to an end, amid mingled cries of disappointment and applause for the fiddler, who bowed and effaced himself. Juliet stood with her family in the entrance hall to bid their guests farewell, for apart from her uncle's family, the Alfords, the Kings, and Lord Barden, their guests were all traveling home.

The carriages were summoned, and the servants were kept busy carrying cloaks and hats and finding outdoor shoes. Juliet yielded her place as eldest daughter to Kitty and stood a little farther back, so that anyone who wished to pretend not to see her could do so. Nobody did. But that may have been Mrs. Stewart's fault, for she went right up to Juliet to shake hands.

"I hope we may meet again, Lady Juliet," she said with a smile.

"So do I. When do you leave Myerly?"

"Wednesday. I have commitments in London. Such a pleasure to meet you, my dear. Goodbye!"

Behind her came Dan.

"How will you all get home?" Juliet asked.

"Will you young men climb onto the roof?"

"I did suggest it, but Colin won't play, and Hugh is too concerned for his coat. So, the carriage will take all our parents and come back for us." He smiled politely, but the soft words breathed through his teeth still reached her. "Meet me." And his eyes flickered to the left. To the side door.

There was no time to reply or even think, for Dan was already wishing Kitty happiness, and the vicar's wife was shaking her hand. "So good to see you, my dear…"

Dan would, surely, have to wait an hour for the carriage to return. His cousins clearly were in no hurry to leave the house for the chill of the evening. But Dan, after seeing his mother into the carriage with her sisters and brother-in-law, would wait outside. For her.

Her heartbeat quickened. Why? Had he learned something important? Was he in trouble of some kind, or just wished to talk? Whatever the reason, she knew she would not refuse him.

When the last of the guests had departed, save the Myerly cousins, Ferdy hailed the young men off to the salon for a final brandy. Her parents and Kitty returned to the drawing room to say goodnight to their overnight guests.

Juliet had been sent to her chamber so often since coming home that no one noticed she did not follow Kitty upstairs. Instead, she walked across the hall toward the back of the house and swept up her old cloak from the stand under the staircase. She turned into the dim passage that led to the side door. Fortunately, there was enough light filtering through from the hall.

She could hear the servants' voices calling to each other as they carried what glass and crockery they could to the kitchen. But they used their own staircase, and there was no one to see her, or even hear her draw back the bolts of the door and ease it open.

She stepped outside, opening her mouth to whisper Dan's name, but without warning, was seized against a man's hard chest, and his mouth devoured hers.

She did not need light to see that it was him. After the first tiny instant of shock, she knew him by his very scent, by his feel, and by the angle of his mouth as it claimed hers. With a gasp that was almost a sob, she threw both arms around his neck and gave herself up to the embrace.

Something was different this time. He wasn't just giving in to sudden impulse. He had planned this; he had arranged it because he wanted to hold her and kiss her. The knowledge was intoxicating. Her mouth opened wide under the onslaught of his, and she adored the caress of his tongue and even his teeth. It was as if he kissed her with all of him. His body wedged intimately with hers, beginning to move, stroking her in the same rhythm as his wild kiss.

Her knees buckled. Only his arms kept her upright. But as he drew back, as if afraid of hurting her, she pulled his head down again and kissed him, pressing herself against him in blind, half-understood need.

Finally, the sounds of voices filtered through her sensual haze. The grooms and stable boys going home... He must have heard them, too, for abruptly, he whisked her back inside the house and closed the door by leaning on it. All without breaking the kiss.

Laughter broke from her, and his lips smiled on hers, slowly releasing them. His arms were under her cloak, one palm flat across her semi-naked back, the other resting intimately on her hip, burning through the thin silk of her gown.

"I have to stop kissing you," he said huskily. "Or we have to talk."

"Talk," she said and kissed him again.

He deepened it for a breathless moment, sweeping both hands over her body, then held her close and pressed his cheek to hers.

"Soon?" he said.

"Soon," she agreed, smiling, for washing through her was the knowledge that had been growing since she'd met him.

His thumb touched her lips, even as he fumbled open the door behind him, and stepped out, drawing it closed behind him.

She blinked at the door, for tears had started to her eyes, and yet she wanted to laugh and run and shout with joy. For this was what she had been struggling with all week. What she had waited for all her life without even knowing.

Love. I love Dan.

CHAPTER SIXTEEN

*H*OW CAN *I not have known before?*
She laughed at herself as she ran back across the hall and up the staircase. *Because I have not yet known him a fortnight! Can one really fall in love so quickly?*

There were no rules. She could not deny the way she felt. She reminded herself that two weeks ago, she had imagined she loved Jeremy. That had been an illusion, pleasant while it lasted. *This*—this overwhelmed her, consumed her.

And yet in another two weeks would this illusion not have faded too?

Her lips, the lips he had kissed, curved into a smile of self-knowledge as she slipped past the drawing room door. Inside, her mother and aunt were talking. Everyone else, it seemed, had gone to bed.

"My dear, it was a long time ago," her aunt's voice soothed. "I cannot imagine him carrying a torch for her still. Not when you and he have a lifetime together, three beautiful children…"

Juliet passed on, a hint of concern for her mother piercing her own selfish happiness. Could the countess truly be concerned by Mrs. Stewart's reappearance in her husband's life? Did she trust him so little?

Juliet had always assumed her parents' love for each other. They supported each other, rarely quarreled, and had always been perfectly comfortable in each other's company—at least according to Juliet's observations and recollections.

But her mother thought she was second best, married only when Jenny Myerly rejected him. And now Jenny was back, still a fascinating woman.

Juliet paused with one foot on the next flight of stairs. A lock of hair had fallen across her neck, and she hastily pulled out the other pins, letting down all her tresses before twisting them into a hasty knot and holding it in place. She blushed and smiled all over again as she remembered how her hair had been ruffled against his arm, his shoulder, his lips…

Further along the gallery, a light shone under the library door. Her father's retreat. Impulsively, she withdrew her foot from the step and walked on to the library. She hesitated a moment outside the door, but hearing no voices, she knocked and went in.

Her father sat in his favorite armchair, his legs stretched out in front of him as he frowned down at his clasped hands. His gaze lifted. "Juliet." His voice sounded pleased, although the frown did not vanish.

"Papa? Is everything well?"

"I think it is. Both Alford and Jeremy are impressed by the dignity you have shown in this difficult situation. And it hasn't hurt that our friends and neighbors have welcomed you back among them as though nothing happened. According to Alford, Jeremy is now prepared to resume the engagement."

It was like a splash of cold water, halting her in her tracks. "But I don't want to marry Jeremy anymore. He does not love me, and frankly, I have come to despise him."

Her father's frown deepened. "Don't be so childish, Juliet. This scandal hangs over you like the sword of Damocles. Marriage with Jeremy Catesby is your best hope. *Our* best hope. It is the only thing that will counter Barden's continued fanning of the flames."

"Barden? The man is a total blackguard. After what he has done, what we *know* he has done, he actually believes I will marry him!"

"Yes, well, if you don't take Jeremy back,

Barden is your only other option," her father said brutally. "If you marry Barden, he'll see the scandal dies, and you'll be a viscountess with a decent home. It will cost me more than I would like to pay, but—"

"What do you mean?" she demanded, advancing to sit on the edge of the chair opposite his. "Why should you pay more than the dowry you have already set aside?"

"Because that is his price for marrying you and ending this. The return of all I won from him ten years ago. Much of that money was plowed into the estates. I won't deny it will be difficult to scrape it back together, but if Barden is your choice, I'll do it."

"*Barden my choice?*" she repeated with revulsion. "The man is an evil snake! I would rather die than marry him."

"Oh, don't be so melodramatic," the earl said impatiently. "Of course, you would not. But I do feel you would be happier with Jeremy, so don't throw him away over pride. I'll find some means or other to silence Barden. It will certainly be easier when you are married to Jeremy, and the Alfords have clearly accepted you."

She sprang to her feet. "But, Papa—"

"That is your choice," he interrupted harshly. "And it's a damned good one considering the scandal around your ears! Jeremy Catesby or Barden. I'll want your answer by the morning."

She whitened, for when her father spoke in that tone, there was no gainsaying him. "You can't," she uttered. "You can't force me to marry one of them! *Either* of them."

His eyes narrowed with temper. "You have a very odd idea of what I can and cannot do. Go to bed. Then take my advice and marry Jeremy. Otherwise, you'll be locked in your room until it's time to marry Barden by special license. Is that clear?"

Agitation forced her to breathe in short, sharp gulps. "I won't," she got out. "I can't. You must... Papa, I don't *care* about my stupid reputation!"

"Out!" he roared.

Once, as a child, she would have fled in frightened disarray when he spoke like that. Now, it still chilled her blood. But more than that, fury and sheer hurt spun her on her heels, and she stormed out of the library, slamming the door behind her.

It was rude, disrespectful, and unladylike, and she meant it all. By the time she found herself in her bedchamber, she had no recollection of how she had got there. Blindly, she seized something from the dressing table—a music box that been a Christening gift—and raised her hand to hurl it.

Then, with a sob, she threw it on the bed, and paced the length of the room instead, prowling like the caged animals at the Exchange in London. How could her father *do* such a thing to her? Force her to choose between the man who had deliberately ruined her from spite and the man who had betrayed her in her hour of need? To lock her in her chamber and force her to marry a man than made her flesh crawl?

When she loved Dan…

Of course, she had not told the earl that. He was in no mood to listen yet alone understand. Besides which, she had not even told *Dan*, did not know for certain what Dan's feelings for her were. Clearly, he liked kissing her, but men kissed easily. They were friends, but…

But nothing. She had been given no time, merely an ultimatum, an unspeakable choice to be made by tomorrow morning.

"I choose neither," she hissed between her teeth, spinning around and striding back the way she had come. "Weasel versus snake! Dan was right! Dan…"

She paused. *Dan will help me.*

There was only one thing to do.

She rushed to the wardrobe and drew out a carpetbag she had used since she was tiny. Into it, she threw a few underclothes, a walking dress, and a morning gown. Then she struggled out of the evening gown she wore and threw that in the bag, too, before reaching up for her riding dress. That, too, was difficult to fasten, but at least it had a little military-style coat that hid her

MARY LANCASTER

improper dress. From habit, she donned the matching hat and then threw a different bonnet into the bag as well. It would be crushed on the ride, but it would survive. She added her toothbrush and toothpowder and closed the bag.

Picking it up, she walked to the window, gazing out to see if any light was reflected from the house. She could get out of the house easily enough. And providing she didn't wake the grooms who lived over the stables, she could saddle her own horse. She would be safe before her father knew she had gone.

⪼⪻

EXCITEMENT ENSURED DAN woke early. Which suited him because he'd been going to walk round a couple of tenant farms with Patrick.

The servants were only just up by the time he ran downstairs to the kitchen, snatched some toast from Cook with a wink and a grin, and ran back up to the front door.

He knew before he pulled back the bolts that it was raining. What he didn't expect was to see the sodden wet figure of Lady Juliet Lilbourne asleep in the corner of the portico.

In sheer alarm, he dropped to a crouch beside her, seizing her by the sodden shoulders. "Juliet! Juliet, in God's name, what is wrong?"

Until her eyes fluttered open and relief paralyzed him, he hadn't realized how far he had fallen. Her bewildered gaze focused on him, and she threw her arms around his neck.

He could only hold her in a rush of tenderness, lift her in his arms as he stood. Then, her breath of laughter pierced his anxiety.

"Oh, let me stand, or you will ruin me all over again."

"Minx," he said huskily, letting her drop to her feet. "But what on earth are you doing here? You're soaking wet." His gaze fell on the small carpetbag behind her.

"I've run away," she blurted. "I have to marry Jeremy or Barden, and I *won't!*"

"Of course, you won't," he said calmly. "Infamous idea." He picked up the bag and ushered her inside.

Griffin stood facing them with a face like thunder.

Dan scowled. "Lady Juliet—"

"I'm aware who her ladyship is, sir. I'm also aware what his lordship's reaction will be to her presence at Myerly."

"Nonsense," Dan retorted. "Even my grandfather would not send a lady away in this condition, and I most certainly will not. Send Susan to us, and she can take Lady Juliet to whichever chamber is still free."

"Very good, sir," Griffin replied stiffly. "And

you will be where, sir?"

"Visiting his lordship, of course, to bring him the good news." With that, Dan ushered the shivering Juliet into the reception room.

"I'm sorry," Juliet blurted. "I didn't mean to bring trouble upon you. I just needed to run, and I knew you would help me, only I didn't think it all through…"

"There's nothing to think about. No one will throw you out."

She shivered, no doubt remembering that the Alfords had already thrown her out of their house. Beside them, what were the chances with a grumpy old man who hadn't spoken to her father in more than twenty-five years?

"We'll sort it out, Juliet," he assured her. "How long were you out there?"

"I don't know. I lost track of time after I spoke to Papa. I was so *angry*…and I hadn't even realized it was raining when I left the house. I didn't want to go back for a cloak. It was still dark when I got here, so I stabled my horse…and then I realized I couldn't knock on the door in the middle of the night, and I had no idea which window was yours. So, I waited for the house to wake up. I didn't mean to be discovered asleep. And now I must look like a drowned rat!"

"Kitten," he assured her. "Or a very beautiful urchin. Either way—"

Susan appeared, and he broke off, probably

for the best. Susan's eyes widened as she recognized Juliet, but she only curtseyed. "If you'd follow me, ma'am."

Dan gave the maid Juliet's bag. "Is my mother up yet?" he asked her.

"I don't know, sir. She hasn't rung."

He nodded and watched them go. Juliet glanced back once over her shoulder as though regretting her hasty decision.

She should have been. *He* should have been. But he wasn't.

He waited until the door of the small chamber on the half-landing closed. Then he walked to the stairs and ran lightly up. But before he reached his mother's chamber, Colin appeared in the doorway of his, in his shirt sleeves and still unshaven.

"What the devil's going on? Please tell me you haven't brought Lady Juliet here!"

"I haven't brought Lady Juliet here," Dan said obligingly.

"Then who did arrive? My man said it was Lady…"

"It is," Dan said and knocked loudly on his mother's door.

"Daniel, for the love of—" Colin began.

Dan ignored him and went in at his mother's yawning command.

She was sitting up in bed, drinking hot chocolate.

"He has chocolate?" Dan said, distracted.

"My father? Lord, no, I brought it from London. Geoffrey gave it to me."

"Of course he did," Dan murmured. "I need your help, Mama." Sitting on the edge of her bed, he told her about Juliet's arrival, impelled by her father's ultimatum.

"Oh, drat the man!" Jenny said with unusual irritation. "Just as we were mending fences between us. Now we will have to quarrel again. Is there nowhere but here she can go?"

"Nowhere that will not immediately summon her father to take her home again."

"*I* shall summon her father to take her home again," his mother said firmly.

"No, you won't, Mama. Her position is intolerable."

"Not half as intolerable as it will be when the old gentleman hears of her arrival."

"You needn't worry about that. I'll deal with him."

His mother blinked. "You will?"

Dan nodded distractedly. "Cosland is the bigger problem."

"He will be if he finds her before he's had time to think beyond his fury."

"What do you mean?"

"I mean Cosland blamed your grandfather's recalcitrance for the fact that I ran away with your father. He thinks if my father had only behaved sensibly, it would all have blown over, and I'd have married him."

"Would it?"

She shook her head with a little smile. "No. But it is, generally, sound advice. Once he remembers it, he'll realize he's gone the wrong way to work with his daughter. He would not force her into a repugnant marriage,"

"Not even to save her from ruin?" Dan asked.

His mother sighed. "There is that added complexion to Juliet's difficulty. But I suppose you're right. We can't send her back until he has at least calmed down. What if he comes looking for her, though? We can't deny she is here. Besides, her poor mother! They will all be worried sick." She sat up straight, her eyes widening. "Dan, she'll have left a note! Runaways always leave notes of their grievances. I should know. The chances are, they'll know exactly where she is. Drat and drat! Go away, and let me get up. I shall shield the girl from my sisters, but as far as her own parents go, you are on your own!"

He left her to it and went along to his grand-father's rooms. Waits was heaving the old gentleman into a sitting position and rearranging his pillows.

"You again!" Lord Myerly snarled.

"Me, again," Dan agreed.

Waits, who had clearly heard the news of

Juliet's arrival, looked terrified and began dementedly shaking his head in warning.

Ignoring him, Dan said cheerfully, "I thought you'd want to hear the good news as soon as you were awake."

"What good news?" the old man demanded. "Did you bring a woman into the house? *They* won't tell me." He flung out one claw-like hand toward Waits. "But I tell you straight, even if my daughters weren't here, I wouldn't have your game birds in my house!"

"Game birds?" Dan repeated, startled. "What the devil do you take me for? Your visitor is a lady, in every sense of the word, and she's someone I thought you'd be particularly pleased to receive."

"You are quite fascinating in your own way," Myerly observed. "Entirely and incomprehensibly wrong. But fascinating. Why on earth would I be glad to receive anyone? I don't even want my family here!"

"Well, to have her here would really annoy Lord Cosland," Dan said with perfect truth.

His grandfather stared at him. "What?"

"His daughter came to seek protection because her father wants to push her into a disagreeable marriage."

Myerly's eyes widened and then began to gleam. His wicked old mouth turned upward. "The devil he does. How...exquisite." He let out a snort of laughter. "Give the girl breakfast, and then bring her to see me. Is she pretty?"

"Very," Dan replied.

"I suppose Jenny made a pet of her."

Dan smiled faintly but said nothing. He rose, bowed ironically to his grandparent, and left the room. Waits stared after him with an expression that was half-stunned, half-admiring.

It was, of course, quite unscrupulous to use his grandfather's ill-nature for his own ends. But it still made him smile as he ran downstairs to the breakfast parlor, where he was sure all the family would assemble most punctually.

As he walked in, Juliet, in a fresh, becoming morning gown, was being assailed from all sides. Colin had got hold of her hand and was gazing at her earnestly. Hetty and Tabetha stood at her other side, looking worried. Hugh, out to one side, seemed to be examining the trim on her gown through his quizzing glass, while Jenny waited patiently to escort the poor girl to the table. Only Hugh's father paid her no attention. He was busy at the sideboard, loading up his plate.

"Indeed, Lady Juliet," Tabetha was declaring, "I must in all conscience advise you to go home as soon as you have breakfasted. Colin and I shall accompany you."

"Of course," Colin agreed.

"I'm afraid I cannot go home," Juliet said

firmly. "But if it is difficult for me to remain here…"

"It isn't difficult at all," Dan said, closing the door. "His lordship is happy to welcome Lady Juliet. In fact," he added, catching her eye, "he wants to see you after breakfast."

Her eyes widened and began to sparkle with curiosity. No one in the neighborhood had seen "Baron Miserly" in years. More to the point, it took the wind out of his aunts' sails, and Colin finally released her hand. Or she drew it away, it was difficult to tell which.

"Come and have breakfast," Jenny said, indicating the sideboard.

Juliet turned with her, though she cast a fleeting glance up at Dan as she went.

"Did you even speak to my father?" Tabetha demanded. "Why would he agree to such a thing?"

"To annoy Lord Cosland, of course. And you, Aunt Hetty, and my mother, are all here to play hostess, so there can really be no objection." He poured himself a cup of coffee and sat down, hoping to God that he was right.

But now that he had done everything practical to ensure she was safe here, he could acknowledge the emotions swirling beneath. She had come straight to him in her trouble. Not to older or better friends. It made him proud, triumphant, and terrified. And more than that, determined to protect her.

CHAPTER SEVENTEEN

JULIET KNEW SHE had not thought this through. She had sought out Dan from sheer instinct, and he had not disappointed her. But she had not considered difficulties like the rest of his family, like the old tyrant in his sickbed who terrified his whole household—with the possible exception of Dan—and had been her father's enemy for more than twenty-five years.

Still, the house and its inhabitants held their own fascination. The interior resembled the outside, in terms of neglect. The carpets and curtains were worn, the windows grimy, the hallways dusty, and the servants sparse and mostly old. But as she climbed the stairs with Dan and Mrs. Stewart to visit Baron Miserly himself, it struck her that beneath the dirt and the mustiness, the house was really rather beautiful. The proportions were pleasing, the wood paneling very fine, and the staircase quite gracious. She imagined herself in a Mrs. Radcliffe novel and smiled.

Which was not, she suspected, the reaction of most people on entering the domain of the fearsome old gentleman.

An ancient valet opened the door and bowed creakily.

The baron was seated in an armchair by the fireplace, dwarfed by the huge, ornate dressing gown he was wrapped in. Only the fierce eyes under shaggy white brows denied the first impression of weakness.

His gaze whipped over Dan, lingered on Juliet, and then he snarled quite unexpectedly, "What the devil is she here for?"

Warned by the entire family, Juliet had been prepared for rudeness, but the injustice of this took her breath away.

"He doesn't mean you," Dan assured her. "He is complaining about my mother's presence, though he knows perfectly well she came to keep the proprieties."

"Ha!" Lord Myerly said with derision. "Jenny playing propriety? Who'd have thought it?"

"I would," Juliet said. "Mrs. Stewart has shown me every kindness."

"Not surprised," snapped the old man. "Two peas in a pod from what I hear."

"We'll come back when he's in a better mood," Dan said, turning and indicating the door. "Although we may have a long wait."

"You will," Lord Myerly agreed, surely with a hint of amusement. "So, you might as well stay. Hmm, so, you are Cosland's girl? Never thought to be giving refuge to one of his brood."

"I'm grateful for your hospitality, sir," Juliet said politely.

"Are you, by God?" He waved a stick at the chair opposite. "Sit and let me look at you... Pretty little thing, aren't you? I suppose they'll all be vying for you now, the way they were for Myerly."

"Don't be vulgar, Grandfather," Dan said. "Lady Juliet is used to a courteous household."

"Then what's she doing here?" the old man demanded. "I don't recall Cosland being so damned courteous, do you, Jenny?"

"Lord Cosland and I are friends," Mrs. Stewart said, sitting in one of the more distant chairs. Juliet found herself glad that Dan stayed beside her.

"I suppose we can expect them all calling here, then? Imagining they're also friends with me? And looking for this chit, I imagine." He glared at Juliet, and it was quite an effort of courage to glare back. "What the devil were you doing in that house?"

Juliet blinked. "I live there."

"Not Hornby! The Princess of Wales's establishment."

"I was doing, as I thought, my duty," Juliet replied stiffly. "Protecting Her Highness."

"She doesn't need protecting from what I hear," Myerly said with an unpleasant chuckle.

Juliet lifted her chin. "Her Highness is a kind and misunderstood lady."

"As I suppose, are you?" Lord Myerly mocked.

"In this matter, yes. I was deliberately tricked and traduced by a so-called gentleman who is now at Hornby, and who is one of the reasons I have sought refuge with you."

"My." The old man sat back, regarding her. "Honesty, at last. I like her. She can stay. I might even come down to watch all you young bucks fight over her. Now, go away. I'm going to rest for a while."

There was nothing for Juliet to do but rise and drop a curtsey before walking out of the room.

"Well done, my dear," Mrs. Stewart murmured. "He actually likes people who stand up to him."

"I'm afraid I was distracted from proper gratitude by temper," Juliet said ruefully.

"No," Mrs. Stewart said simply.

From the floor below, came sounds of scurrying feet. Whether family or servants, they had clearly been waiting to hear how Juliet had been received.

Mrs. Stewart said bluntly. "*Did* you leave a note for your family?"

"Yes," Juliet admitted. "But I just said I was going somewhere safe, and they should not try to find me until I wrote again. They'll never think I would come to Myerly."

Mrs. Stewart nodded. "Well, I am going to lie down for an hour after all this excitement."

"I was going to see Patrick," Dan said, glancing at Juliet. "Care to come?"

"Everyone will know who she is," Mrs. Stewart warned. "Word will get back to Lord Cosland,"

"I shall be discreet," Juliet told her.

"And Patrick won't gossip," Dan said, "The rain's gone off for now, but you can take my cloak until your own dries. Come on then. Gun will be desperate."

Five minutes later, they left by the kitchen door, collected the ecstatic Gun from a very pleasant, if overgrown, walled garden just beyond the vegetable patch and set off over the fields.

"I didn't mean to spoil your plans," Juliet said as they walked.

"You didn't," he replied at once. He cast her a quick smile. "Though I may have to adjust them slightly. So might you. Your father will find you, you know. Even with discretion, he'll know you're here within—what? Two days? No more."

She sighed. "Probably. But presumably, he wanted my answer this morning because Barden did. Hopefully, he'll then give up."

"Barden?" he said doubtfully. "He's gone to a great deal of trouble to give up at the first setback. What I can't understand is why your father is even considering giving you to such a vile man."

"I couldn't understand it either," she admitted. "I was too hurt and too angry that he did. Now that I'm calmer, I think he is simply trying to preserve my reputation to make my life easier. I would not be the first woman to make the best of a bad marriage. Also…he probably feels guilty because he won all that money from Barden in the first place." She shrugged a little wearily. "I've always thought of myself as a dutiful daughter, but I won't pay the price for that folly."

"It sounds like you would both pay the price."

She cast him a crooked smile. "You mean I am doing my father a favor by hiding from Barden? At least he will remain better off. To give him his due, he prefers Jeremy of my two options."

He turned his head. "Do you?"

"Probably. But it doesn't matter. I've no intention of marrying either of them. Or even being *engaged* to either of them until the scandal blows over, which was Kitty's advice. Just to be engaged to *someone*."

She searched his face, waiting for him to speak. To say something about his feelings, his kisses, and an offer that was a natural progression from there.

He didn't.

She swallowed. He was a poor man, and she a wealthy heiress. Of course, he would not speak. She drew her gaze free. "If you like," she said with difficulty, "I could be engaged to you."

He didn't answer for so long that she felt dizzy from holding her breath. She exhaled in a rush, and at last, he turned his stormy gaze back to her.

"Until the scandal blows over?" he said scathingly.

She bent hastily to pet Gun, who had kindly brought her a stick. She picked it up, "Never mind. I was just thinking aloud," She hurled the stick and chased after the dog to hide her burning cheeks.

By the time they caught up with Patrick, Lord Myerly's steward, they were again chatting like old friends. But she could not forget his reaction to her suggestion, which had both hurt and surprised her. She could have more easily understood if he had run screaming from the prospect of marriage or refused to be thought a fortune hunter. But to answer with such withering contempt for the suggestion…it made her want to cry.

Fortunately, she pulled herself together and forced cheerfulness back into her voice and manner until she genuinely felt it. That the day was beautiful and fresh, now that the rain had gone off, certainly helped, as did the scenery and the greetings of Patrick and his son, who were introduced to her and sworn to secrecy.

Although she had little interest in the science of agriculture, she found she was impressed by Dan's knowledge, as much as his curiosity. This was why Lord Myerly had made him his heir. Perhaps it was the old man's act of redemption for neglecting the estates for so long.

Perhaps.

"Are you tired?" Dan asked as they made their way back toward the house. "I can run ahead and fetch the pony and trap? Or your horse, if you prefer."

"No, I like to walk. And I have been trapped for so long, this is wonderful. Though I suspect I shall sleep well tonight."

"We can stop in the hamlet and—" He broke off as a sudden crack rent the air, and his hat fell off.

"Goodness, that gave me a fright!" she exclaimed while Gun bolted toward the noise, barking, then skidded to a halt in bafflement and ran in circles.

Dan frowned, bending to swipe his hat off the ground. "That's the second time this has…" He trailed off, and Juliet saw why.

There was a large tear in his hat, front and back, as though…

"Gunshot! Dear God, Dan, did it hit you?" Desperately, she seized his arm, then dragged down his head to inspect it thoroughly.

"It didn't hit me," he said patiently. "But by God, it was close." He scowled. "And that is my only hat, dash it."

"Your only… Dan, how can you care about such a thing right now?" With difficulty, she refrained from slapping his undamaged head and released him with a little push. "This could have been a terrible accident. Someone nearly killed you!"

He straightened, seizing her arm and moving quickly down the hill, his gaze searching all around. "I know. We need to get off the hill and among more people."

She cooperated fully with this plan. "You think this was deliberate?" she demanded.

"Once could have been an accident. Twice makes me suspicious. Especially when…"

"Especially when what?" she demanded.

"Oh, nothing. Life is a bit strange at the moment for all of us."

She thought about that. "Perhaps someone doesn't like Gun. Perhaps he attacked their sheep or just scared the wits out of them." She looked up at Dan. "Or perhaps it wasn't meant for you but for me."

He glanced down to meet her gaze. "I was hoping you wouldn't think of that," he admitted.

"Then you think it's possible?"

"It crossed my mind, but who would do such a thing? Barden is a snake, and I would not put it past him to shoot someone from a great distance, but you are his means to a fortune. Why would he attack you? Likewise, Catesby wants his alliance—or you—or both. If it was one of them, they'd be more likely to shoot at *me* because they perceive me as a threat to their marriage plans. It's a risky way to beat a rival, though."

"And you said this had happened to you before?"

"Well, I don't know that it did. A gun went off a little too close for comfort, but I wasn't hit, and I couldn't tell which direction it had come from. I assumed it was someone shooting rabbits or birds." He shrugged. "It still could have been."

"And today?"

"An unlucky shot?" he guessed. "Aiming at something else?"

"I suppose that does seem likeliest," she said doubtfully. "But it is shockingly careless!" She shuddered, trying not to imagine what might have happened. He could be lying on the ground where his hat had been, the lifeblood draining from this vital, fun, *necessary* being…

His arm came around her shoulders in a brief hug, although he let her go again almost immediately. She wanted to cling, hide him, keep him safe…

A few minutes later, they came to the hamlet, basically just a few cottages and a tavern. Juliet drew the cloak more tightly about her and pulled the hood up over her bonnet, so that she looked as little like the earl's daughter as possible. A few curious glances were cast at her, but the locals appeared to know Dan, greeting him with nods and the occasional, amiable word. Apart from the man in the red coat who sat outside the tavern and who gazed with unfriendly eyes as they stopped.

"I can bring you a drink if you like?" Dan offered.

"No, thank you," she replied. "I believe I would rather get back to the house." She frowned, finally realizing that the man with the hostile eyes wore a military coat.

Dan seemed to notice him at the same time, for he strolled toward the man. "Beautiful day, is it not?"

"If you say so," the soldier replied insolently.

Dan regarded him for a moment. "My name is Stewart. I'm staying up at Myerly Hall."

"I know exactly who you are," the soldier retorted.

"And you don't seem to care for the knowledge," Dan observed.

Juliet's stomach lurched. Soldiers had firearms... At least he didn't have a rifle slung over his back or a pistol lying on the bench beside him. She refrained from catching at Dan's arm and dragging him off, but only with difficulty.

The soldier curled his lip.

"What's your name?" Dan asked.

The soldier met his gaze with defiance. "None of your business."

Dan shrugged. "As you wish. I just thought you might be Susan Harper's sergeant. Owens, isn't it?"

The soldier jumped to his feet. "If you know about me, you should be quaking in your shoes!"

"I should?" Dan said, startled.

But Juliet suddenly understood and let out a peel of laughter. "Dan, he thinks *you* have led Susan astray! He *is* Susan's sergeant."

"I don't see what's so damned amusing about that!" Sergeant Owens said aggressively.

"Keep a civil tongue in your head when you address a lady," Dan commanded, and rather to Juliet's surprise—and possibly the sergeant's—Owens muttered an apology.

"Thing is, I know she works up there at the big house," the soldier said in a rush. "And I hear you are too dam...*dashed* friendly with her. I know your sort. Think you're a lady's man and don't care about the carnage you leave in your wake. Why—"

"You've got the wrong end of the stick," Dan interrupted before the tirade went any further. "I've never seduced anyone's housemaid, least of all my grandfather's. Does she know you're here?"

Owens shuffled his feet. "Not yet."

"Then we'll tell her where you are," Juliet said sternly. "And if she wants to see you, she will. If she doesn't, you can go straight back to your barracks. And incidentally, Sergeant, do you have a firearm with you?"

The man's mouth fell open. "Firearm? What would I be doing wandering around Yorkshire with a rifle? Don't even have the French to fight anymore."

"Just curious," Juliet replied. "Good day, Sergeant."

"Subtle," Dan murmured in apparent amusement as they walked on.

"Well, I thought I might as well ask."

"And did you expect a truthful answer?"

She glanced at him in dismay. "You think he was lying?"

"Not necessarily. Don't know the man well enough to say." He gazed thoughtfully down the road toward Myerly. "I wonder if it's a good thing or a bad that he came after Susan?"

"He does seem quite an *angry* young man,"

Juliet admitted.

"I might be angry, too, if someone enticed my beloved away."

"Yes, but I don't think anyone did entice Susan, did they? She left the sergeant and got work here, where she met her farmer."

"It's easier to blame other people than yourself," Dan said vaguely. "But it will be easy enough to find out how long he has been sitting outside the tavern."

⟫⟫⟩✳⟨⟨⟨

"SHE IS *WHAT*?" Lord Barden asked, staring at his host. He didn't believe a word of it.

"My daughter is not in the house," Lord Cosland repeated. "She cannot, therefore, give you or I the answer you seek."

They faced each other in the library once more, but this time neither of them sat.

Barden gave his most unpleasant smile. "That is a pity. I had hoped not to bring up the subject of your daughter's sadly fallen reputation, but—"

A knock at the door interrupted him, and he broke off.

"Enter," Cosland commanded.

Catesby came in and looked surprised to see Barden. He addressed himself to the earl. "Sir, she does not appear to be in the garden. Apparently, she walks down to the river sometimes, so Lady Kitty and King are going down to see if they can see her."

"Let us hope they are quick," Barden said, hoping to convey his not-so-veiled threat. "We agreed to an answer this morning, and it is already well after midday."

"You shall have your answer," Cosland said haughtily, which was irritating because there was no need to involve the girl at this stage.

"Answer to what?" Catesby asked, with a smile to offset any incivility in his curiosity.

"Barden's offer of marriage," Cosland replied.

Barden blinked in surprise. He hadn't expected the earl to admit that much. Was he trying to *auction* the girl?

"Marriage?" Catesby repeated, a flush mounting to his cheeks. "My lord, I understood…"

"You're letting the grass grow under your feet, Jeremy," the earl snapped. "My daughter has never been short of suitors, and she never will be."

Oh yes, she will be, Barden thought savagely.

"Such was not my intention, sir," Catesby said earnestly. "You understand this has been difficult for me—"

"And for her!" Cosland snapped.

"Indeed, indeed, my lord," Catesby said quickly. "But I must claim a prior offer."

"Which you withdrew," Cosland pointed

out.

Damn the man, he was enjoying this, setting them against each other. He probably wanted to make them both squirm, but Barden knew which of them held the aces in his hand, which of them would come home with the bride.

At that moment, the door opened again, and the countess rushed in, waving a letter in her hand. "Cosland! I have just this moment been handed this! The stupid maid had it in her apron all morning and only now thinks to—"

"What is it?" Cosland demanded, striding up to his wife as though with some premonition of disaster.

The countess, becoming aware of Barden and Catesby, tried to smile, searching visibly for an alternative topic of conversation.

"Speak," her lord commanded. "If the letter is from Juliet, they had better know."

"She has gone," the countess whispered. "You should not have spoken to her as you did, pushed her as you did!"

"Gone where?" Cosland demanded, snatching the letter from his wife's hand.

For the first time since coming here, Barden began to feel control slipping from his grasp. This was like Brightoaks and Hazel Curwen all over again. He could not afford to lose another stage of his plan, not *this* stage.

"She does not say." The countess sniffed and

reached for her handkerchief. "But we know all her friends in the neighborhood, so…" She broke off, her eyes widening. "Oh, Cosland, she would not have gone back to London, would she? She has friends there…"

"At this time of year? Who?" Cosland demanded.

"Meg Winter for one, and you know she will feel they are in the same boat."

They are, Barden thought savagely.

"She would not go to London," Cosland said impatiently. "She is not so foolish, or so rich in coins! She is somewhere close by, and we will bring her home directly." He stared down his nose at Barden and Jeremy. "I take it this minor delay makes no difference to either of you? For we are all responsible for her flight."

"I will stand by her," Catesby declared.

Barden couldn't help laughing, "As you did before?"

"No, as I will from now on," Catesby claimed.

"My offer stands," Barden said and walked out of the room, proving he was sure of himself, when in fact, those little doubts were back. He should not have pushed her as he did last night, but damn, it was so irresistible. And she would not choose Catesby. Her father wouldn't let her, not when Barden told them in detail about the alternative to marrying *him*.

As he strolled across the hall, he was gratified to hear servants being sent out to various neighbors with discreet inquiries.

Wretched girl, she will pay for this. And Cosland will keep paying!

CHAPTER EIGHTEEN

LORD MYERLY WAS as good as his word and joined his somewhat alarmed family for the evening meal. He sat at the head of the table in an old-fashioned evening coat, smelling vaguely of mothballs, and Juliet was given the place of honor on his right.

"Good to see you so much better, sir," Colin said politely.

"I believe I'm on the mend." The old gentleman's eyes widened with something approaching horror as he saw the size and number of the dishes being set on the table.

Since servants were few in the house, the dishes, much fewer than Juliet was used to, especially for nine people, were placed on the table, leaving the family to help themselves.

"Living like princes," his lordship muttered,

ladling soup into his bowl. "No wonder you're hanging about here instead of going home!"

"Always so hospitable," murmured Hugh in a faintly fawning voice, although Juliet suspected sarcasm.

Judging from the smile flickering on Dan's face, so did he.

Lord Myerly, however, seemed perfectly unaware. He sneered whenever Hugh opened his mouth, snapped at his daughters and Colin, argued with Dan, and ignored Mr. Ames. He condescended to make conversation with Juliet, although this generally took the form of abrupt questions.

"I suppose you have several more courses for dinner at Hornby?"

"It depends if we have guests," Juliet replied diplomatically.

"Who is it your sister is betrothed to?"

"Mr. King, from—"

"I know the family. Bit of a comedown for the Lilbournes, isn't it? Thought your father would have done better for her."

"Mr. King is Kitty's choice," Juliet said firmly.

He might not have heard her. "But then, he's made a few bad decisions recently. Placed you with the Princess of Wales. Ha!" He reached for the plate of beef.

From the master of the house, each dish tended to circulate to Juliet and around the table to Jenny Stewart on his other side. Which meant there wasn't always a great deal left by the time the dishes reached Hugh and Mrs. Stewart. Juliet suspected he had arranged matters that way.

By the time of the beef course, Dan clearly had decided to speed things up. Seated farthest down the table opposite his uncle Ames, he began seizing on some of the vegetable dishes and offering them first to his Aunt Hetty beside him. Which caused the first smile Juliet had seen on Ames's face, even though it meant he and Dan split meager leavings. If Lord Myerly noticed, he chose not to mention it.

"The Kings," Juliet said, "are one of the oldest and most respected families in Yorkshire. They were here before the Lilbournes and the Myerlys."

"Defensive, aren't you?" his lordship observed. He seemed amused. "No need. No one could accuse your sister of a *mésalliance*."

"Indeed, I would hope not," Colin murmured, passing the mushroom dish on to his mother, who took a spoonful and pushed the rest on to Mr. Ames. For once, there seemed to be enough left to serve everyone.

Juliet found it something of a relief when the meal came to a close. Mrs. Cornwell rose to signal the departure of the ladies, a duty which should have been performed by the eldest daughter as hostess. Mrs. Stewart, however, did not appear to object. Scandal, clearly, had demoted her, which was something for Juliet to consider.

By running here, she had avoided marriage with the only men who could save her tarnished reputation. She tried to envisage a time with her mother gone and Kitty taking precedence over her. It seemed so distant and so unimportant that she really couldn't care.

Instead, she curtseyed to the baron and left the table. As she walked out of the dining room, Susan followed with a heavy tray full of dirty crockery and glass.

"Susan," she murmured, "Did you see Sergeant Owens?"

"Ran down before dinner, my lady. I don't know why he's come. He shouldn't have come... And there's my mother now, back at the Black Cat in Kidield!" Flustered and clearly unhappy, the girl scuttled off, considering the weight of her tray, Juliet did not try to keep her. But Susan's distress bothered her. She hadn't liked the sergeant's aggression.

What if Sergeant Owens was shooting at me, thinking I was Susan walking out with Dan? Annoyed with her own speculations, she did her best to banish them.

Away from Lord Myerly, the drawing room was a little more relaxed.

"I hope my father did not offend you by the

way he spoke of your sister," Mrs. Cornwell said, sitting beside Juliet on the sofa.

"Of course not," Juliet replied politely.

"He has grown too used to saying exactly what he pleases," Mrs. Cornwell mourned. "And in truth, he often speaks for effect, to create an argument. For example, suddenly announcing Dan was his heir, just to see if it would cause friction between us."

"There is a little more to it than that, Tabby," Mrs. Stewart said mildly. "He *did* make Dan his heir. It's in his will."

Mrs. Cornwell bridled. "Well, if you imagine he won't change it again before the end of the month and for no good reason, you are deceiving yourself! Is she not, Hetty?"

"I wouldn't be surprised," Mrs. Ames said apologetically. "It's true he doesn't like Hugh, but he's as likely to choose him just to annoy Colin as the other way about…"

It had struck Juliet already that someone in the family could actually have shot at Dan. Her mind still rather boggled at the idea—unless it was a moment of frustration, designed simply to frighten? Well, *she* was frightened, however Dan felt.

On the other hand, she couldn't actually imagine the very proper Colin or the dandy Hugh, let alone Hugh's ineffectual father, risking murder for the dubious pleasure of inheriting a neglected estate hundreds of miles from London.

"Oh, dear," Hetty murmured as they heard the sounds of voices and footfalls approaching the drawing room.

Tabetha cast her a glance of annoyance and squared her shoulders. They really were frightened of their father. And yet, they stayed here when they had his leave to depart.

"Be easy," Hugh said blandly, entering the room just ahead of Colin, who appeared to be lecturing Dan. "His lordship has retired without apology. Waits and Griffin are heaving him up to his chambers."

"Hugh," his mother protested. "Don't be so flippant, my love."

Hugh went over to pat her shoulder. Mrs. Cornwell stood up, and Colin sat smoothly in her place. To Juliet, it almost seemed rehearsed—and in fact, had something very similar not happened at Hornby? She laughed at herself for imagining such a thing. He certainly seemed to have nothing important to say, for he made mere small talk for the first ten minutes, and Juliet's eyelids grew heavy. She had not slept last night, and she began to fear she would give offense by dozing off.

Fortunately, Dan sat at the ancient harpsichord by the window, idly testing how far out of tune each note sounded. The discords were enough to keep her on the edge of her seat.

Then, when the others were distant enough not to overhear either, Colin said quietly, "You were out for a long time with Daniel."

"And Gun," she reminded him.

"He is a large dog," Colin allowed with a quiver of distaste. "I imagine he requires a good deal of exercise. But that is Daniel's business, you know. You need not accompany him. In fact, I did want to just drop a word of warning."

"About what?" she asked, keeping her voice pleasant while she hoped he read the quelling message in her eyes.

He didn't. "About Daniel. I would hate your reputation to suffer while you are our guest. And it is unconscionable of him to put you in this position."

"What position?"

"Of imagining yourself beholden to him or any of us. It is obvious he has made himself agreeable to you since coming to Yorkshire, but I imagine you know nothing of his previous life. He does not really move in our circles."

"So I believe," she said, allowing boredom into her voice.

"But you should know, my lady, he is not at all the thing."

She smiled brittlely. "I have become bored by *the thing.*"

He smiled as though acknowledging a child's attempt at a joke. "Truly, ma'am, he is my cousin, and I am the first to admit he can be amusing and charming. But I cannot in conscience let you live in ignorance of his true character."

Ignoring her freezing gaze, he leaned closer. "I imagine he did not tell you how he lost his only respectable position as a tutor? He...er...compromised his pupil's sister. Barely sixteen years old. The girl had to be sent abroad, and that is why no one else will employ him. I don't tell you this to be cruel but to warn you not to trust him, especially not in the difficult situation you currently find yourself. You have no parent in this house to look after you, but I beg you will look on my mother and myself as your friends and protectors."

"Thank you." She jumped to her feet only because she couldn't be still in the face of his disturbing revelations. "You are very kind." She flitted across to the window and pulled the curtain back as though gazing out at the night. In fact, she merely wanted to be away from Colin, though it was not so easy to escape her agitating thoughts.

She could not believe Colin's tale, and yet, had Dan not hinted at something unsavory about his dismissal from his post? At their very first meeting at the Golden Cross in London?

No, she could not imagine Dan behaving in such a criminally careless way... Which did not mean the seduction never happened, it just meant it wasn't quite as Colin described it. Either way, she was appalled to find jealousy and curiosity among her tangled emotions. If nothing else, Colin's warning served to remind her that she had not yet known Dan for a fortnight. And she had always recognized the charm of his easy-going, friendly manners.

Perhaps friendships meant little to him. Certainly, he hadn't wanted to pretend engagement to her to help her out of this mess. Although he had done everything else to help her, she reminded herself.

It was difficult to think straight when she was so tired. Abruptly, she swung away from the window and saw Dan gazing at her. One eyebrow twitched upward, asking what was wrong. Every instinct urged her to trust this man, whatever he had or hadn't done in the past.

A frown began to tug at his brow. He stood and began to walk toward her. But how could she talk to him about this? Instead, she swung hastily around to his mother.

"Forgive me, but I think I need to retire for the night. I did not sleep at all last night, so…"

"You must be exhausted," Mrs. Stewart said kindly.

"I'll ring for one of the maids to attend you," Mrs. Cornwell added, pulling the bell.

Juliet managed to smile and curtsey to the

room in general before fleeing to the sanctuary of
the little bedchamber on the half-landing. Forcing
her tired mind to concentrate on Susan's issues,
she sat down on the bed and tried to compose her
questions about the maid's old and new lovers,
and about any communication she had with Mrs.
Harper.

But when she answered the door to a respectful knock, it was an older maid, Betty, who
bustled in and set about drawing back the bed
covers and lighting the bedside lamp from the
candle.

"I thought it would be Susan who came,"
Juliet said, turning her back so that Betty could
unfasten her gown.

"Susan is not well, my lady. We had to send
her to bed with a bucket."

"Oh, dear! Have you sent for the doctor?"

"Oh no, my lady," Betty said comfortably. "It
will just be the stomachache, over by morning.
She shouldn't have eaten all those mushrooms,
and so I told her while she was bolting them
down. But young folk never listen to their
betters."

If Juliet had listened to her elders and betters,
she would be betrothed now to Jeremy or
halfway to London in order to marry the
unspeakable Lord Barden. But she merely smiled
noncommittally.

"Give my best wishes to poor Susan and let

me know if I can help. Thank you, Betty, you may go."

Betty curtsied and left, and Juliet climbed into the big, cold bed. She blew out the candle and snuggled down. The sheets smelled fresh, the pillows seemed to hug her, and in no time, she sank into a deep, grateful sleep.

>>>><<<<

LORD BARDEN HAD waited a long time to see the Earl of Cosland look as worried as this. However, *Barden* was supposed to be the cause of this anxiety, not the hoyden of a girl who had, apparently, flown the nest.

"She wrote that she was going somewhere safe," Albright, Cosland's son and heir said, with a hint of impatience. "I don't see why you're so worried."

"Because her idea of safe may not be mine," the countess snapped. "And because it is not right that she is not in her own home, particularly just now."

Her son shrugged. "I'll ride out and look for her again," he offered.

The countess flapped one dismissive hand. "There is no point."

"There, you see?" Lady Kitty said brightly. "You do not really believe she is alone in a ditch somewhere! You know she is safe with friends."

"With respect, Kitty, that isn't really the point," Catesby piped up. As if he still had any stake in the girl.

The drawing room door opened, and a footman brought a silver tray with a folded paper on it to the earl. Everyone sat up straight. Cosland almost snatched the note, broke it open, and scanned it.

"Well?" Lady Cosland demanded.

"She isn't with the Haretons either." Cosland dropped the note, which fluttered to the floor.

"I'm afraid you will have to produce her tomorrow," Barden said, angrily, for the girl was upsetting his schedule. "I have an important appointment in Cheshire."

"No one is standing in your way," Catesby retorted.

"Enough," Lady Cosland pronounced, but when they both glanced at her in surprise, she was not talking to them, but to her daughter. "Kitty, she may not have *told* you where she was going, but you *know*."

"Of course, I don't," the girl protested. "But if I were you, I would heed her letter, which told you not to worry and that she has gone somewhere safe."

"Kitty," her father said sternly, "if you know something…"

"I do!" the girl exclaimed. "I know that you

are all responsible for this, blaming her for something that you must have *known* she had not done and was not responsible for and then *hounding* her to make sickening reparations that drove her to this!"

Everyone regarded Lady Kitty openmouthed, from which Barden gathered that such outbursts were not common.

Only her brother's expression was admiring. "Well said, Kit," he approved.

"Perhaps," Lady Cosland said sternly. "But now is not the time for lectures. Your sister is endangering herself, and it is imperative we know where she went. You must see this damages her, makes everything worse for her, for all of us."

"I see she had no other choice," Lady Kitty muttered. "Though she said nothing to Ferdy or to me."

"But you suspect." The countess actually rose and went to her daughter, taking both her hands. "I hoped to discover myself without forcing you to betray your sister's confidence. But that time has passed. You are not helping her, Kitty. Don't be responsible for this further ruin. If you have *any* idea where she might have gone, you have to say."

Her brother sighed. "I think you do, Kit. She's punished them enough."

Barden held his breath while the siblings exchanged pained looks, and the mother didn't take her eyes off her daughter. Cosland looked as if he were about to explode, and for once, Barden knew exactly how he felt.

Kitty closed her eyes. "I don't *know* this. But I think she has come to regard Daniel Stewart as the only friend who would not let her down. I think she would turn to him for help. And it would be the one place you would never even think to look for her. I think she has gone to Myerly."

Several seconds of silence passed, much to Barden's bewilderment.

"Who the devil is Daniel Stewart?" he demanded.

The earl dropped his head in his hands. "How could she do this to me?" he whispered.

"This is not about you, Cosland," his wife said coldly. "It is about our daughter. Who is at least safe under a respectable neighbor's roof, with adequate chaperones. We will not barge in there to fetch her tonight. That would only cause the kind of talk we have been trying to avoid. Tomorrow, we shall call on Lord Myerly and his family, and we will bring our daughter home."

Relief flooded Barden. All would be well. Perhaps it was all a little more rushed than he had planned, but tomorrow Juliet Lilbourne would become his bride, and his fortune would be restored to him.

CHAPTER NINETEEN

JULIET STRUGGLED UP from a deep sleep, wondering in panic where she was. She could hear whispering voices, footsteps shuffling and running downstairs. For a moment, she couldn't work out why such sounds would be so close, and then she remembered. She was at Myerly, and her bedchamber was right beside the stairs.

But it was too dark for the servants to be up and about already, and from somewhere, she could hear moaning and wails of pain.

Abruptly, she sat up and lit the candle on the bedside table before throwing off the bedclothes. She seized a shawl, threw it around her shoulders, then picked up the candle and hurried to the door.

One of the elderly footmen was vanishing across the hall downstairs in the direction of the kitchen. Betty was climbing laboriously to the floor above with a cup and bottle in one hand and a large bowl in the other.

"Betty? What is happening?" Juliet demanded.

"Oh, it's Susan, my lady. She's been taken very bad, very bad indeed."

Juliet left her chamber and ran upstairs after the maid.

"It's her stomach, my lady," Betty revealed. "Pains like you wouldn't believe, and sicker than a dog..."

"Oh, dear! And what is this?" Juliet took the cup and bottle from her.

"Lady Myerly's recipe for stomach medicine," Betty said. "Can't do any harm."

By candlelight, the liquid was such an evil color that Juliet had severe doubts about it. How long had Lady Myerly been dead?

On the attic stairs, lurked Griffin in his nightgown, holding up a branch of candles to light the way.

"Pardon, my lady," he said anxiously. "Did we wake you?"

"No, well yes, but I would like to help if I can."

Betty led the way into a small bedchamber beneath the eaves. Two beds were crammed into it. One was neatly made. Juliet guessed it was Betty's. In the other, lay the writhing, sweating figure of Susan, panting and groaning in clear distress. Mrs. Stewart knelt beside her, murmuring soothing words while bathing the sick girl's forehead.

She glanced up, and at sight of Juliet, her eyebrows flew up.

"What can I do?" Juliet asked.

"Give me the medicine," Mrs. Stewart said, reaching for it.

"Are you sure?" Juliet said, handing it over.

A distracted smile flickered across Mrs. Stewart's anxious face. "Don't worry, it always looks like that."

"It's only her ladyship's *recipe*," Betty explained. "Cook makes it up, so you needn't worry about it being thirty years old and rancid."

"As I recall, it couldn't taste worse if it *was* thirty years old and rancid," Mrs. Stewart said, "but it took care of all my childish stomach upsets. Juliet, can you just help her sit up a bit more so that she swallows this…"

Obediently, Juliet went to the bed and heaved the shivering girl into a more upright position. Susan took the medicine from the cup Mrs. Stewart held to her lips and swallowed.

"All of it," Mrs. Stewart said, tilting the cup once more, and Susan took the rest. If it tasted vile, she didn't seem to notice.

Juliet eased her back onto the pillows.

A minute later, while Betty, Juliet, and Mrs.

Stewart gazed anxiously down at her, Susan
suddenly heaved herself up, reaching blindly.
Mrs. Stewart snatched the bowl from Betty, and
the maid was violently ill into it.

"Griffin," Mrs. Stewart called. "Send Dan for
Dr. Gorman."

"Dr. Gorman in Kidfield?" Juliet asked. "Susan's mother is in the town, too, at the Black
Cat."

"Send to her, too, by all means," Mrs. Stewart
murmured. "We all want our mothers when
we're sick."

An urgent clatter on the stairs, and Dan's
tousled head came round the door. He seemed to
be fully dressed.

"I'll come with you," Juliet said, pushing past
him. "And fetch Mrs. Harper."

He caught her arm, frowning. "Don't be silly.
I'm riding for quickness. Dr. Gorman has his own
horse, and Mrs. Harper doesn't."

"Besides, you can't gallop around the country
at night with Dan," Mrs. Stewart said prosaically.

"Write her a note," Dan urged, "and I'll drop
it at the Black Cat on my way past." He released
her, looking instead toward his mother. "What
should I tell Gorman about her condition?"

Juliet darted back to her own chamber, fer-
reted out her writing materials from the bottom
of her bag, and scrawled a quick, somewhat ink-
blotted note to Mrs. Harper. It was just about

legible. Hastily, she folded it, wrote the woman's name across the front, and bolted to the door just as Dan's boots thudded their way back down.

He paused on the half-landing with a quick, crooked smile, taking the note from her. "I won't forget."

"Dan," she said urgently. "Be careful. Remember what happened this afternoon."

"I'll be riding like the wind," he said lightly. "No one could touch me if they tried. Which they won't. I'll be back in just over an hour or so, hopefully. If he isn't out on another call."

His eyes flickered down to her lips, and lower, reminding her she wore nothing but the night rail and the open shawl. But even as her whole body flushed, his gaze rose determinedly back to her face, and with another flickering smile, he was gone.

Juliet swallowed and returned to the sick room. Here, she helped Mrs. Stewart change Susan's soiled sheets, while Betty kept the girl warm in blankets. Juliet was disturbed by the spatters of blood across the pillowcase. At last, they half-carried Susan back into her bed. Betty brought over the two clean bowls, which the footman had left outside the bedchamber.

"I don't think you have been to bed," Juliet said to Mrs. Stewart. "Go and sleep, and I'll sit with her."

"I cannot take such advantage of a guest,"

Mrs. Stewart said lightly.

"You would be doing me a favor," Juliet assured her. "I like to be useful. And I owe Dan so much."

"Do you?" Mrs. Stewart said thoughtfully, although she rose to her feet. "You must tell me about that some time. Because obviously, Dan will not."

"I will," Juliet promised, taking her place. "Betty, you should lie down. I'll call if I need help."

Mrs. Stewart vanished in a swish of skirts and could be heard directing Griffin to bed. Betty lay down fully dressed. Juliet squeezed out the cloth and gently bathed Susan's face. The girl was exhausted, not quite asleep, but not truly awake.

She didn't know how much time passed before she heard the clattering of hooves below. Two horses. Until the relief hit her, she hadn't realized just how frightened she had been for Dan's safety, riding alone across country in the dark while someone, perhaps Sergeant Owens at the tavern, still wanted to harm him.

Since she had warning of their approach, she made sure she had her shawl gathered closely about her when she rose to greet Dr. Gorman.

The man blinked. "Lady Juliet? I did not expect to see you here!"

"Oh, I'm staying with Mrs. Stewart for a few days," she said hastily, "but it is Susan here who needs your help."

"So I gather," he said, placing his bag on the floor and taking the space Juliet had just vacated. He picked up her hand to take her pulse and felt the temperature of her forehead.

Betty lumbered up from her bed to supervise and answer the doctor's questions, while he drew back the bedclothes and felt Susan's stomach.

The girl whimpered.

"There was blood, you say?" Dr. Gorman demanded.

"A little."

"What did she eat that the rest of you didn't?"

"Nothing," Betty assured him. "She did wolf the leftover mushrooms, which came down from upstairs. *We* didn't eat any of those, but the family did."

Juliet nodded. "The mushrooms were good. I'm sure it was not something she ate."

"Hmm," Dr. Gorman said. It meant nothing, and yet Juliet had the impression he did not agree. "I need to purge her. Perhaps your ladyship would allow me this space to work?"

Which was a polite way to dismiss her.

"I'll tell Mrs. Stewart," she said, and left the room, taking her stub of candle with her. "Oh, Betty, which chamber is hers?"

"Last door on the left, ma'am, opposite Mr. Dan's."

There was no sign of Dan in the passage. No

doubt he had already fallen into bed after his hard ride to Kidfield and back, and it was almost dawn. After scratching softly at his mother's door, she let herself in, calling softly, "Mrs. Stewart?"

A bundle on the bed reared up.

"It's Juliet," she said hastily, raising the candle to reveal herself. "The doctor is with Susan."

"Oh, thank you." Mrs. Stewart yawned and stretched and clambered out of her bed, crushed but still fully dressed. "What did he say?"

"He's purging her. He seems to think it was something she ate, though apparently, she had nothing other people did not share."

"It would just take one mushroom that was the wrong kind," Mrs. Stewart pointed out. "One that no one noticed before they were all prepared and covered in sauce. Cook is old and no longer sees so well."

Juliet nodded, frowning as something elusive tugged at her memory and her understanding.

"Go back to bed, my dear, and get what sleep you can," Mrs. Stewart said kindly, thrusting her feet into bedroom slippers. "I'm so grateful for your help."

Juliet followed her more slowly back along the passage. *One mushroom that was the wrong kind.* Or one deliberately inserted for Susan after the dish was returned.

Sergeant Owens at the tavern. Had he followed Susan back up the house after she'd been to see him? Somehow, she couldn't actually imagine him sliding a poisonous mushroom into her food. Slapping her, perhaps, even shooting her in a fit of rage, but poisoning seemed...wrong for him.

Besides, it was Dan who had been shot at, and the theory that the shooter had been aiming at her in mistake for Susan seemed somewhat far-fetched.

She paused outside her bedchamber door, her hand gripping the handle as she recalled the progress of the mushrooms around the table. Like several of the side dishes to the main course, Dan had passed them to his aunt Hetty Ames, who took the first serving. They had come all the way around the table, and she could remember seeing the dish passed back to Dan. There had been more than enough left, for once, for one generous helping. Someone had not taken any. And neither had Dan, for he had pushed the dish aside untouched.

Blood sang in her ears. Had someone hoped to poison Dan? Someone who had sat between her—she had eaten the mushrooms and passed them on—and him? There had been no servants in the room. It could only have been Colin, his mother, or Mr. Ames.

Her breath caught.

No, this was foolishness, imagination run riot. It was more likely something dangerous had been spilled by accident into the leftover mushrooms in the kitchen before Susan had seized on them.

And yet, someone had nearly killed Dan on the hill, and it was probably the second time he had been shot at since coming to Myerly. And mushrooms, which he had rejected at the last moment, might have poisoned the maid who'd seized on them belowstairs.

Might have, she reminded herself. But unease was spiraling upward into alarm, into fear. If Dan were to die...

With a gasp, she spun on her heels, rushed back up the stairs, and hurried down the passage once more to the door opposite Mrs. Stewart's. She scratched at the wood, praying he was not yet asleep. Her heart thundered.

She heard no movement in the chamber beyond, except a faint snuffle under the door that was obviously Gun. She wondered if he was still downstairs. She was just about to turn away when the door opened abruptly, and Dan stood there in his mud-spattered pantaloons and shirt sleeves, hanging on to the scruff of Gun's neck.

His eyes widened in clear astonishment before he glanced rapidly up the passage and dragged her inside by the arm. "What the devil are you doing here? If anyone sees you—"

"What if it was the mushrooms?" she inter-rupted, laying her candle down on the table by the door and mechanically fending off the delighted Gun. "What if they were poisoned by someone of your family who really resents you inheriting Myerly? Why didn't you eat the mushrooms?"

He blinked and released her arm. "I don't like mushrooms. Nasty slimy things."

"Does your family know that?"

"My mother does. I don't recall ever discussing it with anyone else. But why are you so concerned with the mushrooms?"

"Because there were some left. More than you didn't eat them. Susan grabbed them as soon as they were taken back to the kitchen."

He frowned down at her. "And you think someone at the table *poisoned* them? Just for me? My uncle Ames?"

Stung by the disbelief in his voice, she said, "Or your aunt, Mrs. Cornwell, or your cousin Colin. You cannot deny both are disgusted by your being named Myerly's heir."

Dan rubbed his stubbly jaw. "There's disgust," he said, "and there's murdering your own blood."

Embarrassment seeped into her bones. "I know. It's a silly idea, and it would never have entered my head if you hadn't been shot at this afternoon. It just seemed too much coincidence."

"I doubt they're related," he said. "I think we should wait to hear what the doctor says. Will

Susan recover?"

"He's purging her. And I should go. I just thought I should warn you, even if it's nothing, and I'm being silly." She turned away, and a splash of color drew her gaze to the chest of drawers beside the door. On it, a watercolor landscape was propped up against the wall. "It's mine," she said in surprise.

"You gave it to me."

She smiled. "I know. But I didn't expect you to keep it. I thought you would screw it up into a toy for Gun."

One startled eyebrow shot up. "You have a very odd idea of your talents. And your effect on people. Especially dressed in no more than a wispy piece of cotton and your hair..." As if he couldn't help it, he reached up and lifted a thick curl of hair from her shoulder.

Her breath caught. Her gaze flew up to his. His lips curved, and his eyes grew warm in that strange, clouded way that set butterflies soaring in her stomach. Held by his gaze, she felt paralyzed, enchanted rather than frightened.

This was Dan, her easy-going friend, and yet in these moments, he seemed suddenly much more—an overwhelmingly physical, handsome man, the man she secretly loved, and yet a stranger with desire in his eyes and her hair in his long, sensitive fingers...

With a nervous breath of laughter, she

reached up, snatching the tresses from his hand, and bundling them up with the rest of her hair as though to pin it up in a respectable manner, although, of course, she had no pins. Her arms fell back to her sides, but not before his hand had dropped lightly to her shoulder. One finger touched the skin of her neck above the shawl, spreading sweet, thrilling awareness, especially when it moved in a light, almost distracted caress.

"You came to warn me," he murmured. "But you do understand you are now alone with a man of dubious reputation, in his bedchamber after dark?"

"It does seem to beat my previous mistakes to flinders," she managed. It was hard to think when his finger continued to stroke her neck, inducing little sparks of pleasure that swept over her skin, reaching through her whole body. She swallowed. "How fortunate that you are my friend."

"I am," he agreed with a hint of ruefulness, although his finger did not stop its sweet, potent arousal. "But I am not a saint."

"So your cousin told me."

His finger did not even pause its caress but moved an inch further back, to her nape. And now his thumb brushed her over-sensitized skin, and she almost gasped.

"Colin?" he murmured, without obvious interest. "What did he tell you?"

"That you lost your position as tutor by seducing your pupil's sister."

"I didn't touch her." His fingers stilled, and something approaching panic filled her.

Don't stop, don't stop.

For once, he looked serious. "Do you believe me?"

She gazed deep into his dark eyes and nodded, "Yes." It wasn't really a surprise. She knew him, this friend whom she loved.

But perhaps it surprised him, for his lips quirked as his finger and thumb moved again. Relief surged along with delicious weakness. How could such a small, light, yet entirely improper caress, affect her so deeply?

"Then you trust me?" he asked.

She nodded again, and with the movement, his finger slid lower, beneath her shawl.

His breath caught on a sound that wasn't quite laughter. "You have no idea of the wicked ideas in my mind right now. Believe me, your trust is all that holds me to one kiss."

His mouth suddenly closed over hers. A flame of sweet, powerful desire curled low in her belly. His kiss was tender, as gentle as his caress, and yet it was so deeply sensual that she trembled.

Slowly, his hand moved, around to her throat and gradually, achingly, his mouth left hers. "Run," he whispered.

She reached blindly for the door latch, and he kissed her again.

"You said one," she reminded him shakily against his lips.

They smiled on hers. "I lied." He raised his head. "But only a little."

His had fell away at last, leaving her cold, and it was he who opened the door a crack, making sure the passage was clear. As if she couldn't help it, her hand followed her fascinated gaze to the strong column of his throat. Her fingertips trailed down it to the pulse that thundered at the base.

He grasped her hand and glanced at her, his eyes laughing and yet behind the amusement, a look of deadly seriousness that thrilled her. Wordlessly, he dropped a light kiss on her hand and drew her outside into the passage, thrusting her candle back into her fingers.

With the cooler air, cooler sense washed over her, and she fled. She only glanced back once, and he was still watching her. Somehow, that was thrilling, too.

CHAPTER TWENTY

LEANING ONE SHOULDER against the door frame, Dan watched her glide along the passage in the glow of her candle. She looked ethereal, almost other-worldly. Beneath the sheer fabric of her night-rail, where the shawl did not reach, the tantalizing shape of her legs glued him to the spot. His mouth was dry.

Turn back. Come back to me now. Where would be the harm?

She glanced back once, then vanished down the stairs. Only when he heard the faint click of her door closing, did he move back inside his chamber.

The harm, of course, would be in her uncertainty. So many other people were trying to force her into marriage that the last thing she needed was a man seducing her and forcing the issue in another direction. She had already offered to be engaged to him just to discourage everyone else. The hurt of that had surprised him, as had the strength of his desire to be betrothed to her in reality.

To call Juliet his wife…

Unthinkable…

And yet to have the right to protect her, the joy of being her husband, living with her, loving her…

Dan had never had the means or the desire to even consider marriage, but with Juliet, it would be *fun*. His breath caught. He groaned, dragging his tortured body to the bed and throwing himself down. He lay, staring up at the ceiling, the back of one hand across his forehead. Gun leapt up and lay at his feet.

Juliet. My Juliet.

Yes, but she isn't mine. Maybe one day…

Determinedly, he dragged his mind away from such fantasies, and searched around for a subject to distract his lust.

Susan, mushrooms, shots that had so far missed him.

Juliet's warning touched him. And though he didn't want to think about it, she had made the point he had been avoiding. The Cornwells and the Ameses were his family by blood, but they barely knew each other. A few duty meetings when he had first come home, and when his father had died. And he had met some of them here, the few times he had been summoned to his grandfather. They were not friends, and they were not family in the way Juliet and her cousins clearly were.

To Dan's family, he was the product of a scandalous marriage, a poor interloper threatening their chances of inheritance. Well, more than threatening now. Of course, his grandfather could, and probably would, change his mind again, but until then, Dan was everyone's enemy.

Would they—would one of them—really try to be rid of him for good? Did they know or care what such a loss would do to Jenny? Could they really be so cruel and unfeeling and *greedy*?

In truth, he knew them as little as they knew him. Perhaps he should ask his mother... And scare the wits out of her? *No.* But neither could he sit and wait and do nothing. If Susan *had* been poisoned and a gunshot had almost torn his head instead of his hat, then he had to do *something*.

Still wide awake, he bent his mind to the problem, imagining and discarding several ideas before he found one that might just unmask a scoundrel. If such a being existed. If he didn't, then Dan had lost nothing except a little time.

Gun, of course, would be devastated, but he could make it up to the dog later.

Accordingly, he stood up, much to Gun's excitement, and went to dunk his face in the washbowl. After washing, shaving, and dressing, he picked up his battered hat, which was almost beyond mending as it was. He sighed and spoke to Gun.

"Wait here. I'll be back in a moment."

Dawn was breaking. This was the time he had used to set out toward Hornby to meet Juliet, being very careful not to think of it as an assignation. But that was no reason to assume she would be awake this morning. She had had two disturbed nights in a row. The girl deserved to sleep.

But he did want someone to keep an eye on the comings and goings from the house. And distract Gun from his absence.

He veered to the attic stairs and climbed. He could hear the servants moving and talking sleepily as he knocked on Susan's door. Betty opened it almost at once, and he saw Juliet sitting awkwardly on the end of Susan's bed, her back against the headboard. She was dressed now, but her eyes were closed. And Susan wasn't moving.

"How is she?" he asked Betty quietly, aware from the corner of his eye that Juliet immediately sat up straight.

"Better, sir," Betty said. "She's sleeping, and the pains seem to have gone. Dr. Gorman says she almost died, but she should recover now. What a strange thing!"

"It is," Dan agreed. He looked over to the

bed. "Juliet? May I have a word?"

"You go, my lady," Betty said. "I'll stay with her a while, but I think she's safe to leave alone now."

Juliet nodded and walked across the room, brushing past Dan at the door. She walked downstairs in front of him, but from there, he diverted her to Myerly's dusty library, which was largely unused and so never cleaned.

Carefully, he left the door open, to counter both his own temptation and any spread of gossip.

"What did the doctor say about Susan?" he asked abruptly.

"That she had eaten something she should not and that a mere surfeit of mushrooms or any overindulgence would not have caused such a reaction. He thought rat poison or some such must have got accidentally among whatever she's eaten. Cook is outraged."

"*Rat poison?*" he exclaimed, startled. He dragged his hand through his hair. "Look, I was thinking about what you said, and this has to be brought into the open before someone actually dies."

She nodded eagerly. "So, I think."

"Well, I have a plan. I'm going out, and I want you to tell everyone who will listen that I'm going via Patrick's house, and from there to look at the boundary with Hornby land."

"The river?"

"The river. You could mention a pleasant spot on this side where I could eat breakfast, just before the bridge."

Her eyes widened. She even reached out to seize his arm before she checked herself. "You are setting yourself up to be murdered!"

"Not at all," he said cheerfully. "In fact, I shall be somewhere else, quite safe, watching who comes and what they do."

She searched his eyes, her own brilliant with worry and extraordinarily beautiful. He couldn't look away. "You will need a witness," she declared. "I shall come with you."

"Oh, no," he said at once, for he had come prepared for such a suggestion. "I need you here to tell everyone where I've gone. And to take care of Gun, if you would be so good."

She frowned, as though still suspecting she was being kept out of the way. Fortunately, she seemed to see it necessary, for at last, she sighed with resignation. "Then you will take Patrick? Or better still, young Pat? He can be added protection as well as a witness."

He hesitated, unwilling either to lie or to take this beyond the family. "I'll speak to Pat," he said at last.

She nodded decisively. "Then I'll do it. But, Dan?"

Halfway to the door once more, he paused

and glanced back over his shoulder.

"Be careful," she pleaded, and he was almost undone.

For the first time, he wondered if she actually loved him. Rather than simply being intrigued by a different kind of friendship with a taste of passion.

He managed to smile. "And you."

❯❯❯❯❮❮❮❮

IN THE END, he did speak to both Patrick and his son about the various members of his family now residing at the house. But they knew nothing of Colin or Hugh except his lordship's derogatory comments. Old Patrick at least remembered their mothers as children. Jenny had been his favorite, but unexpectedly, he also harbored a soft spot for Tabetha.

"She looked after Miss Hetty," he recalled. "Even when she didn't need to. It revealed a kinder spirit than she often showed the world."

It was interesting, but not terribly helpful, and when young Pat spoke of an appointment at some distant farm that morning, Dan gave up, with relief, any lingering obligation to confide in him or ask his help.

Instead, he left the father and son to their duties and remounted to ride toward the hamlet.

He had wondered whether or not to ride this morning, for the place he had in mind for his trickery was within easy walking distance of the house. But in the end, he took the horse, more as proof of his presence to leave standing around for any watcher to see. And the horse was Lord Myerly's, not his own. No one would willingly harm it, which was not the case with poor old Gun.

It also meant he could move across the country more quickly, and he had time to call in at the tiny tavern.

"About your guest," he said when he had returned the tavern keeper's cheerful greeting, "Sergeant Owens."

"What about him?" the man asked with a wary glance toward the narrow stairs.

"He had a visitor yesterday afternoon."

"Young Susan, from the house."

"Did they quarrel?"

"They walked outside. Didn't seem to quarrel."

"Really? Interesting. Did she go back to the house alone, or did he walk with her?"

"Must have gone alone, because he came back here without her after only a quarter of an hour or so."

Boots thudded heavily on the steps, and the sergeant himself appeared, glowering. "What's it to you?" he demanded.

"I was just wondering whether or not it was safe to tell you," Dan said, already walking to the door. "Susan was taken very ill last night. She seems to be on the mend, but if her mother isn't there already, she soon will be. The rest is up to you, but don't make the servants—or my cousins—throw you out."

With that, he left and made for the river. There, he spent some time examining the ground along the Myerly bank and working out what could be seen from where. When he had decided on the likeliest spot, he walked over the bridge to the Hornby woods until he found a branch of about the height, thickness, and strength he needed.

Armed with his stick, he returned to the Myerly side and his chosen spot, climbed down to the water's edge, and rammed the stick into the mud. Then he placed his now thoroughly disreputable hat on top of it and climbed up the bank. From the top, it looked exactly what it was—a hat on top of a stick. But when he had walked a few yards back from the river, in the direction one would approach from the house, he could no longer see the stick, just the hat. Now, he hoped, it looked as if someone was sitting by the water's edge, perhaps dozing, perhaps watching the fish while munching some breakfast coaxed out of Lord Myerly's cook. Which everyone knew he did.

Leaving his horse tied to the side of the bridge, where it would surely catch the attention of anyone looking for him, he settled down *under* the bridge and waited to see if anyone would come.

The next stage of his plan was flexible. In fact, it was downright vague, for it depended so much on who the culprit was and what they intended to do. He was not an angry man by nature, but the thought of someone trying to put a period to his existence over something as trivial as money and an estate no one else gave two hoots for....that did arouse his ire. And something akin to hurt that he didn't want to acknowledge, for his own sake or his mother's.

Even now, he didn't truly believe in what he was doing. He was merely ruling out the possibility in the face of some serious and dangerous events. And when he saw someone walking briskly across the meadow from the direction of Myerly, his heart sank.

Part of him even cringed inside. But he would face it as he had faced everything else in his life. Head-on.

And so, he waited to see who the approaching man was, for it definitely was a man. A gentleman by the outline of his dress and the way he walked. So at least he didn't need to confront his Aunt Tabetha.

Of course, it was perfectly possible this man

had nothing to do with him. He might not be family, and if he was, he might have come to talk to him. Even when Dan saw the gun, he harbored the same hope.

Until his Uncle Ames paused and raised the fowling piece, taking clear aim at Dan's hat.

※

JULIET, HAVING DONE her first duty of informing Mrs. Stewart, in the company of the entire family, where Dan had gone for the morning, retreated to the walled garden where Dan had left Gun.

The dog was delighted to see her, and she soon took up position on the mossy old bench which had been built on a raised dais. From there, she could throw sticks for the dog and see who left the house from the front, the back, or the side.

She saw the doctor arrive, presumably to see Susan, and leave again. Colin strode out of a side door, making her sit up straight, but he only walked briskly around the house twice and then vanished back inside. Tomorrow was Wednesday, the day they should all be leaving. If Mrs. Stewart went, too, she could no longer stay here.

But then, it had only ever been a short-term strategy. She would have to go home eventually and face the music. But hopefully, the unspeakable Barden would have left, enraged, and Jeremy would be too appalled with her behavior to wish any resumption of their engagement.

As for the scandal, it would no doubt get worse with Barden fanning the flames. Her ruin would be utter, and no one would want to marry her. That would not please her parents. Or Kitty. But Kitty's Lawrence would stand by her. And Juliet did not want to marry anyone anyway.

Apart from Dan.

The laundry maid was hanging out sheets to dry at the back of the house. Between that and her own dreamy thoughts, she almost missed the man leaving by the front door. He wore a cloak over one shoulder. Mr. Ames. And he was crossing the drive, toward the fields that led to the river.

She stood up in sudden panic. She had promised to stay here, but she had done as Dan had asked and had seen who left the house.

What if someone else left after him, and Juliet was not here to see? Besides, she was being silly. Dan would take care of himself. He had a plan, and what threat could the vague, sickly uncle possibly be to a fit young man?

And then the wind caught his cloak and blew it back, and she saw the gun he carried over one arm.

She was already at the gate, shutting poor Gun in again before she knew fully what she was doing. At the other side of the gate, she hesitated, for Gun would provide both excuse and protection on her walk. But Dan had left him behind deliberately, and it was Dan who was in danger. So, she left him, seized her bonnet from the washing line where it was still airing after her night's adventure in the rain, and tied it on while she hurried toward the river.

She knew the countryside better than Mr. Ames, who was taking the well-worn path over the fields to the bridge. Juliet ran directly to the river itself and followed its bank so that she could support Dan by coming at Ames from a different angle.

And if I'm wrong? If he's just gone shooting birds?

He probably had. She could not really imagine him shooting anyone, let alone his wife's nephew… And yet it was he who had passed the mushrooms to Dan.

And if I'm wrong, and someone else comes, then I'll see them as well from here as from the garden. And here I can do something if I have to.

What that something was, she had no real idea. Until she rounded the bend in the river and saw she was about to intercept Mr. Ames.

She stopped dead, but the man didn't see her. He was striding across from the meadow toward the bridge. And then something caught his attention, and he stopped. At once, she saw what it was.

Someone had scrambled down the riverbank to the side of the water. From the stillness of his head, he had fallen asleep. And from the shape of the hat, she knew who it was.

Asleep!

The stunning realization hit her almost at the same moment as she saw the gun emerge from Ames's cloak. She began to run, coming at him from behind. He raised the weapon to his shoulder, taking slow, careful aim at the head of a man who could not even see him.

In pure terror, she screamed out a wordless warning, both to Ames and Dan, and launched herself through the air to land on Ames's back.

⟫⟫⟪⟪

WATCHING AMES WITH as much sadness as anger, Dan couldn't quite believe his eyes when the tiny figure hurled herself out of nowhere, screaming like a banshee as she landed on Ames's back.

His heart in his mouth, Dan popped out from under the bridge, pounding toward the two-headed spinning creature that was made up of his uncle and Juliet. She had landed on him with such force, that Dan was actually surprised Ames didn't immediately fall forward on his gun. Instead, he spun around, trying to dislodge her, which gave her the opportunity to wrest the weapon from him and hurl it away.

Ames reached over his shoulder, grabbed her by her clothing, and sent her flying to the ground.

Dan emitted a sound of fury and cannoned into his uncle, flattening him beneath his body on the ground.

Ames stared up at him in utter bafflement, jerking his head around to see the hat and then back to the man who should have been wearing it. "What... what..."

Dan rose, hauling his uncle to his feet and started desperately toward Juliet.

She might have been winded by the force with which she hit the ground, but she was all spirit. She staggered to her feet, stumbling in the direction of the fallen gun. And then she saw Dan and Ames and behind them, the hat.

Her mouth fell open.

"I told you I had a plan," he said apologetically. Dragging Ames with him, he picked up the gun, and only then let his uncle go. He unloaded the weapon.

By then, Juliet had stormed closer to the hat and seen enough to understand what he had done. She spun back on her heels, strode straight up to Dan, and slapped him across the face. With that, she burst into tears and hurled herself into his arms to kiss him full on the mouth.

"I thought I was saving you!" she cried.

Dan was enchanted. He closed his free arm around her. "You did, you are."

"No, I almost got you killed instead! And now I've struck you for my own idiocy, and you'll hate me, and I'll never—"

He stopped all that by simply capturing her mouth once more. Which at least seemed to convince her that he was not angry.

Ames uttered a snort of disgust. "You'll spread colds and diseases of all kinds."

Dan drew back to stare at him. "You're worried I'll get a cold when you just tried to shoot me?"

"That's the third time." Ames sighed. "The first time, I didn't really try very hard, wasn't sure I wanted to do it. But even so, you have the luck of the devil."

"Why?" Juliet demanded helplessly. "Why do you want him dead?"

"Hugh," he said simply. "I don't have very much, let Hugh run through what little there was... Thought old Miserly would leave him at least something, but I soon saw the way the wind was blowing. The old man loves you." He gave Dan a smile that was incongruously sweet from a man who had tried several times to kill him. "As I love Hugh. I don't have long for this world. It's time for me to face the clouds and stay away... And then who will look after Hugh? I had to do it first."

"Hugh is six-and-twenty years old," Dan pointed out, "Don't you think he can shift for himself?"

"Didn't work so well for you, did it?" Ames said, quite without anger. "Until the old man decided to favor you. I think it's time to go. Tell Hugh…"

"*You* can tell Hugh," Dan said, taking his arm and beginning to walk.

Ames frowned at him. "Aren't you taking me to the magistrate?"

"To charge you with what? Being a rotten shot? Aiming at an empty and already destroyed hat?"

"Or putting rat poison in the mushrooms?" Juliet said severely.

Ames sighed. "A moment of madness. I picked up the tin someone had left in the back hall, put some in my snuff box. No one noticed at the table when I tipped it into the mushrooms. Dan didn't even eat them."

"Susan the maid did," Dan said shortly.

"Oh," He looked quite alarmed. "Is she…is she dead?"

"No, but it was close," Dan said.

"Madness," Ames murmured. "It's the clouds. Can't think straight. But I'm glad *she* didn't die."

Which left him ambiguous at best about Dan's survival. They walked on in silence as Dan tried to come to terms with the danger lurking beneath his uncle's vagueness.

"You will look after Hugh and Hetty, won't you?" Ames said suddenly.

Dan stared at him. "Why the devil didn't you ask me that before all this...palaver?"

Ames shrugged. "Didn't know you and didn't like you much. Didn't think you would share. Perhaps I was wrong."

"You *were* wrong," Juliet said fiercely. "Very wrong."

CHAPTER TWENTY-ONE

Juliet's bolt to the house of her father's enemy gave Lord Barden the clue that she would not be so easily managed as he had assumed. Therefore, he rose early in order to accompany Cosland in retrieving her and was glad to find the earl alone in the breakfast room.

"I want the matter dealt with as speedily as possible," he told the earl briskly. "I have already spent more time than I had intended on this matter. Therefore, I shall accompany you to Myerly, and I have taken the liberty of sending my man to your vicar with instructions to meet us there."

Cosland blinked. "I'm not sure instruction is the correct way to deal with a respected clergyman like Mr. Coates. I do know that even more piling into his home will arouse the ire of

Lord Myerly. He will be angry enough to see me."

"His sister told me he was bedridden," Barden said carelessly. "He need not see any of us."

Cosland paused. "Sir, I do not think it advisable that you accompany us. It was largely because of you that my daughter fled in the first place. Your presence will merely make the matter more difficult."

"We are agreed it was your handling of her that caused her to bolt," Barden retorted. "Thus, forcing my hand. Most men would withdraw an offer of marriage after such a vulgar start, particularly considering she is already ruined. I, however, am still prepared to take the girl on the conditions we agreed, providing it is done today."

Cosland's face spasmed.

Which warmed Barden's heart. He had waited a long time to insult the proud aristocrat who had cost him everything. He rubbed salt in the wound. "I brought a special license from London. If you can control her, she may stay with you until my return from Cheshire, by which time I shall expect our business arrangements to be complete."

"You are running ahead of yourself," Cosland said abruptly. "My daughter has not yet chosen, and Catesby also wishes to press his suit."

Barden laughed. "I trust he knows there will

no saving the reputation of his would-be wife. Without me, she will not be received in society. People will snigger behind their hands as he walks past, the husband of a—but there," he finished hastily, catching the murderous glint in Cosland's eye, "you understand me perfectly."

"I do," Cosland said grimly. "And it's my belief that if she chooses Catesby, the power of the Alfords and the Coslands will easily counter your vulgar innuendo. Particularly once we prove you placed that disgusting piece in the newspaper."

"But I didn't," Barden said amiably. "I learned a lot, made a lot of useful…acquaintances in my years of servitude to His Highness. You will find me above suspicion."

"The Regent's snake is above no suspicion," Cosland snapped, though before Barden could do more than flush with anger at the insulting nickname, he rose to his feet, holding up one hand as though to prevent a tirade. "However, I have said I will allow her to choose between you, and I will. But Barden? If she chooses you, you will treat her with the respect due to her birth and rank, or I will tear you down at any cost. If you insist on coming, we leave in ten minutes."

"We" turned out to be not only the earl but the countess. And Jeremy Catesby.

"There is no point in your going," Barden said irritably as he came face to face with his rival in the carriage. "I have a special license and mean to marry her immediately."

"What you mean may not matter to Juliet," Catesby said with an oddly deprecating laugh. "At least I know I have behaved badly."

"We have all behaved badly," Lady Cosland uttered. "The test now is if we can manage better." She did not look at her husband as she spoke, but it was he who bit his lip.

Oh, yes, the matter needed to be finished today before the earl got cold feet and Barden lost any control. It struck him he had allowed triumph to get in the way of the cold good sense that had first formulated his plan. He had made mistakes in dealing with both the earl and his daughter. But he held the special license, and he undoubtedly held the upper hand still. The girl would choose him. There was no other viable choice.

Besides, he would make it easy for her. He could be conciliatory when he chose.

It was not a long journey to Myerly. The house unnerved him slightly because of its general air of neglect and several windows appeared to be shuttered.

"Good God," he murmured. "Why did she come here?"

"To annoy me," Cosland said without heat. He alighted first and handed down his wife.

The place hardly looked as if it was used to

receiving visitors, and yet the door was opened almost immediately after Cosland's sharp rap.

An elderly butler gazed at them. He did not seem surprised but bowed without immediately standing back to admit them. "My lord."

"Good morning, Griffin. I imagine his lordship is at home if he is able or chooses to receive us. But it is my daughter I've come to see."

That didn't seem to surprise the butler either. He sighed and stood back, opening the door wide. Lady Cosland sailed in, and the others followed.

The ancient butler closed the door and tottered toward a door on the right of the entrance hall. "Please follow me, and I shall inform the ladies."

"Lady Juliet, if you please," Cosland reminded him.

The old man bowed and opened the door to a musty-smelling room. The shutters were still closed, letting in a few beams of sunlight through the cracks. While the butler retreated, a middle-aged footman entered and opened the shutters.

"Why would she come here?" Catesby asked uneasily. "How could she live like this?"

"Oh, it isn't all this bad," a vaguely familiar lady said, bustling into the room. "I'm so sorry they put you in here. It *is* the reception room, but as you see, there hasn't been much call for it. Come up to the drawing room."

"Jenny—Mrs. Stewart," the earl said, striding up to her. "Where is my daughter?"

"I have sent for her," Mrs. Stewart assured him.

"Why did you not tell us she was here?" the earl burst out.

Mrs. Stewart glanced ruefully from him to his wife. "I'm sorry. I can only imagine your anxiety, but she assured us she had left you a note to say she was safe. She asked us particularly not to inform you, and to be frank, I was afraid she would bolt again if we insisted. She was…upset when she arrived, and I for one thought you would rather she stayed here than went anywhere else less…safe."

"You were right," Lady Cosland said, following her from the room while Barden and the others trailed after her. "Thank you for looking after our daughter."

"Actually, it has been a pleasure, although she has been looking after us. We had something of a household emergency last night, and Juliet was most helpful."

"Myerly?" Cosland asked quickly.

"No, no, one of the maids. My father appears to be indestructible."

"He won't like you receiving me," Cosland warned.

Jenny laughed. "Then he has changed his tune since the last time we discussed it."

Barden neither understood this sally, nor cared to, but it caused the earl to emit a bark of laughter, and the countess to cast a sour glance at Mrs. Stewart.

In the drawing room, which was at least clean if faded, they discovered Mrs. Stewart's sisters and the stiffly upright Colin Cornwell, all of whom Barden knew slightly from London as well as the dinner at Hornby. They all looked anxious and embarrassed, and Cornwell, who bowed very low, said in a rush, "I hope you know, my lord, that keeping Lady Juliet's presence here from you was at no point my idea. Nor did it have my app—"

"Content yourself," Cosland interrupted wryly. "I know full well whose idea it was."

An elderly maid stood in the doorway, panting slightly. "Lady Juliet's not in her chamber, ma'am. Nor with Susan."

"Oh." Mrs. Stewart seemed genuinely surprised. "Perhaps she has gone for a walk with Dan and the dog. She will be back directly. Are they making tea, Betty?"

"If they've gone for a walk," Cornwell said grimly from the window, "they haven't taken the dog. It's digging up a tree in the garden."

How would you tell? Barden wondered with amusement as he glanced at the window and the wilderness beyond.

"Oh, no, they haven't gone together," Mrs.

Ames pronounced in her irritatingly nervous way, clutching at the shawls, which fell continuously from her arms and shoulders. "Dan went early, if you recall, to meet with Patrick—the Myerly steward, you know—and I did see Lady Juliet in the garden after breakfast. Playing with the dog."

Why did people keep harping on about the dog?

Cornwell frowned. "Why didn't Dan take the dog? He always takes him when he's tramping the estate."

"Oh, no," Mrs. Cornwell blurted, exchanging glances with her sisters and then gazing at Lady Cosland. "He wouldn't have."

"Wouldn't have what?" Mrs. Stewart asked with a hint of irritation.

"If Juliet isn't in the garden, where is she? Why did neither of them take the dog? What if they have...?"

"Eloped?" Mrs. Ames said in horror.

"Oh, don't be ridiculous!" Mrs. Stewart uttered. "Dan would not elope with her!"

"Well, he was clearly making up to her," Cornwell retorted with more than a hit of bitterness.

"You are thinking of yourself there, I think!" Mrs. Stewart shot back.

"I find it offensive," Lady Cosland interrupted, "that you assume my daughter would elope with anyone. I understand from my younger daughter that Juliet considers this young man a friend."

"They *are* friends," Mrs. Stewart agreed cordially. "And neither has the reason nor the character for elopement."

"Ha!" uttered a cadaverous old gentleman shuffling into the room with an ancient valet at his side, bearing two cushions and a bottle of smelling salts. "What on earth makes you imagine that? Dan's your son, isn't he? Handsome young devil, too. Wouldn't be surprised if the ladies didn't take a shine to him." He looked directly at Lord Cosland and smiled. "Your girl certainly did."

Cosland took one step toward him, then seemed to remember himself and bowed jerkily. Barden didn't blame him for the stiffness. All this talk of elopement was making him uneasy, too.

"I hope you forgive the intrusion," Cosland said frostily. "I have to thank you for caring for my daughter, but we have come to take her home."

"If they can find her," Barden couldn't help murmuring.

One would have assumed such an old gentleman to be deaf, but apparently, he was not, for he turned at once on Barden. "Who the devil are you?"

"Papa," Mrs. Cornwell protested in clear

embarrassment. "This is Lord Barden."

"Lady Juliet's betrothed," Barden said, bowing gracefully.

The old man's eyes widened gratifyingly.

"Allow me to preset Lady Cosland," the earl added, "and Mr. Catesby."

"Catesby?" Myerly pounced. "Alford's boy? Weren't you engaged to the girl, too?"

"Yes," Catesby admitted, tilting up his chin. "And I have hopes she will still marry me."

"Bah," Barden said derisively.

Lord Myerly admitted a crack of laughter. "Well, looks like you're both too late if she's off to the border with Dan."

"She is *not* off to the border with Dan!" Mrs. Stewart exclaimed. "How can you even think such a thing?"

"Because you did it, of course," the old man snapped.

"I had no choice," Mrs. Stewart claimed. "Dan has every choice."

"And perhaps, it's not marriage he has in mind," Barden said nastily, for he already disliked this so-called friend.

"Best run off after them, then," Myerly snarled unexpectedly. "No one wants you here, and I'd quite like Dan to punch you in the nose, even if I'm not there to see it."

Mrs. Stewart made a strangled sound in her throat, which she turned into a cough, just as the elderly maid and footman carried in tea trays.

"Tea," she said shakily. "Thank goodness. Please, sit down..."

Just as things were easing back into tense civility with the pouring and receiving of tea, someone else wandered into the room. Hugh Ames, who fancied himself a dandy and had excruciating taste. This morning, his coat was pink, and it quite clearly caused a spasm to cross his grandfather's face.

However, he looked preoccupied, and his eyebrows shot up to see so many people in the room. He bowed with his usual flourish. "Enchanted, enchanted," he exclaimed. "But no, I don't believe I will have tea, Aunt Jenny. I just thought my father was in here?"

"Oh, no," Mrs. Ames said, looking guilty for some reason. "I have not seen him since breakfast. I thought he was with you."

"For God's sake, who cares?" Lord Myerly interrupted, and Barden tended to agree with the sentiment. "He's a grown man, isn't he? Let him off the leash!"

After a faintly nervous glance at his grandfather, Hugh returned his gaze to his mother. "I fell asleep," he admitted. "Bit of a disturbed night, with one thing and another. I'll just head off and look for him."

"No need," Cornwell said abruptly from the window. A look of profound relief covered his face. "He's just come back with Daniel and Lady Juliet."

Barden did his best to hide his own relief. They had almost had him believing in this ridiculous elopement. But the girl was not a fool. She would not elope with a *nobody*.

"They're in the garden," Hugh Ames said, having walked over to join his cousin. "Playing with that monster Dan insists is a mere dog. Perhaps I *shall* have a cup of tea, Aunt."

"They're not bringing the animal into the house, are they?" Colin said in obvious alarm.

"Why shouldn't they?" Lord Myerly demanded, presumably from sheer devilment. "I already told Dan he could, if he keeps it under control."

They must have come into the house with a key, for Barden heard no knocking, no creaking of ancient footsteps before bright laughing voices and the quick *clip-clip* of a dog's claws on the wooden floor.

"Griffin, is my cousin Hugh about?" called a young man.

"In the drawing room, sir. But, sir, my lady, you should know—" The butler clearly meant to warn them about the visitors, but with the impetuosity of youth or sheer foolishness, Lady Juliet walked into the room. And stopped dead.

Close on her heels came the elder Ames, who, in fact, walked into her. Behind him came the hugest, hairiest, worst-bred dog Barden had ever had the misfortune to lay eyes on. And holding onto its threadbare leash, the equally shabby figure of the young man who had stolen Juliet for the waltz while Barden was still tormenting her. So that was Daniel Stewart.

Barden had neither the time nor the inclination to put up with tantrums, though judging by Juliet's face, he suspected he was going to have to grit his teeth with boredom and put up with one.

"Well, Juliet?" her father said heavily.

And Juliet actually sprang forward, hugging her mother and then kissing her father's aloof cheek. "I am so sorry to have worried you! I was wrong to go as I did, so please forgive me."

In that moment, Barden actually admired her. She had managed to take the wind out of her parents' sails and thus made his own intentions quicker and simpler. It was a good omen. This was the match that was meant to be.

She turned, politely greeting both himself and Catesby, without favoring either, but he could see the curiosity on her face.

Lord Myerly explained it to her, a malicious glint in his eyes. "Apparently, they are both engaged to you."

"Whoever told you that was utterly mistaken," Juliet said calmly.

"Thought they must be," Myerly agreed. "Which one *do* you favor, then?"

"Neither!" Juliet exclaimed at the same time as the earl said haughtily, "That is none of your business, sir!"

The huge dog, meanwhile, had dragged its master far enough to be able to lay its head on Mrs. Stewart's lap, to the imminent danger of the tea table.

"Good morning to you, too, Gun," the lady murmured, patting the hairy head. "Watch him, Dan, or he'll upset everything."

"Dan," however, seemed to be trying to hold a low-voiced conversation with young Ames, and Juliet was asking her mother if she could not stay at Myerly until tomorrow, if his lordship did not object.

"Stay as long as you like," Myerly said expansively, merely to stir the pot, Barden was sure. "You cheer up these tired old eyes."

Barden had had enough. The whole ridiculous situation was beginning to spread out of control once more. He dragged it back to heel.

"I expect you are wondering why I chose to accompany your father upon the visit," he said loudly to Lady Juliet. "The truth is, I have arranged for us to be married right away."

Her eyes widened with undisguised horror, and in spite of everything, all that beauty afraid of him was both gratifying and arousing.

"Don't be ridiculous, man!" Catesby exclaimed. "You cannot rush the lady into something of that nature."

"As you would know, having so markedly dragged your heels," Barden snapped. "Lady Juliet knows all the advantages she and her family will receive from marriage with me." He smirked. "And the pariah she would remain with you."

"Rubbish!" Catesby blustered. "Juliet and I understand each other very well. Tell me now, Juliet, that you forgive me and accept me, and I promise I will make all this go away."

Everyone gazed at Juliet, who looked at first desperate and hunted. And then, to Barden's surprise, her lip twitched, and a spark of humor gleamed in her eyes. "Actually, I think Lord Myerly is the one to do that."

"In the meantime," Dan Stewart said, easing the dog carefully away from the tea table, "I'm afraid Lady Juliet will not be marrying either of you today or any other day. She is, in fact, engaged to me."

"For God's sake, Daniel!" Cornwell exploded.

Lord Myerly snickered.

Barden wanted to throw something.

Juliet, however, cast a sudden, brilliant smile at the shabby young man, whose lips quirked upward. "If she still wants to be."

Unexpectedly, Juliet dashed to his side, snatched the leash from his fingers, and handed it to Mrs. Stewart. "If you please, just for a moment," she said breathlessly, and seizing

Stewart by the arm, she dragged him out of the door.

Instinctively, Barden started after them. So did Catesby, Lord and Lady Cosland, and Cornwell.

CHAPTER TWENTY-TWO

A S SOON AS they were out of the room, Dan pulled the door shut and held onto the handle.

Juliet hung onto his free arm, giving it a little shake to get his attention, for someone was clearly trying to open the door from the other side, and Dan was exerting considerable strength to keep it shut.

"Thank you for saying that," she said in a rush. "But before we go back, I want you to know that I'll never hold you to it. As soon as this nonsense is done, I'll jilt you quite heartlessly. If that's what you want. But Dan?"

His eyes had never left her face, even when the door rattled and pulled behind him. "Mmm?"

"Before… I didn't ask you then just to get me out of trouble. I won't ever want to marry anyone *except* you. But I would die rather than make you marry me from some kind of false responsibility."

"I have no responsibility," he said.

She smiled, "Yes, you do, Dan. Sometimes you hide it, but it's there, behind the fun. It's one reason I love you so much."

"Love?" He swallowed. "You…love me?"

"Oh, Dan, of course I love you! But if you don't l—"

The rest of her speech was lost in his mouth as he kissed her. With a sob of joy, she flung both arms around his neck and abandoned herself to the wild, hard kiss.

His arm dragged her against him, so closely, they could have been one.

"Of course *I* love *you*," he muttered against her lips. "How could I not, you—"

And the words vanished again into another deep, wondrous kiss.

He loved her. Dan loved her, and now, *now*, everything would be not just fine, but wonderful. Joy stretched out before her.

At some point, it seemed, Dan forgot about the door, for both his arms were around her. And people, including her parents, spilled out the room in shock.

Juliet gasped and whisked herself out of Dan's arms, though she seized one of them back again before anyone could separate them. "I'm going to marry Dan," she said happily.

Her father groaned. Barden looked furious enough to be dangerous. Jeremy, oddly, looked devastated.

"Come back inside," her mother instructed.

Juliet obeyed, but she realized, suddenly, she was not afraid, and she would not run. Because Dan stood by her side, and together, they could do anything.

But Lord Barden took the floor, drawing all eyes, although to Juliet suddenly, he looked more like a stage villain than a real threat. Mrs. Stewart released Gun's leash, and the dog trotted happily up to Dan and Juliet. She patted his big head, and he gratefully licked her hand while she regarded Lord Barden with only faint interest.

"I believe you know and understand the power I wield in society," Barden said. "You would be ill-advised to throw that away on a passing fancy for a handsome face. Even Catesby would be better than him, you know. But neither will bring you the...salvation that I will. Tell her, Cosland."

Her father was scowling. "Look, Juliet, I know, I understand why you are doing this, but truly it is not the way out. Barden *is* your best hope of recovery in society, although if you would rather Jeremy, I have already agreed, I will respect that."

"I have chosen Dan." She smiled. "And Dan

has chosen me."

"God help me, I shall be sick," Barden muttered, and Juliet laughed, which seemed to throw him.

"No," her father said firmly. "He will do you no good, Juliet. I will not allow it."

"Then, I shall wait until I am twenty-one and marry him anyway."

"Juliet," her mother pleaded.

But Barden, clearly, had had enough. He took a step nearer her. "Stop playing games, you *silly* little girl," he snarled. "You will marry me today or be ruined beyond all possibility of saving."

Beside her, Dan stirred. "And you will see to that, will you?" he said gently. "Personally?"

Barden curled his lip, giving up all pretense. "Yes."

Dan's hand clenched, but before he could move, Juliet caught the dog's head and pointed his nose straight at Barden in the center of the room. Dan paused, his breath catching as he realized what she was about.

"Gun," she said happily. *"Fire!"*

She had no idea what would happen, or if the dog would obey someone other than Dan. But even if he just sat there, it would have been worth it, just for the suddenly terrified look on Barden's face. However, Gun outdid himself.

With one of his brutally sudden barks, he shot out of her hands like a ball from a rifle, sending a side table flying in a hail of crockery and silver teaspoons. Dan's aunts squealed.

Barden staggered backward in a futile attempt to escape, but Gun landed on him, with all four paws, bringing him down like a hunted deer.

Barden yelled. "Get it off, get it *off* me!"

Dan strolled forward. "Then you'll withdraw your insolent offer of marriage and attendant threats?" he inquired casually.

Gun snarled, slavering over Barden's throat.

"Dear God, Dan," Mrs. Stewart said, awed. "I didn't know he did that. Is he quite safe?"

"No, not really." Dan smiled. "He's a street cur, and he's had no breakfast. In fact, I might have forgotten his dinner last night."

"Very well, very well!" Barden screamed. "Get the monster off me, and I'll agree to anything."

Dan appeared to think about it while everyone watched him in fascination. "You'd better keep to it. Otherwise, he'll find you. Enough, Gun." Dan hauled the dog off. "Let him stand."

As Barden staggered to his feet unaided, something fell from his coat. Dan picked it up, and Barden immediately snatched it from him.

"You're welcome," Dan said wryly. "What is so precious?"

Barden's lips twisted angrily. "A special license that would have saved a lady's reputation."

"Instead of which, the dog appears to have

saved it. But since you don't need the license…"

Hastily, Barden whisked it out of the way, and Juliet, propelled by sheer mischief, plucked it away from him, just as the door opened, and Griffin announced Mr. Coates, the vicar, in an increasingly faint voice.

The vicar halted in mid-step, regarding the carnage open-mouthed. Gun wagged his tail and loped toward the new visitor, who backed toward the door.

Hastily, Dan caught the leash. "Sorry, sir. He's quite harmless, really."

"No, he is not!" Barden exclaimed in high, outraged tones. "The dog is an evil, dangerous cur that should be shot!"

The evil cur rubbed his head against Dan's leg and wagged his tail. He looked as if he was smiling, and the vicar's face softened visibly.

"Lord Myerly, I will bid you good day," Barden said between his teeth.

"About time," his lordship said, scowling. "Never asked you here in the first place."

Barden bowed stiffly. "Sir, come with me," he said to the vicar. "Your services are no longer required."

"Dan, get him out of here!" Myerly roared suddenly. "How dare he dictate which guests come into my house! Coates, sit down, have a cup of tea!"

Since Dan had told her Myerly frequently

denied the vicar access, this sudden invitation was somewhat surprising. Barden merely sneered, but Juliet's mother added insult to Barden's injury.

"My lord, I really believe you have stepped beyond the line of what is pleasing, or even permitted, by a guest. Please take our carriage back to Hornby. The servants will help you pack while the carriage returns for us. Goodbye, my lord."

Barden spun on his heel and walked out of the room, leaving the door open.

Juliet, still holding the special license, met Dan's gaze. His lips quirked. His eyes gleamed in invitation, and her breath caught. Mischief surged along with excitement and a much more basic feeling of rightness, of completion.

"Papa." She stepped up to her father and took his hand. "Please consider this. Because if necessary, I will wait for him, and I will marry him on my twenty-first birthday. But I would so much rather do it with your blessing."

Her father snatched his hand back. "Look, there is Jeremy, who once you eagerly promised yourself to. What has changed?"

"*I* have. Papa, Jeremy does not love me. Dan does."

"Loves your money more like," Colin muttered. Hugh nudged him ungently with a sharp, pink elbow.

"That isn't true, Juliet," Jeremy said desperately. "Oh, perhaps once I took you for granted. I behaved ill, as though you could be exchanged for someone else of similar birth and influence. But the truth is, you can't be, because you've made me realize….oh the devil, in short, Juliet, I *do* love you, and it would be my profound honor to call you my wife."

"Why, Jeremy," she said, touched in spite of herself. "That was a genuinely handsome speech, and I'm grateful for the sentiment. But the truth is, I am at fault, too. I didn't realize it before when we were engaged, but I didn't love you, either. I was wrong. I love Dan."

To Juliet's surprise, her mother took her father's hand. He frowned down at her, reading her unexpected, silent plea. Juliet began to smile.

Her father groaned. "This is madness! You barely know him! He has nothing! And your reputation—"

"He is the heir to Myerly, and my reputation means nothing without him."

The earl continued to scowl.

"Cosland, allow her this," her mother said, low. "It is her happiness."

"Oh, for the love of—" He threw up both hands. "Very well, have him, marry him."

"Oh, thank you, Papa!" She hugged her father and mother together and turned, laughing, back to Dan.

"Ha!" uttered Lord Myerly. "Got round the

great Lord Cosland, did you? Well, you won't get round me. I forbid it!"

All eyes turned on him in dismay. Silence filled the room, and the old man sat back and enjoyed it.

"You can't," Dan said. "I'm well past the age of majority."

"True. But I can take Myerly away again, give it to Hugh!"

"That's not such a bad idea," Dan said seriously, and with a jolt, Juliet remembered the bizarre revelations of the morning.

Lord Myerly stared at Dan. So did Hugh and Mr. Ames.

"Why?" Myerly barked.

"Hugh will tell you later. If you don't shout. Mr. Coates, I have a special license here. Would you be so good as to marry Lady Juliet and me?"

»»»«««

LORD BARDEN SAT in the bumping Cosland carriage, stunned and entirely at a loss.

And yet, this had happened before. Only four days previously, his plans for Hazel Curwen had been thwarted by his humiliating ejection from Brightoaks. And he still felt that previous failure must have contributed to this one. With Hazel as his acknowledged mistress, his social power would have been that much more apparent.

Damn Cosland, damn him! And damn that puppy and his monstrous hell-hound...

To hell with all of them. He had recovered from worse, and it was undeniably true that his initial revenge held true. Hazel Curwen and Cosland's daughter were both ruined. He had that much satisfaction.

But now, he had to look ahead, not backward. He might have hurt Cosland, and he certainly would do his best to hurt Juliet further, but he did not have his money back. His estate was still mortgaged and rented out. He lived in inferior rooms in London instead of the gracious family townhouse. To get those things back, to live in luxury, he needed another wealthy bride. One of even higher standing than Juliet Lilbourne.

He sat up. *Oh, yes.* With a few tweaks to his original plan, he could still salvage everything. He hesitated, wondering whether it would be best to concentrate now on Meg Winter... Or stick to his original schedule and go to Deborah Shelby in Cheshire to cover his back.

Yes, Cheshire would be best. And while he was there, he could set the other matter in motion.

He was almost cheerful by the time he returned to Hornby Park, where he took great pleasure in revealing nothing to Juliet's avid siblings.

>>>≫≪<<<

JULIET WAS IN awe. She could not quite believe this was happening, that she was marrying Dan. Breathless laughter bubbled just below the surface as she stood beside the man she loved and made her vows of marriage before Mr. Coates, witnessed by her parents and Dan's family. And Jeremy, who seemed both stunned and devastated, but who shook hands manfully with Dan afterwards and wished them both happy.

Bizarrely, the man who had just tried to kill Dan remained in the room to witness his wedding. Seated by Mrs. Ames with Hugh standing behind them, he watched in silence. But when Juliet and Dan approached them, tears were running down his face. He looked terrified.

"It's time, Hetty," he said agitatedly. "It's time."

"Time for what, dear?" Mrs. Ames asked, patting his hand. "Congratulations, Dan. I wish you both the best of everything in your marriage."

Hugh stuck out a hasty hand. "All the best, old fellow. Lady Juliet, you have broken my heart by marrying this lout, but funnily enough, he's the best of us."

"Time, Hugh!" Mr. Ames insisted.

"Yes, Papa." Hugh patted his shoulder. "It is

time. We won't come to your wedding breakfast, though it is most kind of your mother to invite us. I think we'll head back to Hertfordshire."

"Will you manage?" Dan asked bluntly. "What will you do?"

"It's been planned for a while. A couple of strong footmen and a kind nurse already work in the house on different duties. They will now care exclusively for my father. It's what he wants, as you hear. He has frightened himself as much as me by what he did. I'm sorry. I only took my eyes off him for an hour a day." His eyes flickered. "For my own sanity. Never imagined what he was getting up to in that hour." Hugh's smile was lopsided. "Will you take it amiss if I say I'm glad it was you, Dan? Anyone else would have had him arrested. I shouldn't have let him come at all, but he was so eager."

Dan gripped his shoulder briefly. "You're not alone, Hugh. Call on me for anything. If I can help, I will."

Half an hour later, as they waved the Ameses off, Juliet said, "You never know what people carry with them, do you? Poor Hugh has been bearing the entire weight of his father's deterioration, covering for him, looking after him, and all anyone ever said about him—all *I* ever said about him—was that he wore a pink coat."

Dan's fingers slipped through hers. "He does have a pink coat. I expect its brightness cheers him up. But it's far from an empty coat. Shall we ride to Hornby?"

Laughter surged up to the surface. "We are married. No one will raise an objection."

No one did. They were more concerned with persuading Lord Myerly that he should come to Hornby.

"We haven't spoken in a quarter of a century," the old gentleman growled at Juliet's father. "And now you want me to dine with you?"

"It's customary," the earl said gravely. He hesitated, then, "And it's past time we stopped being stubborn. I've always known in my heart you were not to blame for Jenny's elopement. She would always have married Stewart. I'm sorry I spoke to you as I did."

Myerly glowered at him. "And I suppose you expect me to say I should have let you apologize sooner?"

"No," her father said with the glimmer of a smile. "I will give you that one. If you join us to celebrate your grandson's wedding to my daughter."

>>><<<

TEN MINUTES LATER, changed into her riding habit with Betty's aid, she emerged from her chamber on the half-landing to hear some commotion going on at the foot of the attic steps. Since Susan was supposed to be sleeping up there, Juliet frowned and hurried along to sort out the trouble.

Two men, neither of them servants at the house, were quarreling, shoving at each other, while a familiar older lady stood guarding the steps with an umbrella held like a sword before her.

"Mrs. Harper!" Juliet exclaimed.

The men stopped arguing at once, and both turned toward her. Susan's farmer and her sergeant. Presumably, both had come to see her, and Mrs. Harper was preventing them.

Mrs. Harper's face lit up. "Miss Smith! How amazingly fortunate! Is it within your power to have these brutes thrown out of this house and kept from my daughter?"

"Well, yes, probably," Juliet said. "But...how is Susan?"

"Weak as a kitten, but so glad to see me. She wept, Miss Smith. Wept."

"I'm not surprised," Juliet murmured, wondering how to explain that her name wasn't Smith. "But...has Susan said whether or not she wishes to see either of these gentlemen?"

Mrs. Harper's jaw dropped.

"You have to ask her," Juliet said gently. "You can't protect her from everything, or you'll make her run away again."

Mrs. Harper looked outraged and then miserable. Without a word, she turned and hurried up the attic steps. Immediately, Owens charged after her, and the farmer grabbed him by the arm.

"I don't think so!" Juliet cried, incensed. "Stay exactly where you are! There will be no fighting in this house unless you want to be barred from it for good. You will wait to be invited, and if you are not, you will leave. Is that clearly understood?"

The farmer gulped and tugged his forelock. "Yes, m'lady."

She glared at the silent sergeant who eventually gave a reluctant grin. "Yes, ma'am, m'lady, whoever you are."

"Mrs. Stewart," Dan said severely, from behind her. Keeping his eyes on the love rivals, he drew her farther back. "Well?"

"You might need to deal with Sergeant Owens's disappointment. Susan is making up her mind."

Dan looked skeptical, which surprised her until Mrs. Harper reappeared at the top of the stairs. "Sergeant, she will give you five minutes. No longer."

An expression of utter relief broke out on the sergeant's face, softening it into something close to fatuous as he dashed upstairs, unhindered by his crestfallen rival who turned away, head bowed.

Juliet turned to Dan, open-mouthed. "How did you know?"

He shrugged. "He followed her here. He was angry, but never with her. There just seemed more feeling than either Susan or her mother credited him with. Such feeling usually has a reason, in my experience."

"The reason being Susan actually loved him?"

"Perhaps. Come and look at this. They're wheeling out the most ancient coach you've ever seen. And our horses are saddled."

The ride to Hornby was just what Juliet needed—time alone with Dan to come to terms with the astonishing knowledge that he was her husband.

Her heartbeat quickened with more than the exercise of riding as they entered Hornby woods, and their horses slowed to a halt. While his mount cropped at the undergrowth, he reached out for the bridle of Juliet's horse, drawing it close enough to his own that he could lean across and kiss her.

Somewhere, she was aware the birds still sang in the trees, that other small creatures scuttled beneath. The scents of the wood did not change. But his kiss, the first as her husband, seemed so momentous that everything else faded.

"Afraid?" he whispered.

"Of what?"

"Of what we've done."

She smiled, shaking her head so that her lips brushed back and forth across his. "No. Are you?"

"I think I should be. But all I know is that you are my wife, and I have never been so happy in my life."

>>>><<<<

THE ALFORDS WERE stunned, although there was no time for them to work up to offense. After all, it was their son who had broken the engagement. They had claimed to have come to Hornby through mere friendship, with no promises, so they could hardly take it amiss when Juliet chose elsewhere.

Kitty wept and laughed and hugged her. "I was so afraid you would hate me for telling them where I thought you were! But *of course,* you married your Daniel!"

Ferdy just laughed and clapped Dan on the back hard enough to make him stagger.

"I hope that was affection," Dan protested.

"It was," Juliet assured him.

Considering the mix of guests at this very peculiar wedding breakfast, it passed with surprising joy. At least, if others were not joyful, Juliet was far too happy to notice. The air was even cleared between her mother and Dan's, as before the dining room was ready, Mrs. Stewart came and sat beside them.

"I hope you won't take this amiss, Lady Cosland, and I have no hesitation in speaking in front of Juliet. But I want to say how pleased I am to make your acquaintance, and to finally make peace with your husband." She smiled rather ruefully at the countess's sudden stiffening. "He and I would have made each other miserable, you know. *He* certainly knows. I behaved badly to him, but I hurt mainly his pride. He is lucky to have you, and I believe we are all lucky to be allied through our children."

It was a handsome speech, and Jenny Stewart hadn't needed to make it. Juliet's mother acknowledged everything with a brief clasp of her hand.

❧

IT SEEMED BOTH strange and wonderful to dance into her bedchamber with Dan that evening. He was humming a popular waltz tune and pushed the door closed with his shoulder as he spun her. They whirled dizzyingly across the room and landed, laughing, on top of the bed.

"What shall we do now?" Juliet asked as he leaned over her.

His eyes darkened. He swept his hand down

MARY LANCASTER

the length of her body, leaving her breathless.

But she caught his hand, smiling. "No, I mean tomorrow, the next few weeks, the rest of our lives. It's not as if we've had any time to plan this."

"Unplanned fun is nearly always the best." However, he seemed to bend his mind to it. "Tomorrow, we should rescue Gun from the garden at Myerly. Or, alternatively, rescue Myerly from Gun. Then...wedding trips are traditional. Your parents seem to want you to go to London to buy clothes."

"Well, that is always fun. You should do the same."

He sat up and shrugged off his somewhat threadbare coat. Tossing it aside, he said, "Perhaps you are right. And I would like to go to the theater with you."

"And Vauxhall Gardens! Ranelagh!"

"Why do you want to go there? They're hardly fashionable anymore. Or respectable."

"That's why," she said happily. She caught his hand and held it to her cheek. "You are not a poor man anymore, Dan," she said with difficulty. "Even without Myerly."

"I know. Your father spoke to me. Apparently, we have an estate in Lincolnshire. And my grandfather, inspired by his determination to keep up with the generosity of his old enemy, has said I shall still have Myerly. Plus, a small allowance now. Apparently, my aunts and cousins have always had one. Now my mother and I will, too. He even said he would increase Aunt Hetty's, for their…difficulty. And when he dies, he will divide his fortune between us."

"And you will still have Myerly. I think you would have given up the rest for Myerly."

"Except you," he said, tossing his cravat and waistcoat carelessly on the floor. He leaned over her once more, tracing the outline of her lips with his fingertips, then trailing them down her chin and throat.

His lips followed, and her arms came up of their own volition to hold him. His hand slid beneath her, unlacing her gown even as he began to speak, rapidly and breathlessly.

"I will make light of things that are important. I will, from time to time, behave badly, though never unfaithfully. I may wander off forgetting to tell you and miss engagements, though I will try not to. I will laugh inappropriately and fail to be polite to supposedly important people who annoy me. Occasionally, or quite often, I am bound to annoy you. We will quarrel. But through it all, Juliet, never doubt that I love you, that I will always protect you, and love you, support you, and love you…"

"I am seeing a pattern," she managed, and stopped his lips with her own. "Don't apologize for crimes you have not yet committed. I love *you*, Dan, not some silly idealized version of what a husband should be."

He smiled, tugging the gown and undergarments from her shoulders until her arms were free and then the rest of her, and she lay quite naked in his arms. "You are quite wonderful..." His eyes, thrillingly hot and clouded, devoured her. "My God, what did I do in my life to deserve you?"

She caressed his stubbly cheek and throat and tugged at his shirt. "You made that nasty porter give me a ticket for the stagecoach. You helped me and believed me. But it's never a matter of *deserving*, is it?"

"No," he agreed, obliging her by pulling his shirt up over his head. "And it's probably as well you didn't know exactly what was in my head at the time."

"What?" she asked, just before he kissed her mouth long and deeply.

"This," he said huskily, trailing kisses across her cheeks and shoulders and breasts. "And this, this, and this..."

All the delicious heaviness she remembered from previous encounters seemed to intensify. His lips, his hands, trailed fire and sweetness, coaxing, arousing her to bliss and increasingly powerful desire. His breath coming in short, hard pants, he dragged her hand to his body, encouraging her, showing her where to caress him. And his pleasure fed her own, like wind to a wildfire.

She cried out when he entered her, but it was more relief than pain. And then he was moving above her, and his caresses were inside as well as out. And this, *this* was the culmination of her love and his. Finally, they were one.

And when the groans of ultimate joy escaped him, they carried her, too, seizing all the abandoned, glorious pleasures and hurling them together into a wave that consumed her, that would always consume her.

Later, holding her in his arms, close against his body, he murmured, "It's as well you married me, you know, for I'm not sure how much longer I could have kept my hands off you."

She thought about that. "I didn't want you to. Keep your hands off me, I mean. I've never met anyone like you, Dan Stewart."

"Nor I anyone like you, Juliet Stewart." He smiled into her hair. "Will you stay with me?"

"Always," she whispered. "Will you love me?"

He turned her, moving over her once more. "Always," he breathed.

EPILOGUE

Three months later...

HAVING PRUNED THE last of the revived rose bushes at the front of Myerly Hall, Juliette straightened and shaded her eyes against the low autumn sun. She smiled and waved, for two figures on horseback were riding up the drive toward her.

Dropping her basket and knife, she hurried across to meet them. "How wonderful! You're early!"

"Well, we didn't go to Hornby first," Kitty confessed. "We came straight here and thought we could go to Hornby tomorrow." She slipped to the ground unaided to hug Juliet. "I am so glad to see you after all these weeks!"

Juliet hugged her back. "How was the wedding trip?"

"Wonderful," Lawrence said fervently, kissing Juliet's cheek. "Though I'm sorry about Lord Myerly."

Juliet nodded. "Thank you. He died quite gracefully at the end. Not bitter, as he would have been when he summoned everyone to his so-called deathbed in August. I like to think Dan and I made him laugh and eased his last few days in this world."

Kitty nodded. "I'm sure you did. He obviously loved Dan. And you."

"Where is Dan?" Lawrence asked as they walked to the front door, leaving the grooms to take the horses.

"Oh, out in the fields. There is much to do before the new planting begins if they are going to make all the changes they want to. But he shouldn't be long. He's been looking forward to seeing you both."

Kitty had paused, gazing up at the house in wonder. "But Juliet, what have you done with the place? It's a *beautiful* house beneath all that grime! We almost didn't recognize it."

"We just had the stone cleaned and repaired, and the chimneys. And we've opened and aired all the rooms. It is not yet all as we want it, so you must excuse the chaos, but we have a few decent rooms."

She was still showing them around, and they were still exclaiming over the lightness of the rooms and the beauty of the polished old carvings and the new carpet in the drawing room, when Dan shouted upstairs and strode in to join them like a fresh wind.

He wore his old clothes, somewhat muddied, but he grinned at his guests, kissing Kitty's proffered cheek and shaking hands cordially with Lawrence.

"I am disappointed," Kitty pronounced. "I had hoped to see you in a smock!"

"You can, some days," Juliet assured her. "It depends how much laboring he plans to do."

"It does," Dan agreed, catching her round the shoulders and kissing her full on the lips. "But I have several coats now that even Hugh has pronounced acceptable, and a couple of natty waistcoats that he secretly envies. Give me ten minutes to change, and I'll join you!"

"He seems happy in his new life," Lawrence observed.

"He is. It's as if he has come home."

"And you?" Kitty asked, searching her face.

She smiled, knowing her sister would read the answer in her face. "Oh, one moment," she said. "I have to tell the kitchen..."

But she did not go to the kitchen which, with several more servants, now ran itself without any interference on her part. Instead, she hurried

ABANDONED TO THE PRODIGAL

upstairs, to the completely gutted and redecorated rooms she shared with Dan.

His hair was wet and his skin, scrubbed. He had donned a clean pair of pantaloons and was struggling into a fresh shirt when she came in.

She walked right up to him, flung her arms around him, and kissed him. His arms closed around her, and he cooperated fully.

He was smiling when he raised his head. "What was that for?"

"Just because I had the sudden urge. And I've never been so happy in my life."

For an instant, his eyes were serious, and then his smile returned, and he kissed her again.

Somewhere in the house, a dog barked in delight, and someone squealed.

They broke apart. "*Gun,*" they said as one and fled back downstairs to rescue their guests.

About Mary Lancaster

Mary Lancaster lives in Scotland with her husband, three mostly grown-up kids and a small, crazy dog.

Her first literary love was historical fiction, a genre which she relishes mixing up with romance and adventure in her own writing. Her most recent books are light, fun Regency romances written for Dragonblade Publishing: *The Imperial Season* series set at the Congress of Vienna; and the popular *Blackhaven Brides* series, which is set in a fashionable English spa town frequented by the great and the bad of Regency society.

Connect with Mary on-line – she loves to hear from readers:

Email Mary: Mary@MaryLancaster.com

Website: www.MaryLancaster.com

Newsletter sign-up: http://eepurl.com/b4Xoif

Facebook: facebook.com/mary.lancaster.1656

Facebook Author Page:
facebook.com/MaryLancasterNovelist

Twitter: @MaryLancNovels

Amazon Author Page:
amazon.com/Mary-Lancaster/e/B00DJ5IACI

Bookbub:
bookbub.com/profile/mary-lancaster

CPSIA information can be obtained
at www.ICGtesting.com
Printed in the USA
LVHW021550130121
676402LV00011B/1186

9 781953 455031